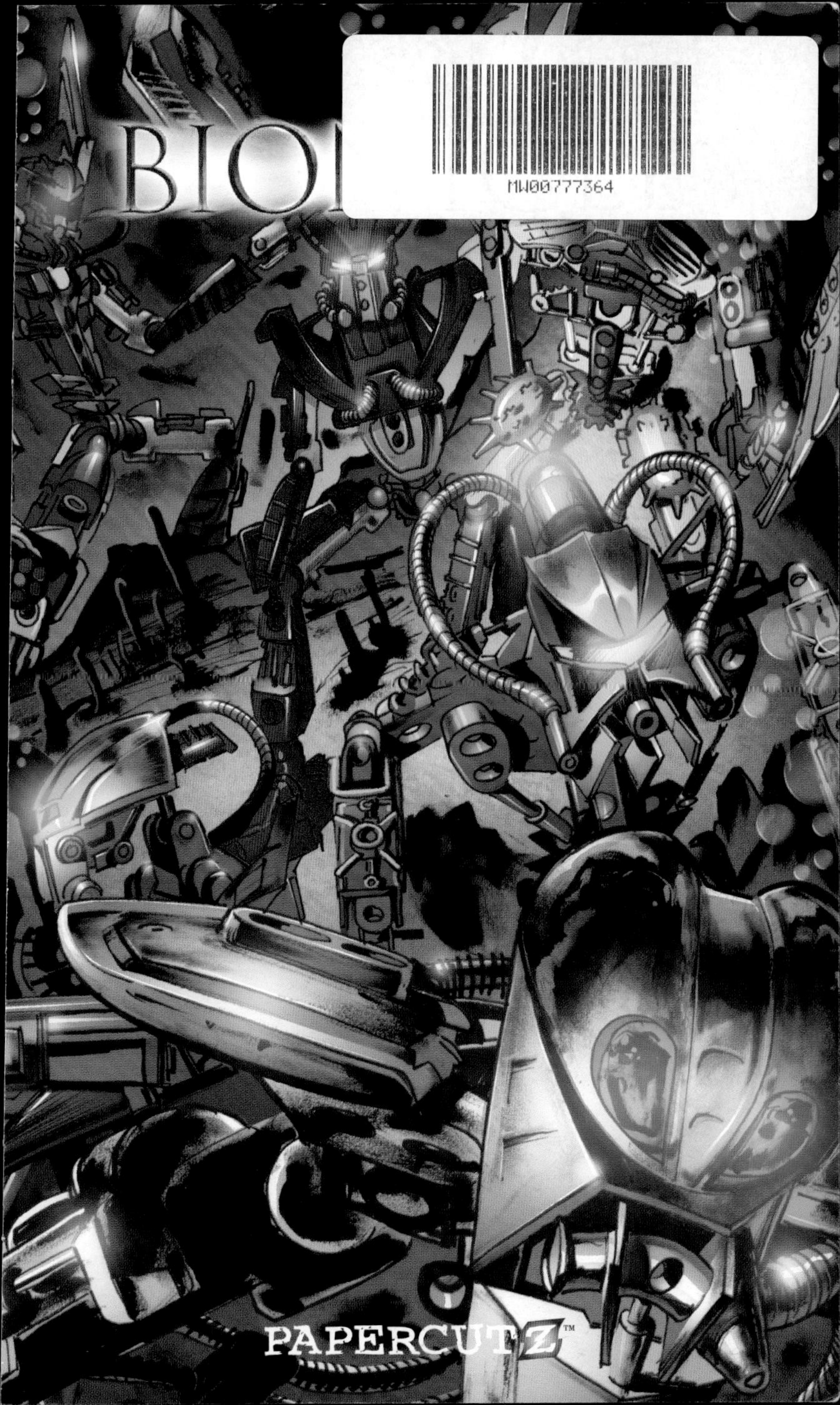
BIO
PAPERCUTZ™

BIONICLE® GRAPHIC NOVELS AVAILABLE FROM PAPERCUT

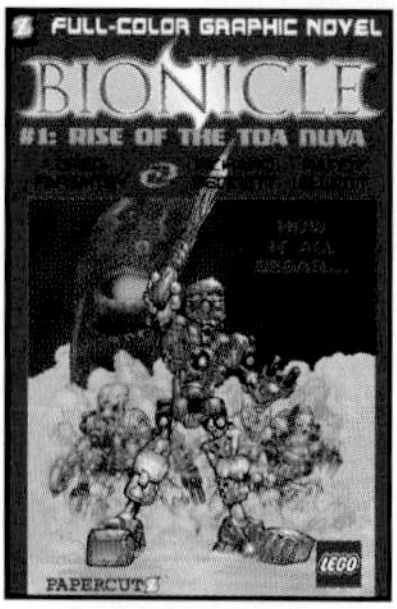
FULL-COLOR GRAPHIC NOVEL
BIONICLE
#1: RISE OF THE TOA NUVA
PAPERCUTZ
LEGO

Graphic Novel #1
"Rise of the Toa Nuva"

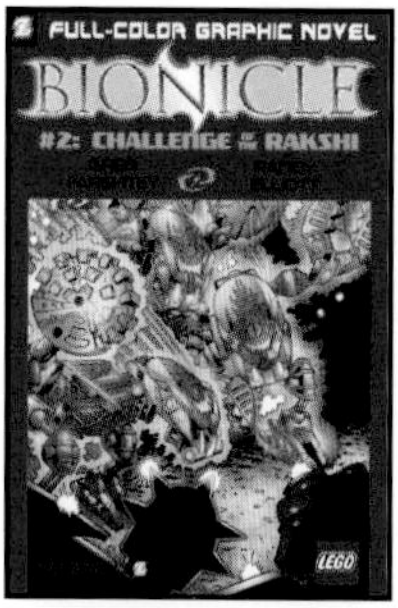
FULL-COLOR GRAPHIC NOVEL
BIONICLE
#2: CHALLENGE of the RAKSHI
LEGO

Graphic Novel #2
"Challenge of the Rahkshi"

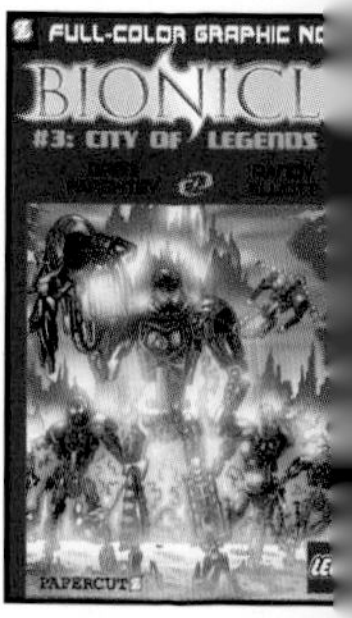
BIONICLE
#3: CITY OF LEGENDS
PAPERCUTZ

Graphic Novel #3
"City of Legends

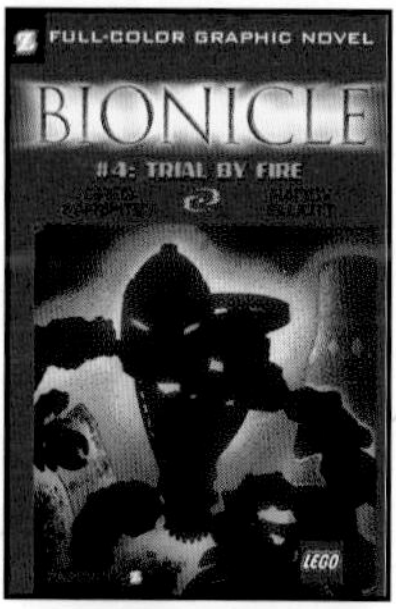
FULL-COLOR GRAPHIC NOVEL
BIONICLE
#4: TRIAL BY FIRE
LEGO

Graphic Novel #4
"Trial by Fire"

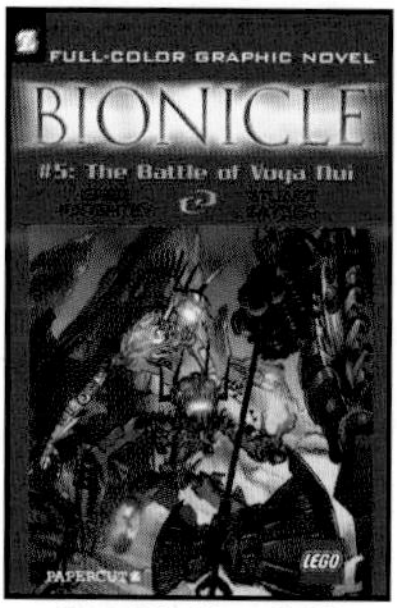
FULL-COLOR GRAPHIC NOVEL
BIONICLE
#5: The Battle of Voya Nui
PAPERCUTZ
LEGO

Graphic Novel #5
"The Battle of Voya Nui"

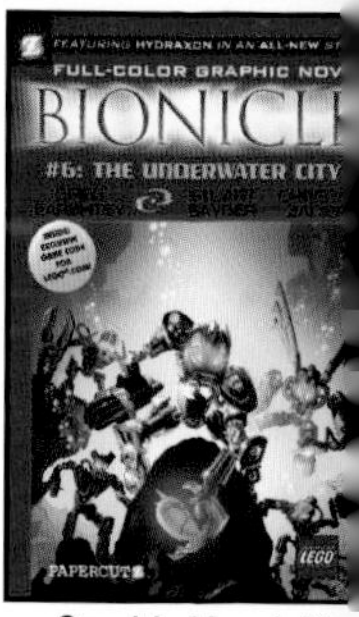
BIONICLE
#6: THE UNDERWATER CITY
PAPERCUTZ

Graphic Novel #6
"The Underwater Ci

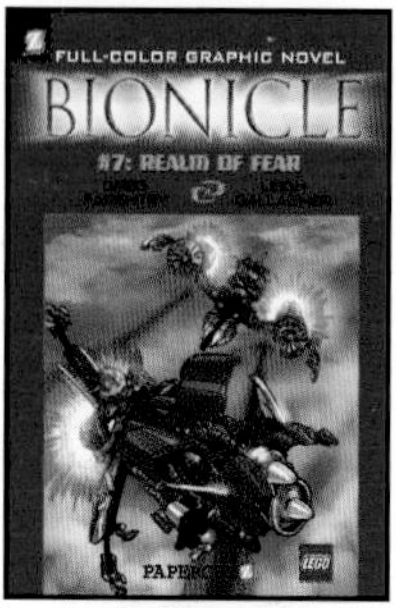
FULL-COLOR GRAPHIC NOVEL
BIONICLE
#7: REALM OF FEAR
LEGO

Coming in November 2009:
Graphic Novel #7
"Realm of Fear"

$7.95 each paperback, $12.95 each in hardcover. Please add $4.00 for postage and handling for the first book, add $1.00 for each additional book. Please make check payable to NBM Publishing. Send to: Papercutz, 40 Exchange Place, Suite 1308, New York, NY 10005 1-800-886-1223

www.papercutz.com

BIONICLE®

#6 The Underwater City

GREG FARSHTEY
Writer
STUART SAYGER
CHRISTIAN ZANIER
Artists

New York

THE UNDERWATER CITY

GREG FARSHTEY – WRITER
STUART SAYGER, CHRISTIAN ZANIER – ARTISTS
TOBY DUTKIEWICZ – ART DIRECTOR/DESIGN
JENNIFER REDDING – ASSISTANT ART DIRECTOR
ALEX BLEYAERT – COLORIST
PHIL BALSMAN, TRAVIS LANHAM, ROBERT CLARK JR., BRYAN SENKA – LETTERE
RYAN NOBLE – CHAPTER FOUR COVER DESIGN
MICHAEL WRIGHT – ORIGINAL EDITOR
JESSICA NUMSAWANKIJKUL – ORIGINAL ASSISTANT EDITOR
JOHN McCARTHY – PRODUCTION
MICHAEL PETRANEK – EDITORIAL ASSISTANT
JIM SALICRUP
EDITOR-IN-CHIEF

ISBN: 978-1-59707-156-7 PAPERBACK EDITION
ISBN: 978-1-59707-157-4 HARDCOVER EDITION

ALL STORIES, EXCEPT "HYDRAXON'S TALE," ORIGINALLY PUBLISHED AS
COMICBOOKS BY DC COMICS AS BIONICLE IGNITION #7-11.

PRINTED IN CHINA MAY 2009 BY 1010 PRINTING
26/F 625 KINGS ROAD, NORTH POINT, HONG KONG
DISTRIBUTED BY MACMILLAN.
10 9 8 7 6 5 4 3 2 1

THE UNDERWATER CITY: PROLOGUE

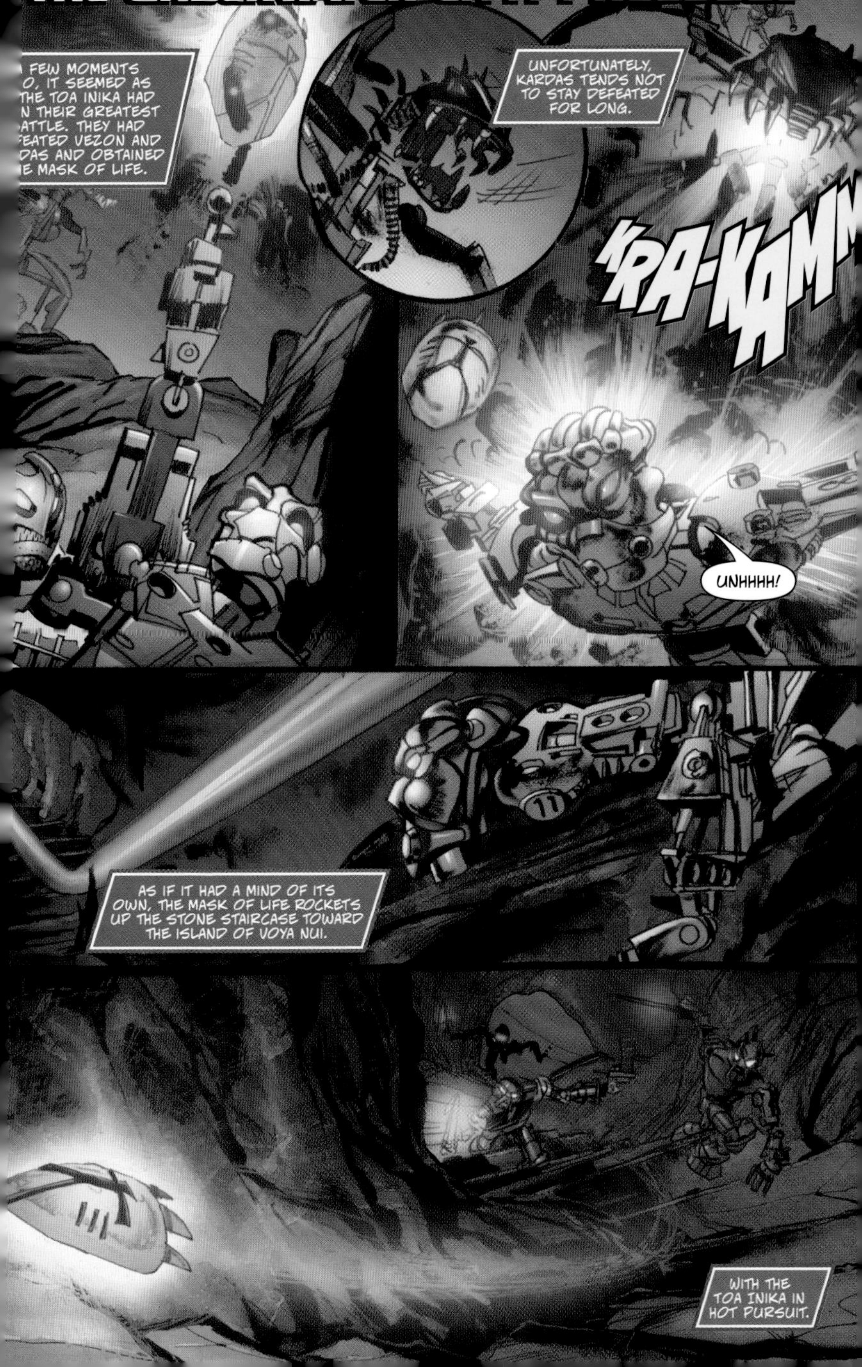
FEW MOMENTS
O, IT SEEMED AS
THE TOA INIKA HAD
N THEIR GREATEST
ATTLE. THEY HAD
FEATED VEZON AND
DAS AND OBTAINED
E MASK OF LIFE.
UNFORTUNATELY, KARDAS TENDS NOT TO STAY DEFEATED FOR LONG.
KRA-KAMM
UNHHHH!
AS IF IT HAD A MIND OF ITS OWN, THE MASK OF LIFE ROCKETS UP THE STONE STAIRCASE TOWARD THE ISLAND OF VOYA NUI.
WITH THE TOA INIKA IN HOT PURSUIT.

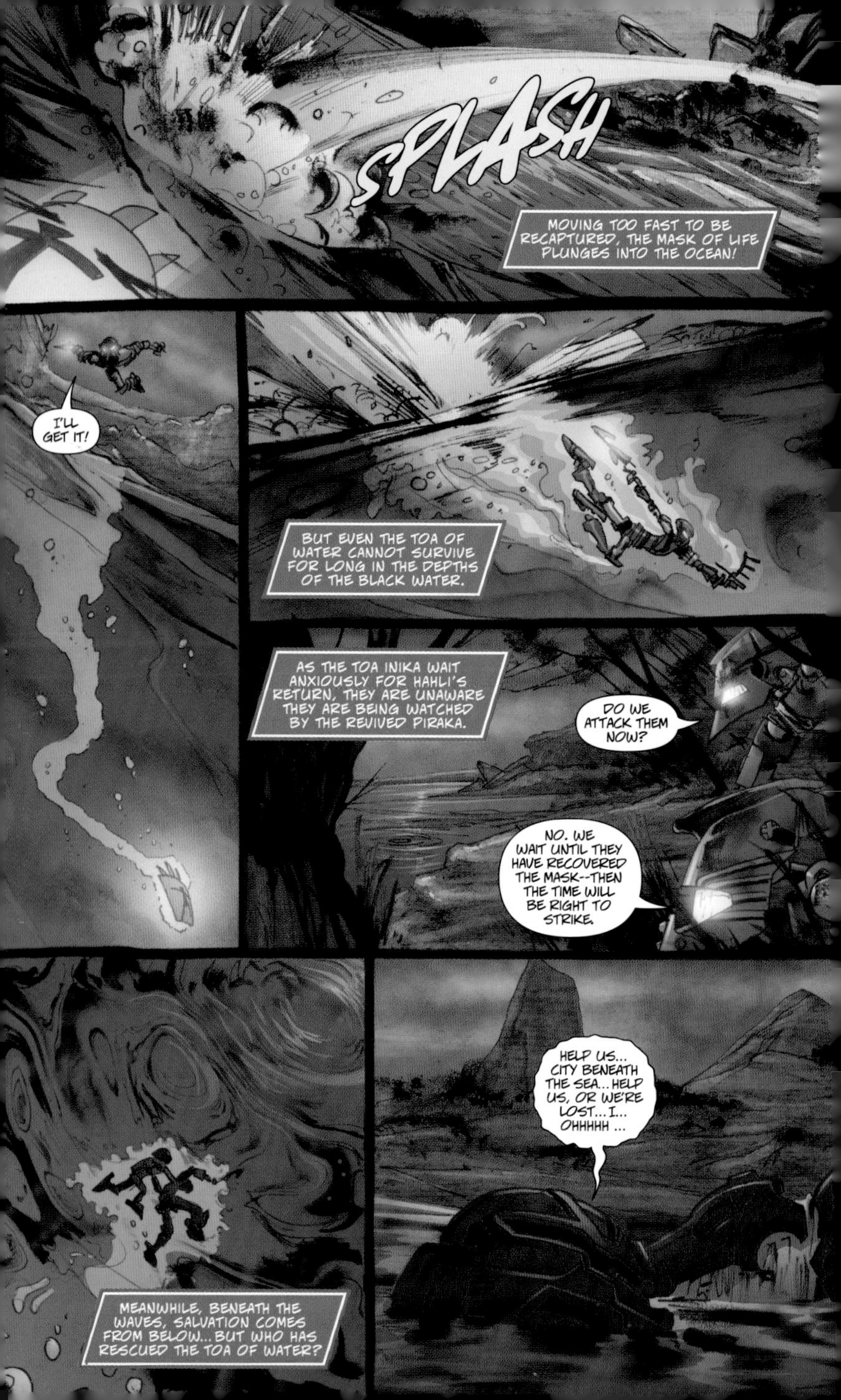
SPLASH
MOVING TOO FAST TO BE RECAPTURED, THE MASK OF LIFE PLUNGES INTO THE OCEAN!
I'LL GET IT!
BUT EVEN THE TOA OF WATER CANNOT SURVIVE FOR LONG IN THE DEPTHS OF THE BLACK WATER.
AS THE TOA INIKA WAIT ANXIOUSLY FOR HAHLI'S RETURN, THEY ARE UNAWARE THEY ARE BEING WATCHED BY THE REVIVED PIRAKA.
DO WE ATTACK THEM NOW?
NO. WE WAIT UNTIL THEY HAVE RECOVERED THE MASK--THEN THE TIME WILL BE RIGHT TO STRIKE.
MEANWHILE, BENEATH THE WAVES, SALVATION COMES FROM BELOW... BUT WHO HAS RESCUED THE TOA OF WATER?
HELP US... CITY BENEATH THE SEA... HELP US, OR WE'RE LOST... I... OHHHHH ...

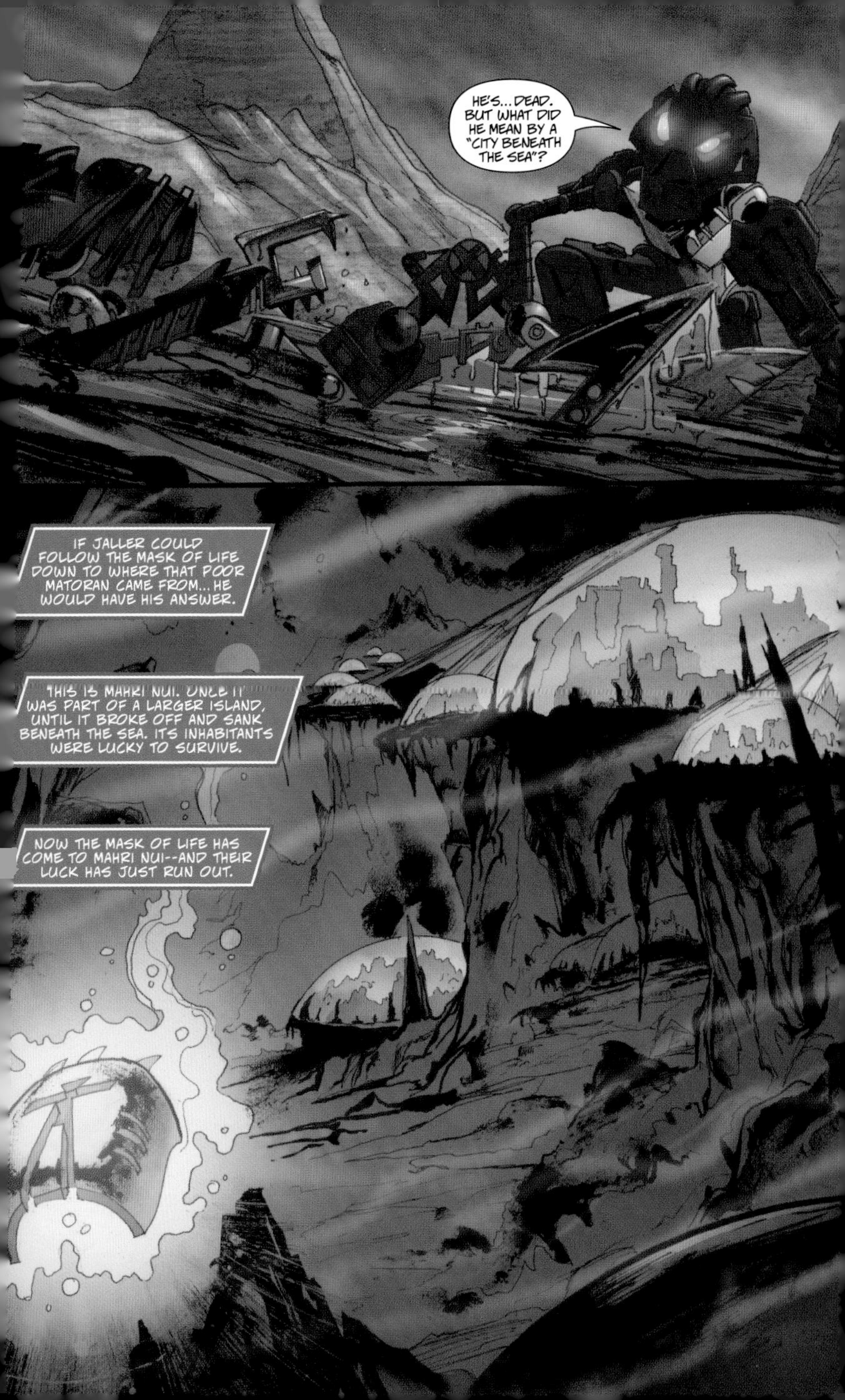
HE'S...DEAD. BUT WHAT DID HE MEAN BY A "CITY BENEATH THE SEA"?
IF JALLER COULD FOLLOW THE MASK OF LIFE DOWN TO WHERE THAT POOR MATORAN CAME FROM... HE WOULD HAVE HIS ANSWER.
THIS IS MAHRI NUI. ONCE IT WAS PART OF A LARGER ISLAND, UNTIL IT BROKE OFF AND SANK BENEATH THE SEA. ITS INHABITANTS WERE LUCKY TO SURVIVE.
NOW THE MASK OF LIFE HAS COME TO MAHRI NUI--AND THEIR LUCK HAS JUST RUN OUT.

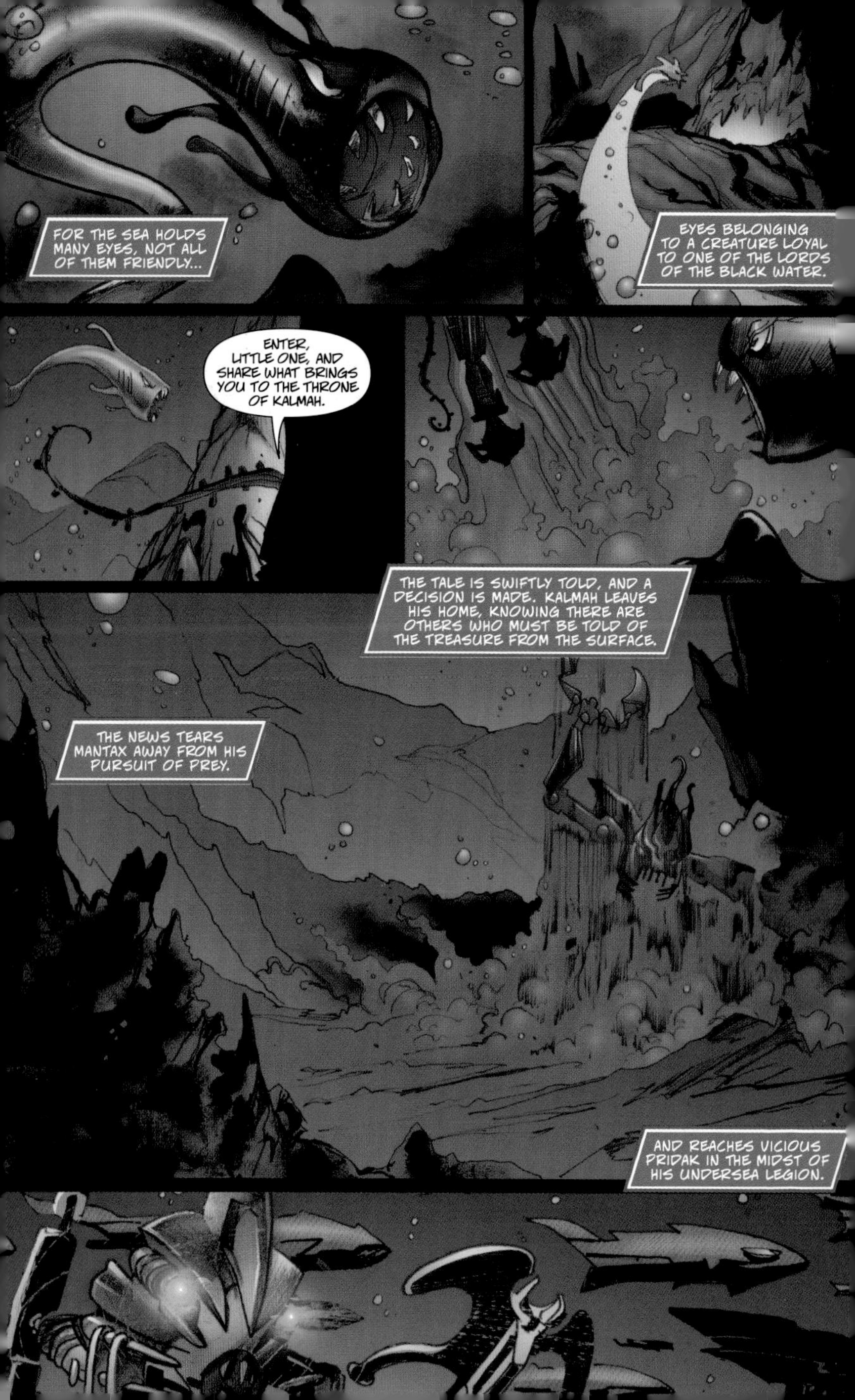
FOR THE SEA HOLDS MANY EYES, NOT ALL OF THEM FRIENDLY...
EYES BELONGING TO A CREATURE LOYAL TO ONE OF THE LORDS OF THE BLACK WATER.
ENTER, LITTLE ONE, AND SHARE WHAT BRINGS YOU TO THE THRONE OF KALMAH.
THE TALE IS SWIFTLY TOLD, AND A DECISION IS MADE. KALMAH LEAVES HIS HOME, KNOWING THERE ARE OTHERS WHO MUST BE TOLD OF THE TREASURE FROM THE SURFACE.
THE NEWS TEARS MANTAX AWAY FROM HIS PURSUIT OF PREY.
AND REACHES VICIOUS PRIDAK IN THE MIDST OF HIS UNDERSEA LEGION.

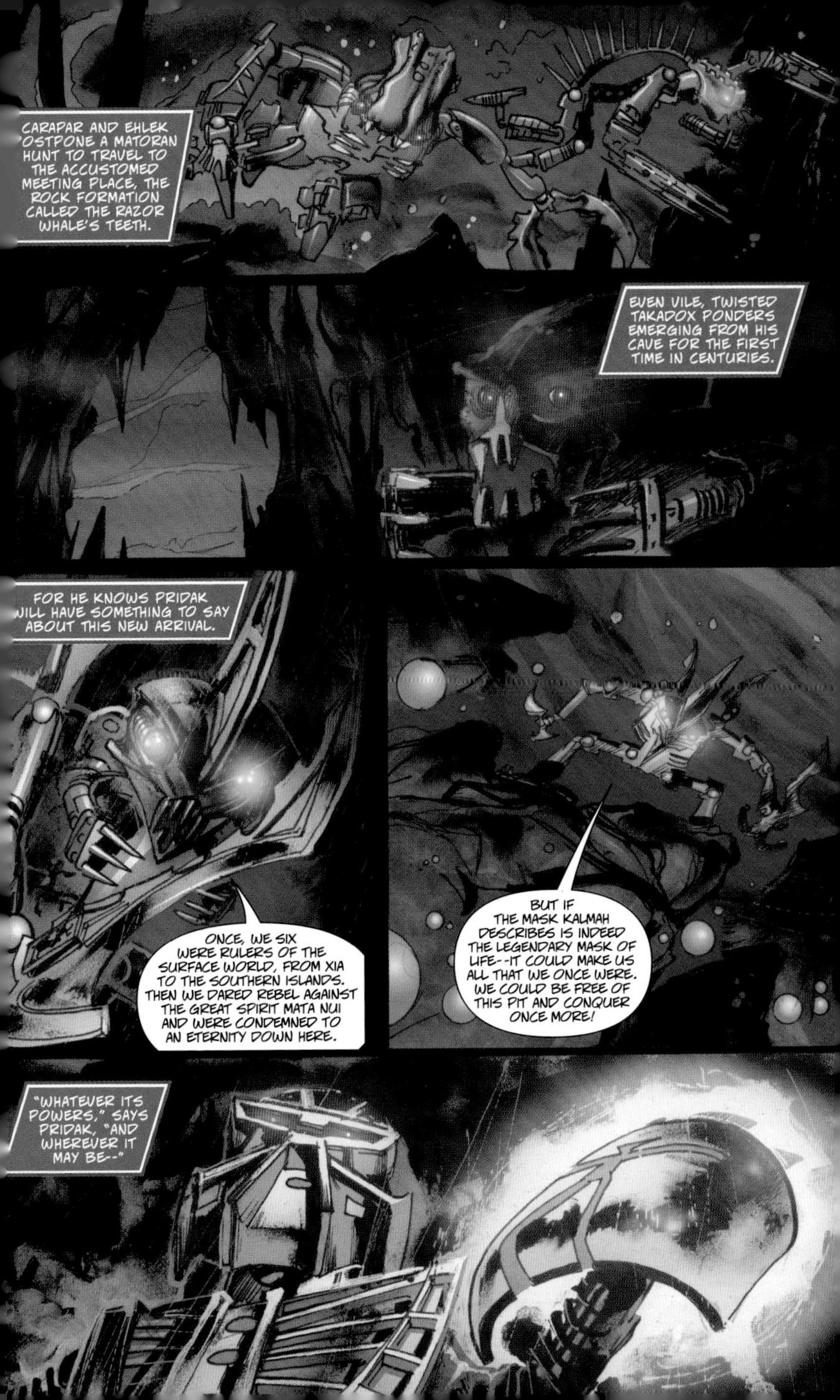
CARAPAR AND EHLEK POSTPONE A MATORAN HUNT TO TRAVEL TO THE ACCUSTOMED MEETING PLACE, THE ROCK FORMATION CALLED THE RAZOR WHALE'S TEETH.
EVEN VILE, TWISTED TAKADOX PONDERS EMERGING FROM HIS CAVE FOR THE FIRST TIME IN CENTURIES.
FOR HE KNOWS PRIDAK WILL HAVE SOMETHING TO SAY ABOUT THIS NEW ARRIVAL.
ONCE, WE SIX WERE RULERS OF THE SURFACE WORLD, FROM XIA TO THE SOUTHERN ISLANDS. THEN WE DARED REBEL AGAINST THE GREAT SPIRIT MATA NUI AND WERE CONDEMNED TO AN ETERNITY DOWN HERE.
BUT IF THE MASK KALMAH DESCRIBES IS INDEED THE LEGENDARY MASK OF LIFE--IT COULD MAKE US ALL THAT WE ONCE WERE. WE COULD BE FREE OF THIS PIT AND CONQUER ONCE MORE!
"WHATEVER ITS POWERS," SAYS PRIDAK, "AND WHEREVER IT MAY BE--"

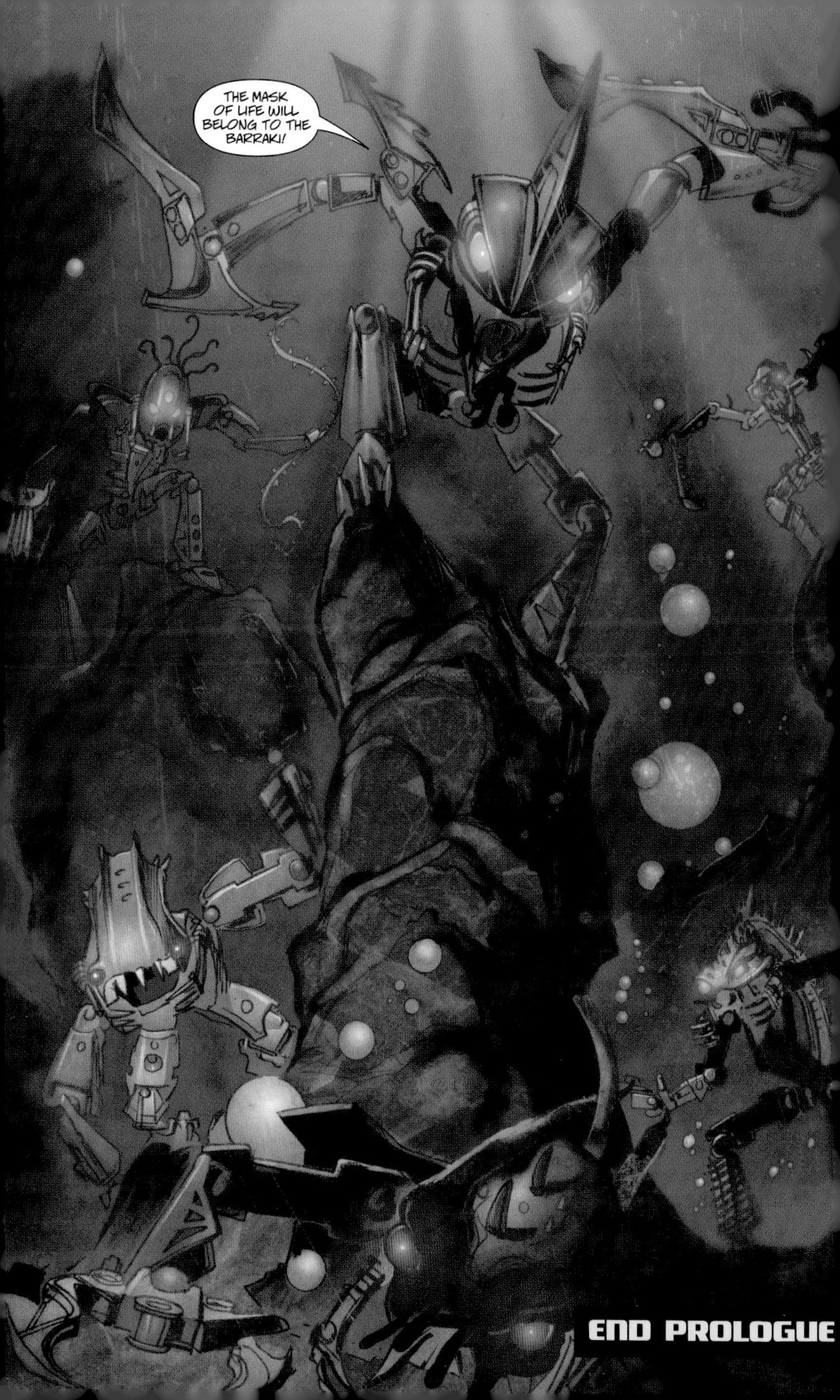
THE MASK OF LIFE WILL BELONG TO THE BARRAKI!
END PROLOGUE

THE UNDERWATER CITY
CHAPTER ONE

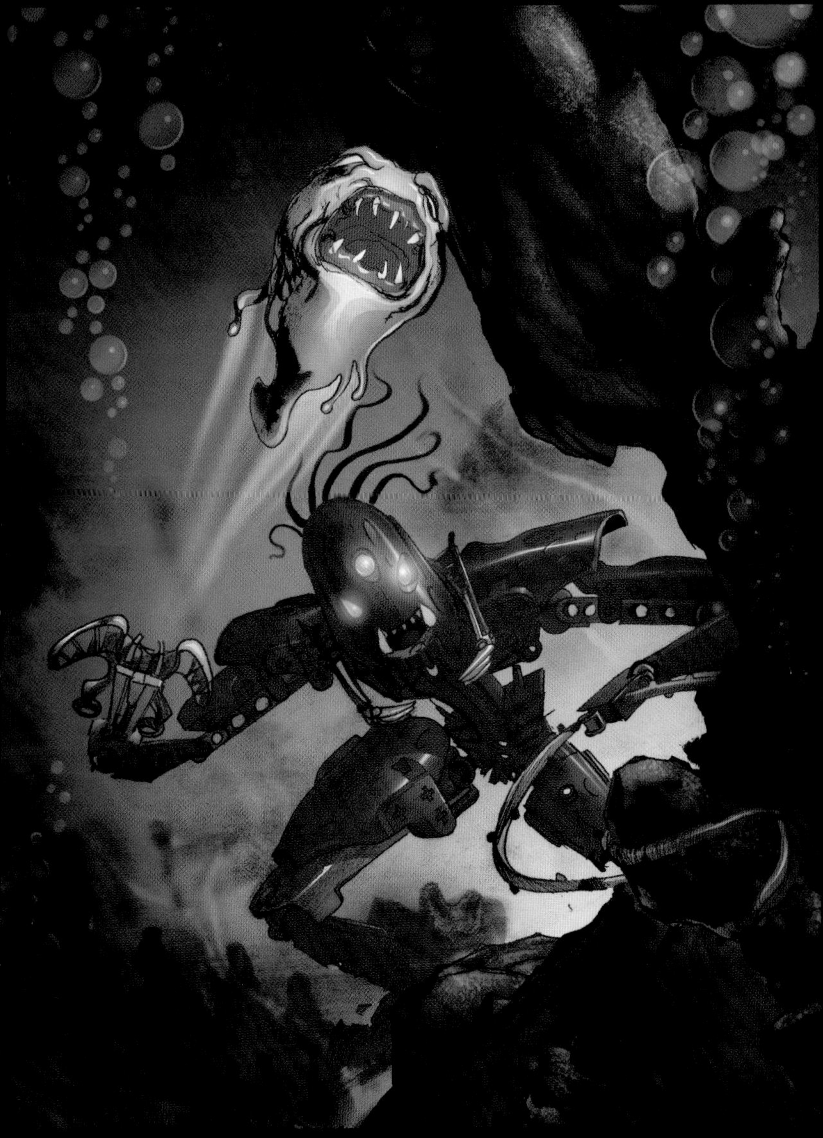

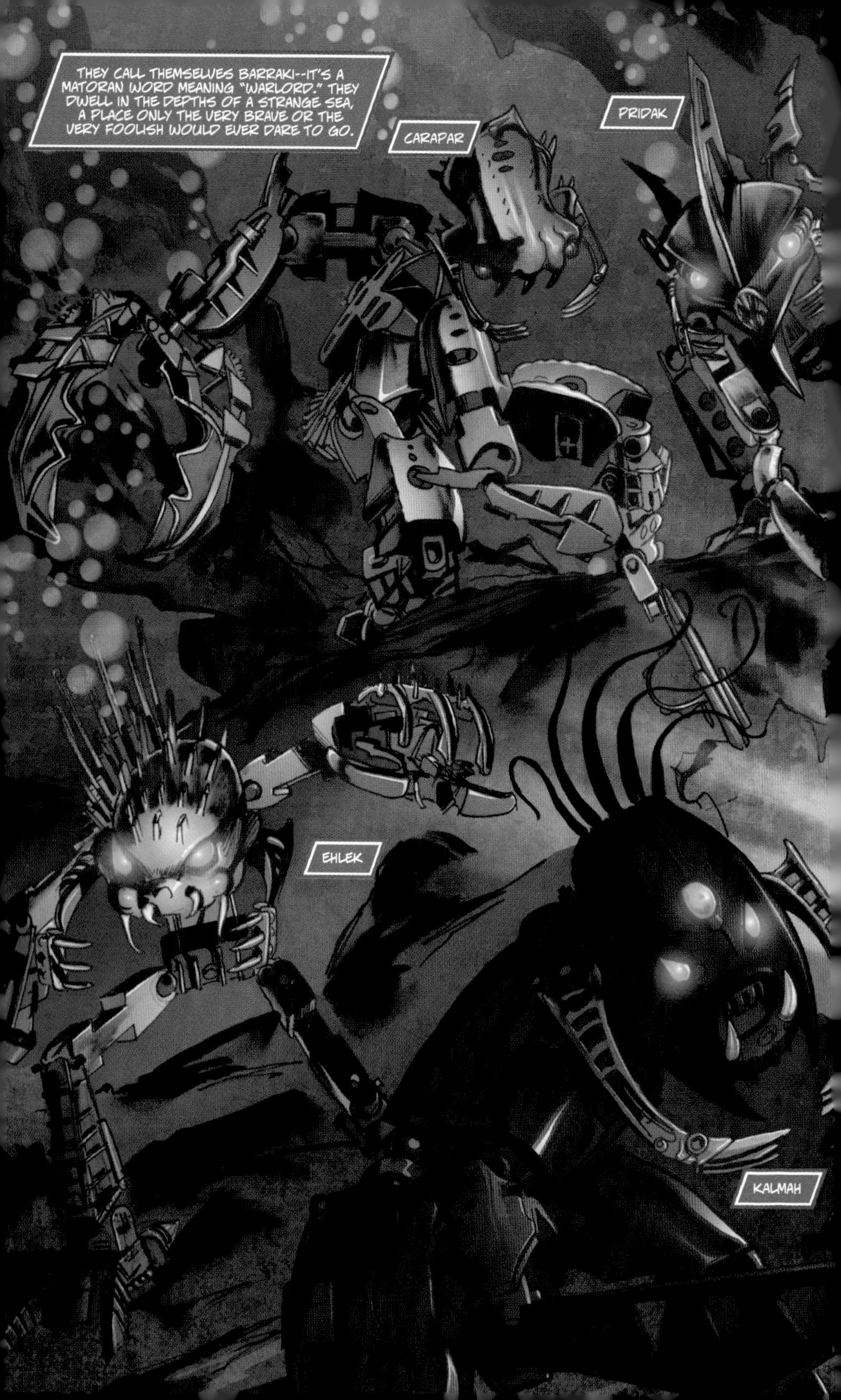
THEY CALL THEMSELVES BARRAKI--IT'S A MATORAN WORD MEANING "WARLORD." THEY DWELL IN THE DEPTHS OF A STRANGE SEA, A PLACE ONLY THE VERY BRAVE OR THE VERY FOOLISH WOULD EVER DARE TO GO.
CARAPAR
PRIDAK
EHLEK
KALMAH

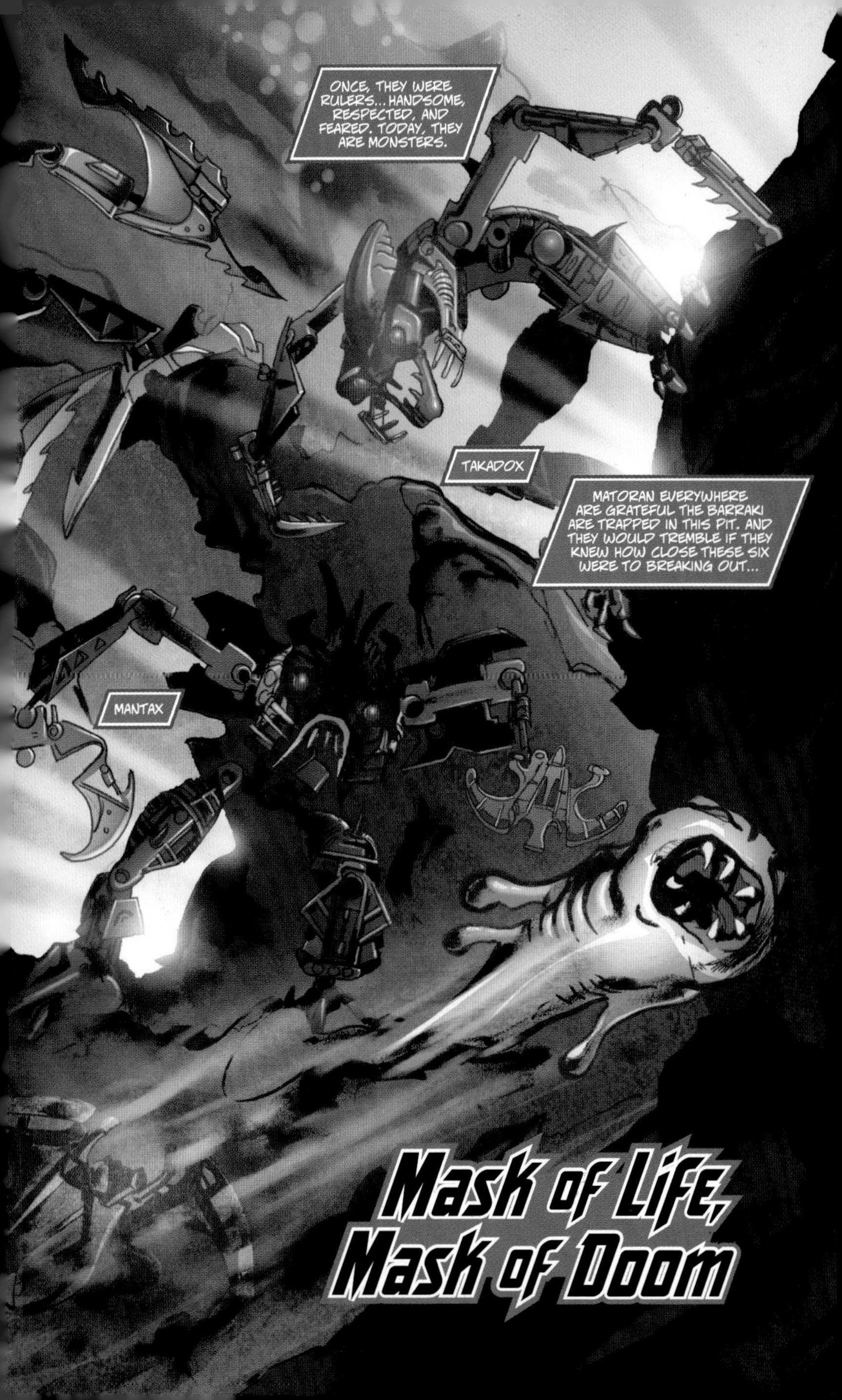
ONCE, THEY WERE RULERS... HANDSOME, RESPECTED, AND FEARED. TODAY, THEY ARE MONSTERS.
TAKADOX
MATORAN EVERYWHERE ARE GRATEFUL THE BARRAKI ARE TRAPPED IN THIS PIT. AND THEY WOULD TREMBLE IF THEY KNEW HOW CLOSE THESE SIX WERE TO BREAKING OUT...
MANTAX
Mask of Life, Mask of Doom

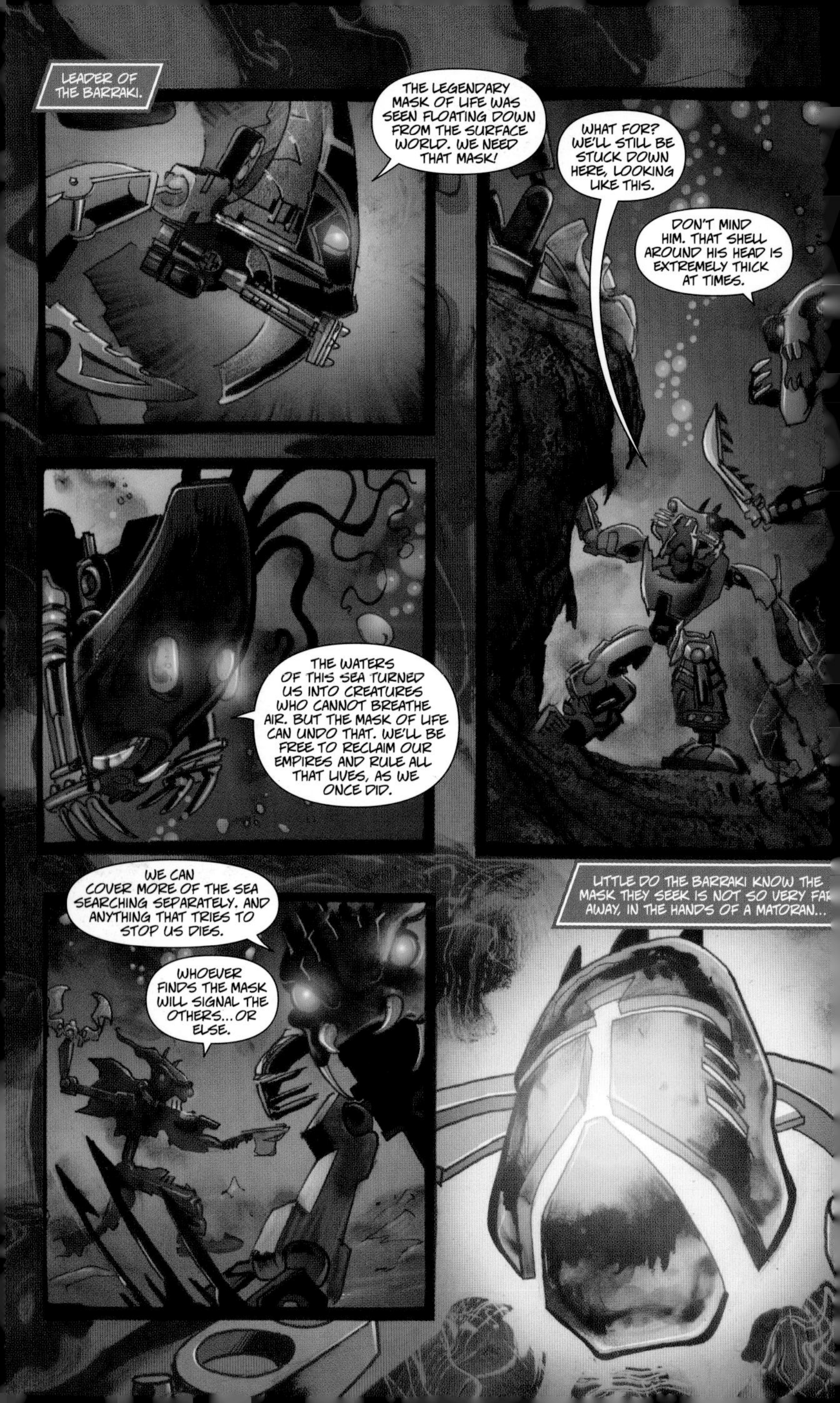
LEADER OF THE BARRAKI.
THE LEGENDARY MASK OF LIFE WAS SEEN FLOATING DOWN FROM THE SURFACE WORLD. WE NEED THAT MASK!
WHAT FOR? WE'LL STILL BE STUCK DOWN HERE, LOOKING LIKE THIS.
DON'T MIND HIM. THAT SHELL AROUND HIS HEAD IS EXTREMELY THICK AT TIMES.
THE WATERS OF THIS SEA TURNED US INTO CREATURES WHO CANNOT BREATHE AIR. BUT THE MASK OF LIFE CAN UNDO THAT. WE'LL BE FREE TO RECLAIM OUR EMPIRES AND RULE ALL THAT LIVES, AS WE ONCE DID.
WE CAN COVER MORE OF THE SEA SEARCHING SEPARATELY. AND ANYTHING THAT TRIES TO STOP US DIES.
WHOEVER FINDS THE MASK WILL SIGNAL THE OTHERS... OR ELSE.
LITTLE DO THE BARRAKI KNOW THE MASK THEY SEEK IS NOT SO VERY FAR AWAY, IN THE HANDS OF A MATORAN...

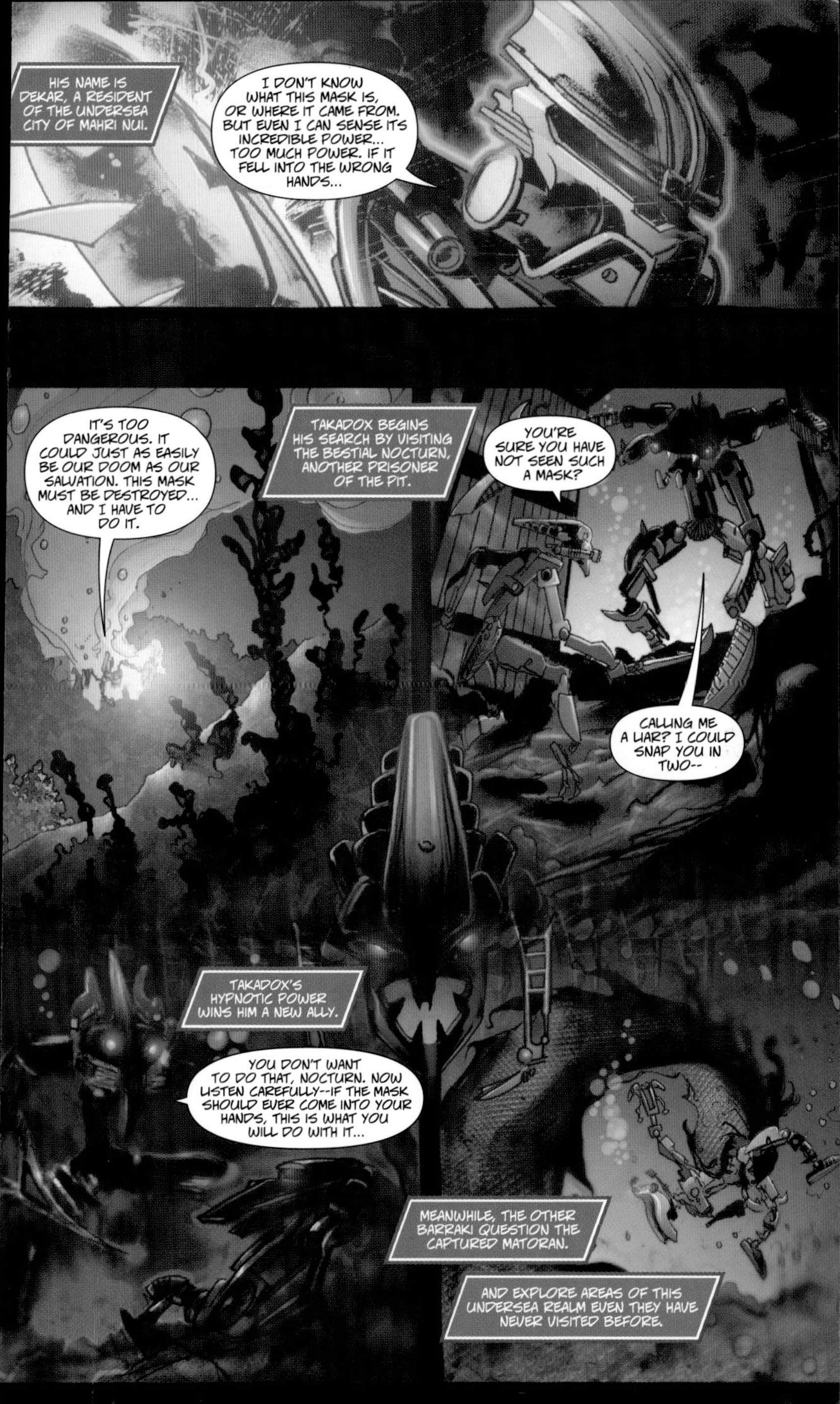
HIS NAME IS DEKAR, A RESIDENT OF THE UNDERSEA CITY OF MAHRI NUI.
I DON'T KNOW WHAT THIS MASK IS, OR WHERE IT CAME FROM. BUT EVEN I CAN SENSE ITS INCREDIBLE POWER... TOO MUCH POWER. IF IT FELL INTO THE WRONG HANDS...
IT'S TOO DANGEROUS. IT COULD JUST AS EASILY BE OUR DOOM AS OUR SALVATION. THIS MASK MUST BE DESTROYED... AND I HAVE TO DO IT.
TAKADOX BEGINS HIS SEARCH BY VISITING THE BESTIAL NOCTURN, ANOTHER PRISONER OF THE PIT.
YOU'RE SURE YOU HAVE NOT SEEN SUCH A MASK?
CALLING ME A LIAR? I COULD SNAP YOU IN TWO--
TAKADOX'S HYPNOTIC POWER WINS HIM A NEW ALLY.
YOU DON'T WANT TO DO THAT, NOCTURN. NOW LISTEN CAREFULLY--IF THE MASK SHOULD EVER COME INTO YOUR HANDS, THIS IS WHAT YOU WILL DO WITH IT...
MEANWHILE, THE OTHER BARRAKI QUESTION THE CAPTURED MATORAN.
AND EXPLORE AREAS OF THIS UNDERSEA REALM EVEN THEY HAVE NEVER VISITED BEFORE.

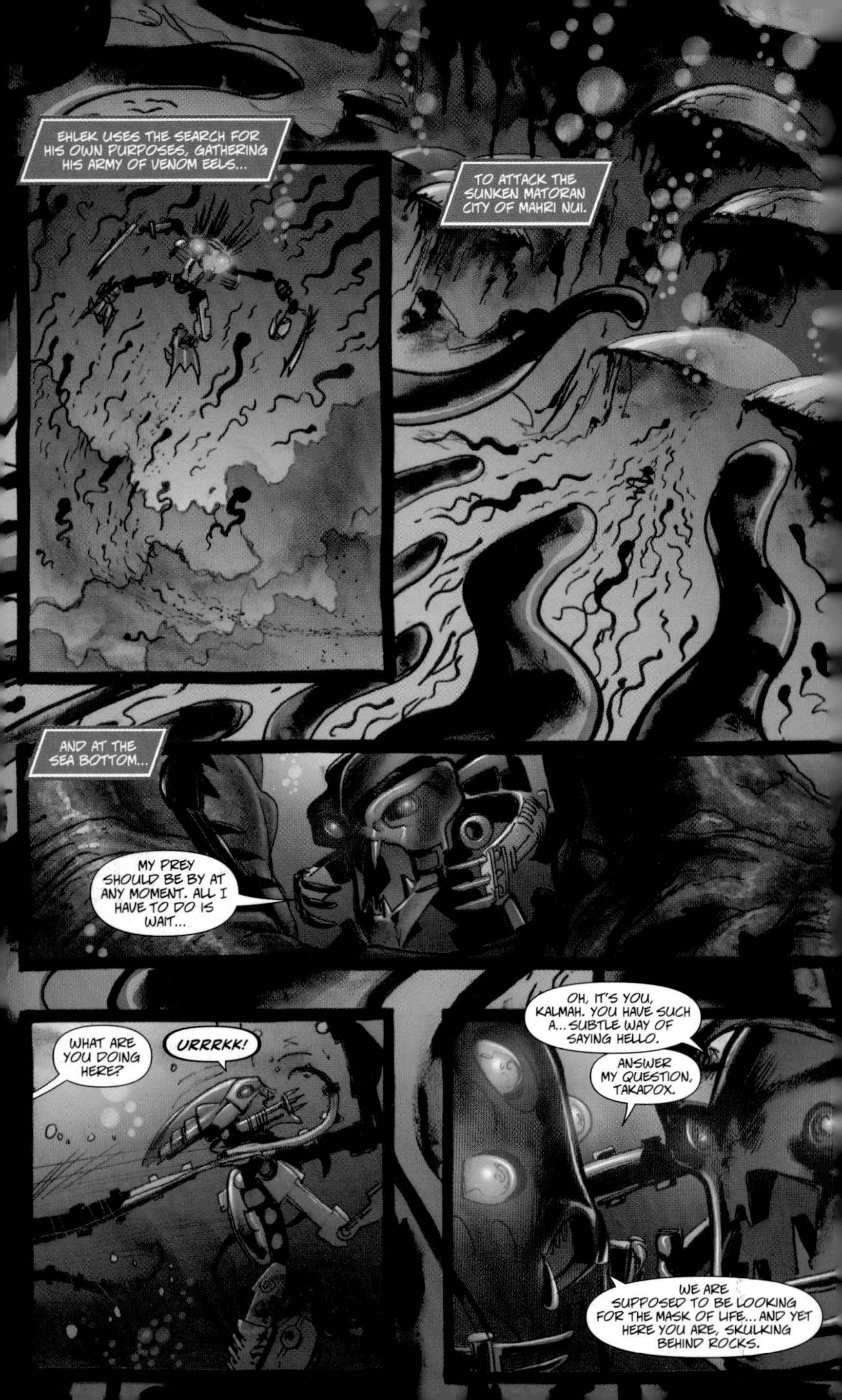

EHLEK USES THE SEARCH FOR HIS OWN PURPOSES, GATHERING HIS ARMY OF VENOM EELS...
TO ATTACK THE SUNKEN MATORAN CITY OF MAHRI NUI.
AND AT THE SEA BOTTOM...
MY PREY SHOULD BE BY AT ANY MOMENT. ALL I HAVE TO DO IS WAIT...
WHAT ARE YOU DOING HERE?
URRRKK!
OH, IT'S YOU, KALMAH. YOU HAVE SUCH A... SUBTLE WAY OF SAYING HELLO.
ANSWER MY QUESTION, TAKADOX.
WE ARE SUPPOSED TO BE LOOKING FOR THE MASK OF LIFE... AND YET HERE YOU ARE, SKULKING BEHIND ROCKS.

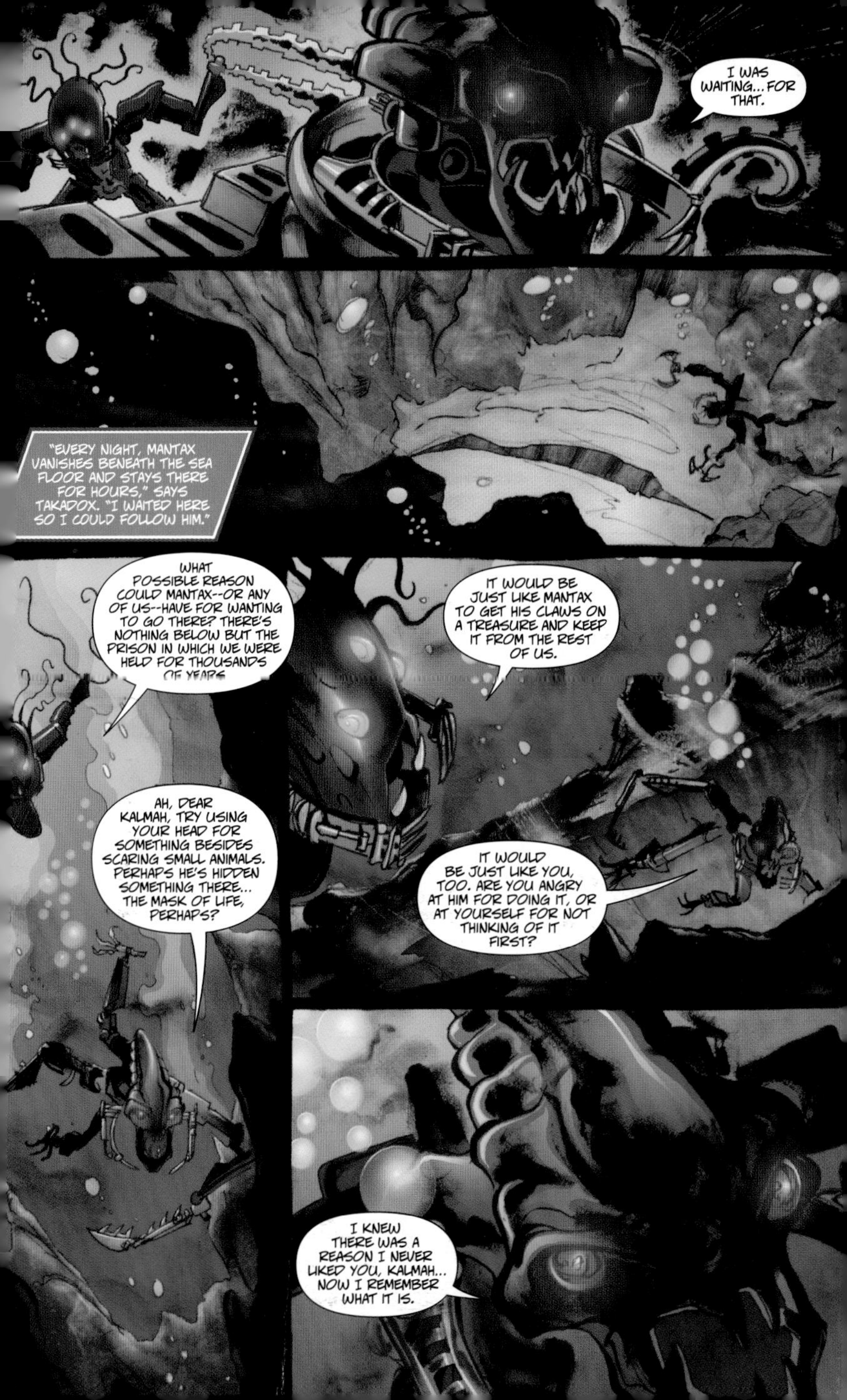
I WAS WAITING... FOR THAT.
"EVERY NIGHT, MANTAX VANISHES BENEATH THE SEA FLOOR AND STAYS THERE FOR HOURS," SAYS TAKADOX. "I WAITED HERE SO I COULD FOLLOW HIM."
WHAT POSSIBLE REASON COULD MANTAX--OR ANY OF US--HAVE FOR WANTING TO GO THERE? THERE'S NOTHING BELOW BUT THE PRISON IN WHICH WE WERE HELD FOR THOUSANDS OF YEARS
IT WOULD BE JUST LIKE MANTAX TO GET HIS CLAWS ON A TREASURE AND KEEP IT FROM THE REST OF US.
AH, DEAR KALMAH, TRY USING YOUR HEAD FOR SOMETHING BESIDES SCARING SMALL ANIMALS. PERHAPS HE'S HIDDEN SOMETHING THERE... THE MASK OF LIFE, PERHAPS?
IT WOULD BE JUST LIKE YOU, TOO. ARE YOU ANGRY AT HIM FOR DOING IT, OR AT YOURSELF FOR NOT THINKING OF IT FIRST?
I KNEW THERE WAS A REASON I NEVER LIKED YOU, KALMAH... NOW I REMEMBER WHAT IT IS.

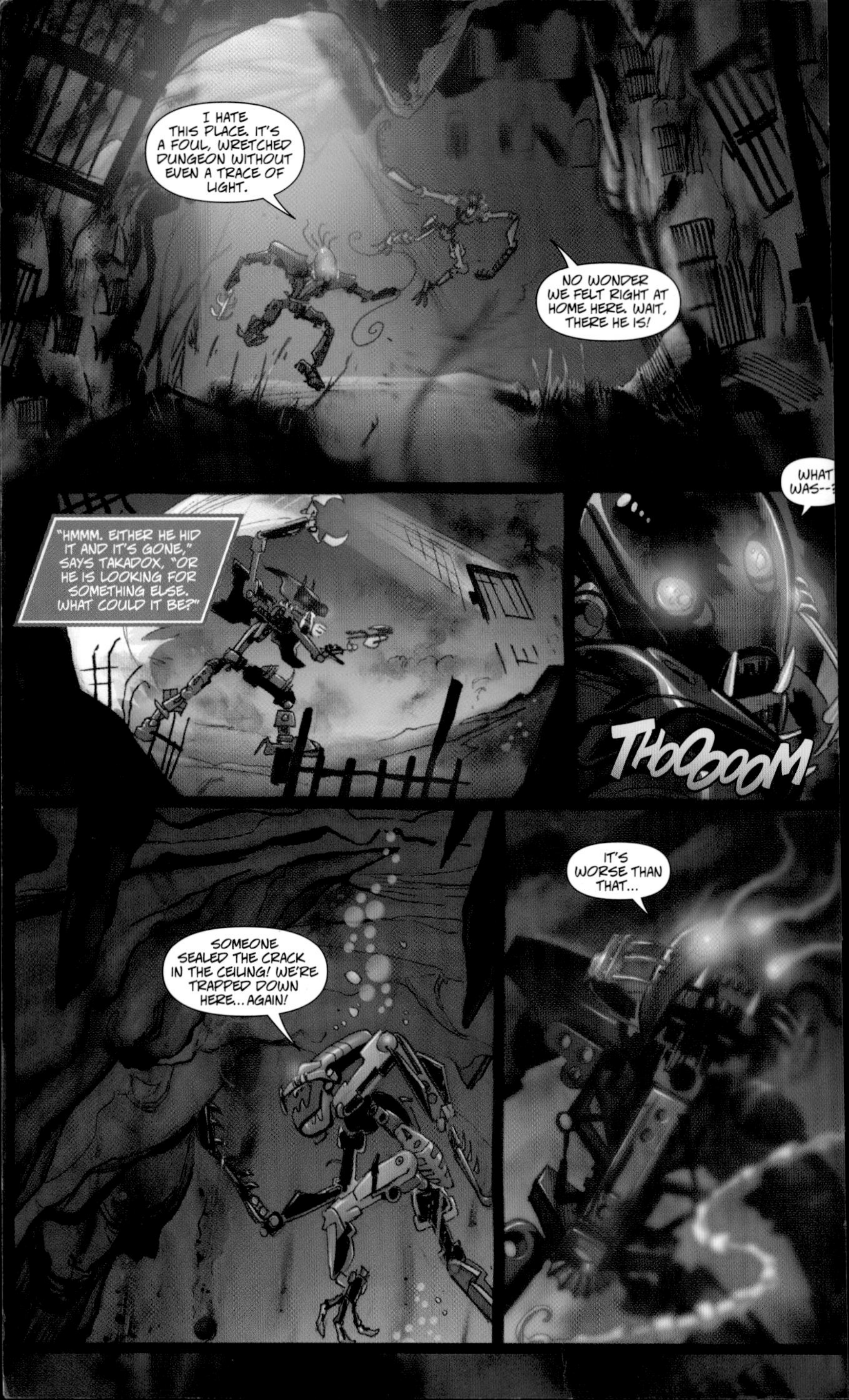
I HATE THIS PLACE. IT'S A FOUL, WRETCHED DUNGEON WITHOUT EVEN A TRACE OF LIGHT.
NO WONDER WE FELT RIGHT AT HOME HERE. WAIT, THERE HE IS!
"HMMM. EITHER HE HID IT AND IT'S GONE," SAYS TAKADOX, "OR HE IS LOOKING FOR SOMETHING ELSE. WHAT COULD IT BE?"
WHAT WAS--?
THOOOOOM.
SOMEONE SEALED THE CRACK IN THE CEILING! WE'RE TRAPPED DOWN HERE... AGAIN!
IT'S WORSE THAN THAT...

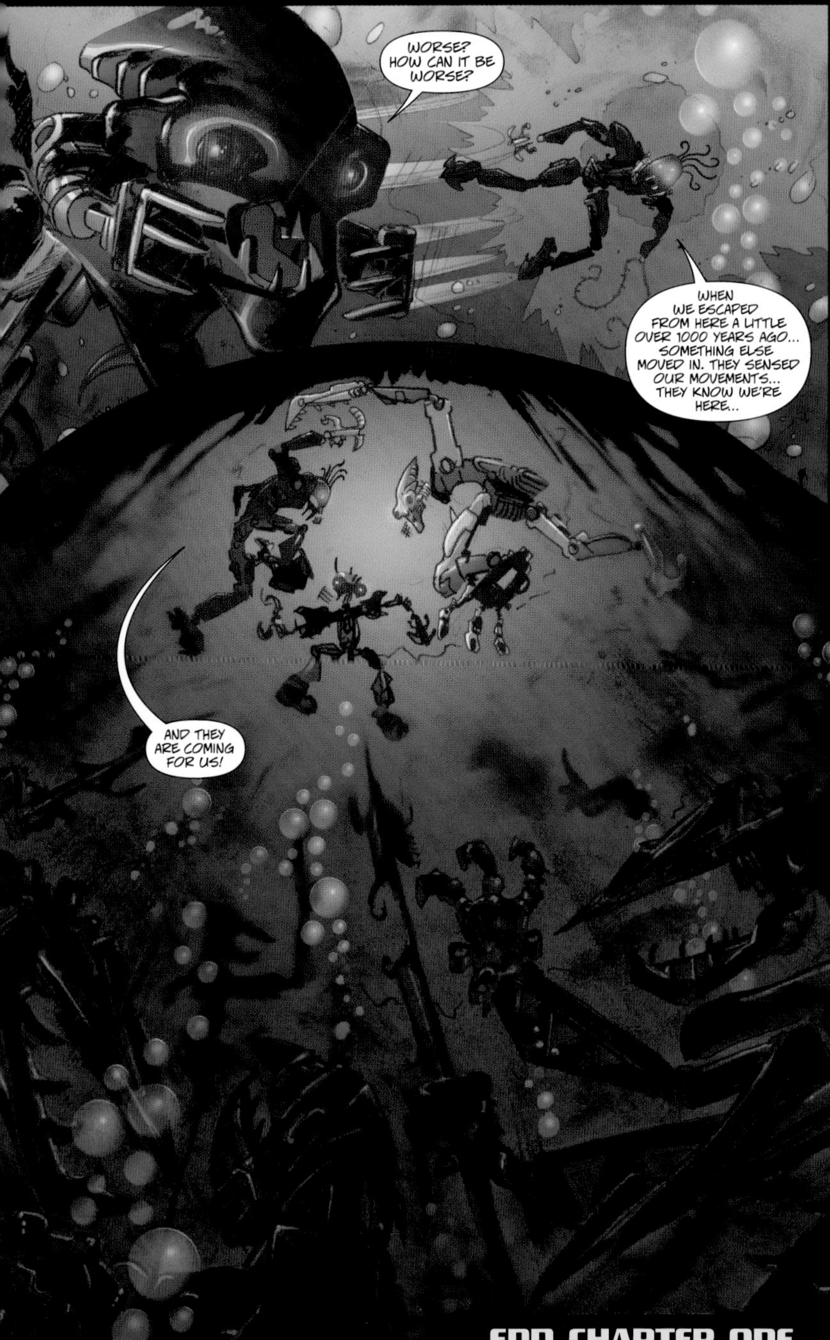
WORSE? HOW CAN IT BE WORSE?
WHEN WE ESCAPED FROM HERE A LITTLE OVER 1000 YEARS AGO... SOMETHING ELSE MOVED IN. THEY SENSED OUR MOVEMENTS... THEY KNOW WE'RE HERE...
AND THEY ARE COMING FOR US!

END CHAPTER ONE

THE UNDERWATER CITY
CHAPTER TWO

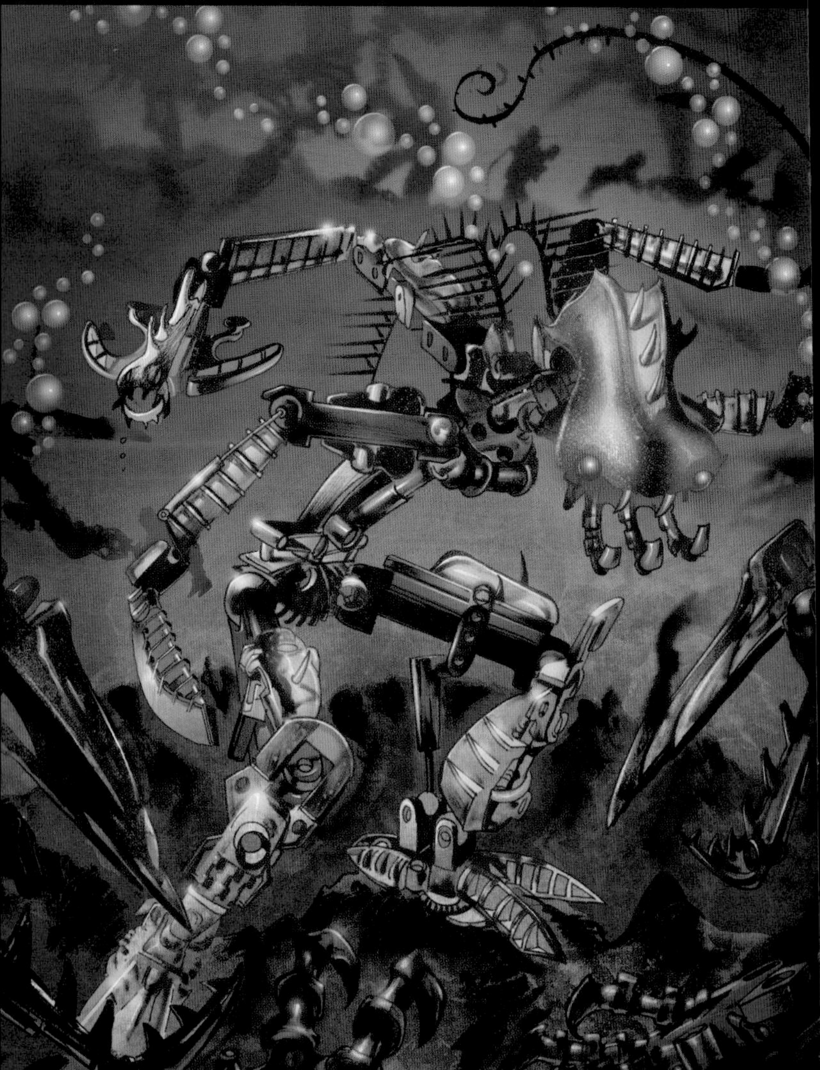

“Sea of Darkness”

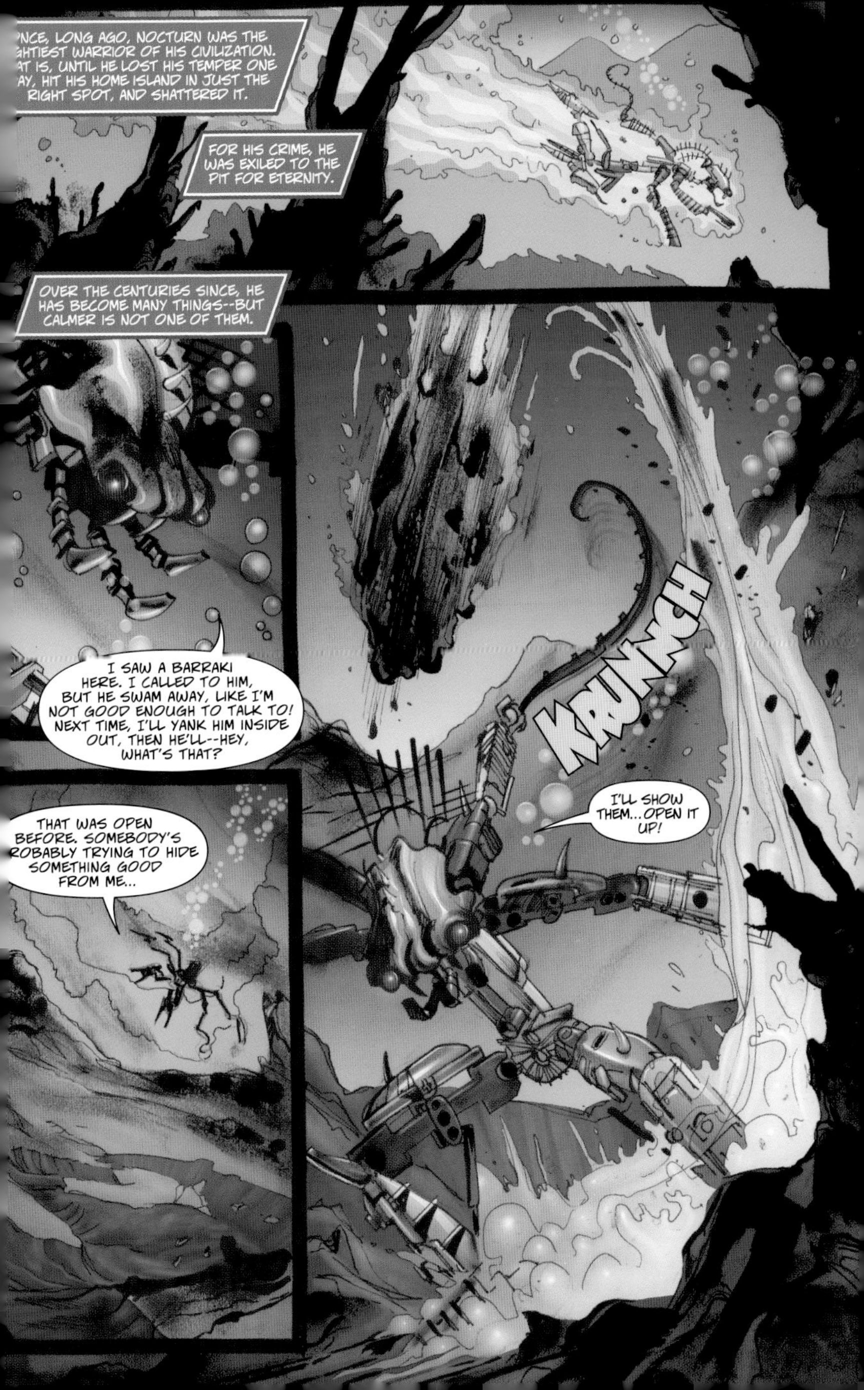

ONCE, LONG AGO, NOCTURN WAS THE MIGHTIEST WARRIOR OF HIS CIVILIZATION. THAT IS, UNTIL HE LOST HIS TEMPER ONE DAY, HIT HIS HOME ISLAND IN JUST THE RIGHT SPOT, AND SHATTERED IT.
FOR HIS CRIME, HE WAS EXILED TO THE PIT FOR ETERNITY.
OVER THE CENTURIES SINCE, HE HAS BECOME MANY THINGS--BUT CALMER IS NOT ONE OF THEM.
I SAW A BARRAKI HERE. I CALLED TO HIM, BUT HE SWAM AWAY, LIKE I'M NOT GOOD ENOUGH TO TALK TO! NEXT TIME, I'LL YANK HIM INSIDE OUT, THEN HE'LL--HEY, WHAT'S THAT?
THAT WAS OPEN BEFORE. SOMEBODY'S PROBABLY TRYING TO HIDE SOMETHING GOOD FROM ME...
I'LL SHOW THEM...OPEN IT UP!
KRUNCH

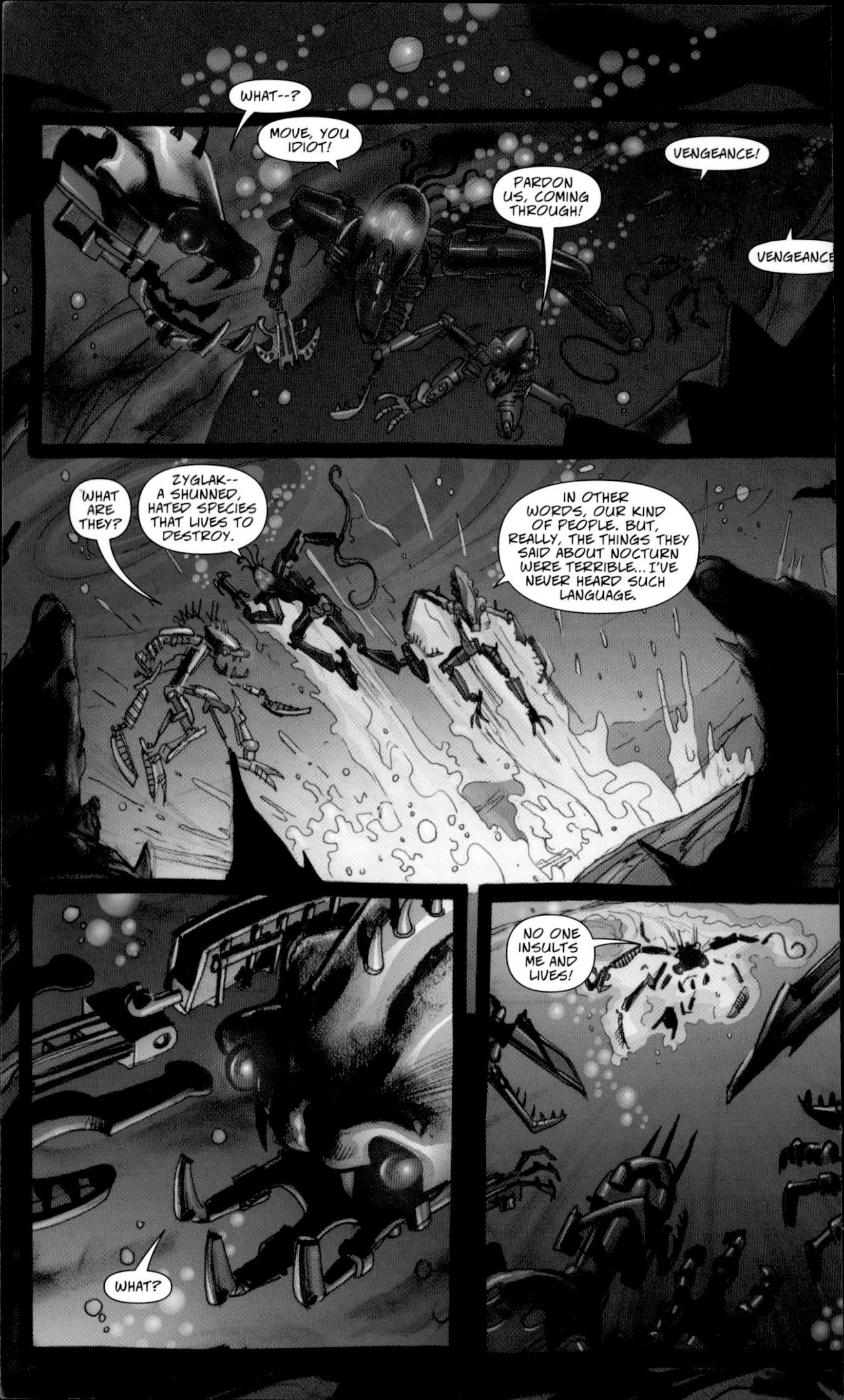
WHAT--?
MOVE, YOU IDIOT!
PARDON US, COMING THROUGH!
VENGEANCE!
VENGEANCE
WHAT ARE THEY?
ZYGLAK-- A SHUNNED, HATED SPECIES THAT LIVES TO DESTROY.
IN OTHER WORDS, OUR KIND OF PEOPLE. BUT, REALLY, THE THINGS THEY SAID ABOUT NOCTURN WERE TERRIBLE... I'VE NEVER HEARD SUCH LANGUAGE.
WHAT?
NO ONE INSULTS ME AND LIVES!

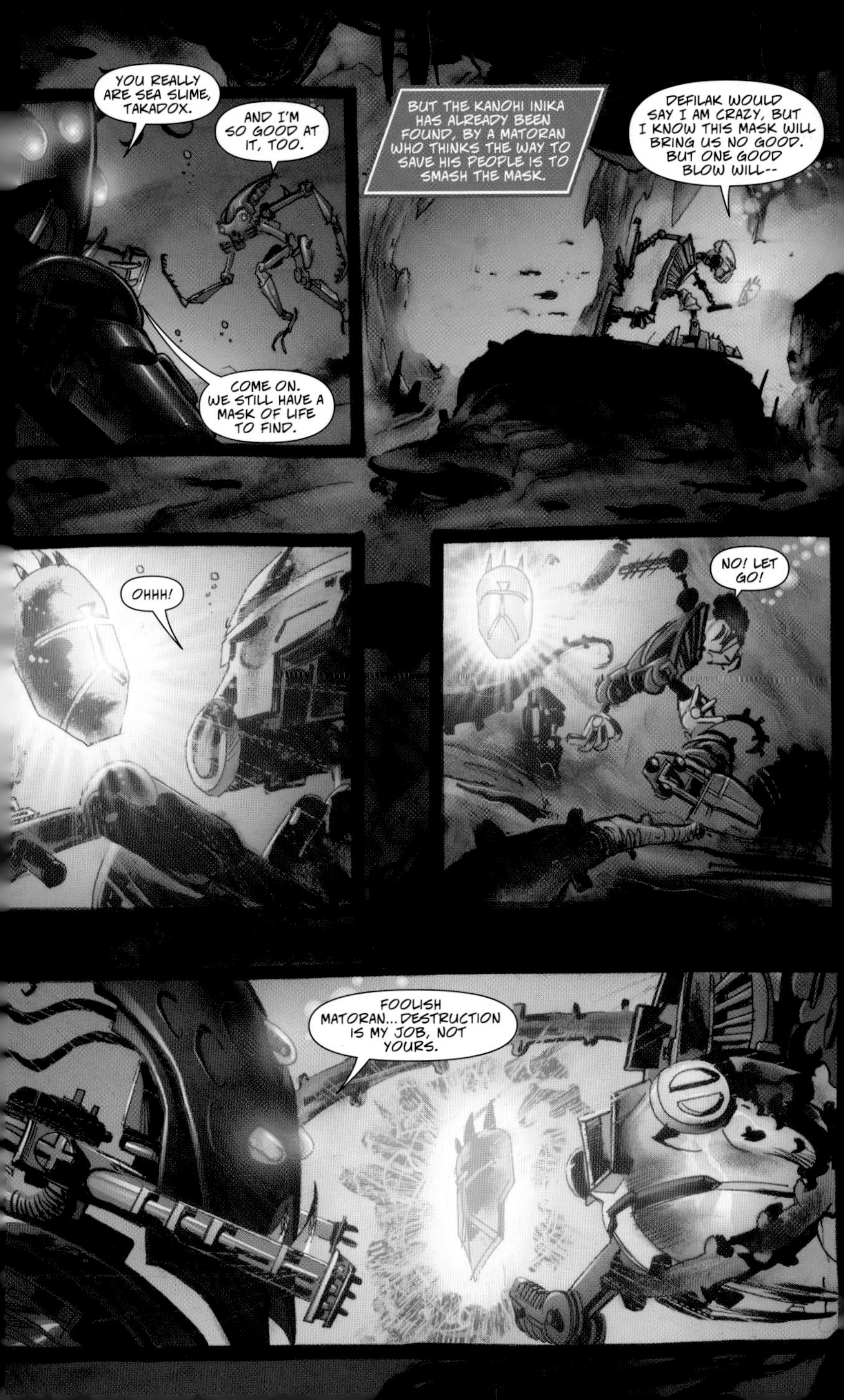
YOU REALLY ARE SEA SLIME, TAKADOX.
AND I'M SO GOOD AT IT, TOO.
COME ON. WE STILL HAVE A MASK OF LIFE TO FIND.
BUT THE KANOHI INIKA HAS ALREADY BEEN FOUND, BY A MATORAN WHO THINKS THE WAY TO SAVE HIS PEOPLE IS TO SMASH THE MASK.
DEFILAK WOULD SAY I AM CRAZY, BUT I KNOW THIS MASK WILL BRING US NO GOOD. BUT ONE GOOD BLOW WILL--
OHHH!
NO! LET GO!
FOOLISH MATORAN...DESTRUCTION IS MY JOB, NOT YOURS.

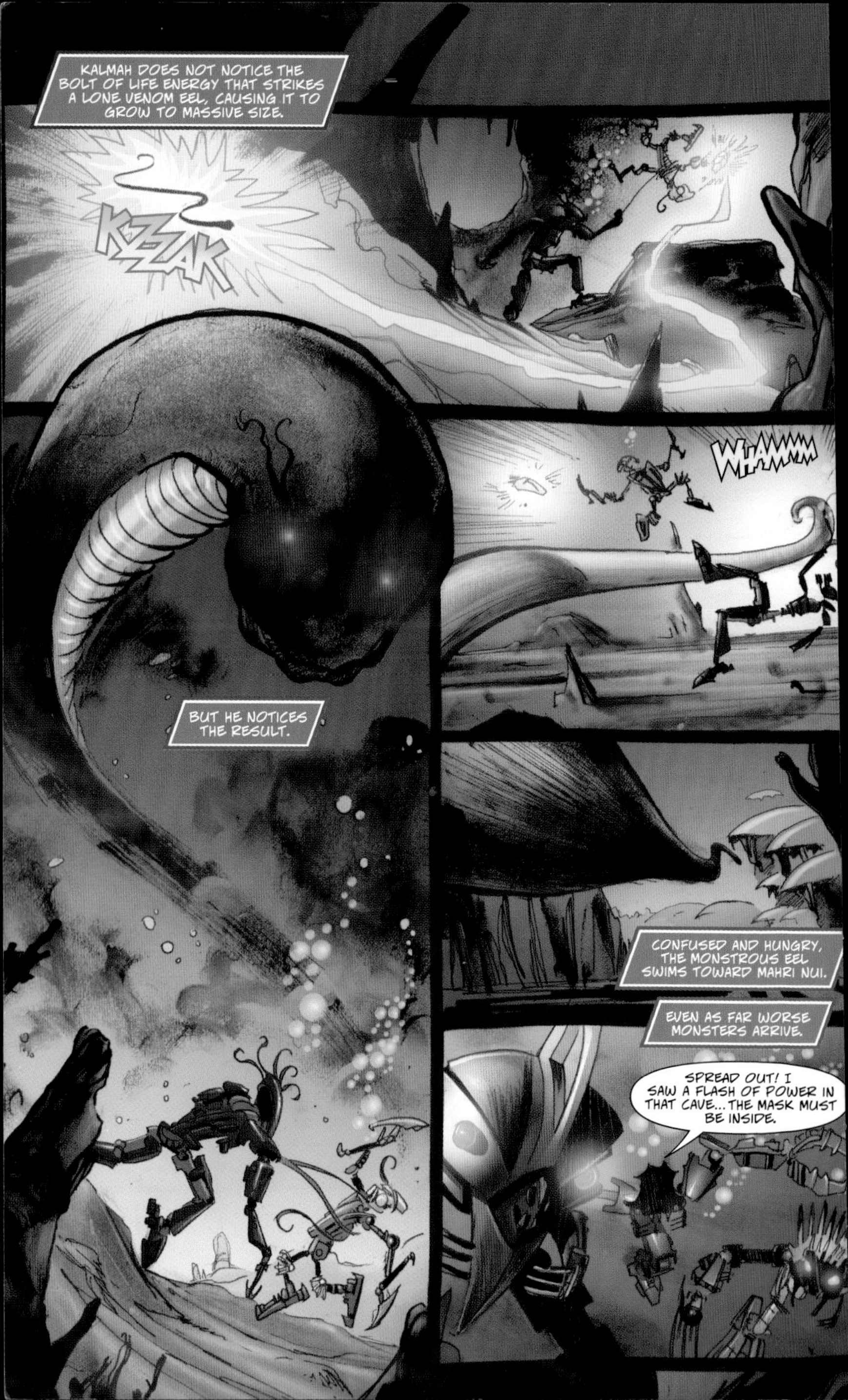
KALMAH DOES NOT NOTICE THE BOLT OF LIFE ENERGY THAT STRIKES A LONE VENOM EEL, CAUSING IT TO GROW TO MASSIVE SIZE.
KZZAK
BUT HE NOTICES THE RESULT.
WHAMMM
CONFUSED AND HUNGRY, THE MONSTROUS EEL SWIMS TOWARD MAHRI NUI.
EVEN AS FAR WORSE MONSTERS ARRIVE.
SPREAD OUT! I SAW A FLASH OF POWER IN THAT CAVE... THE MASK MUST BE INSIDE.

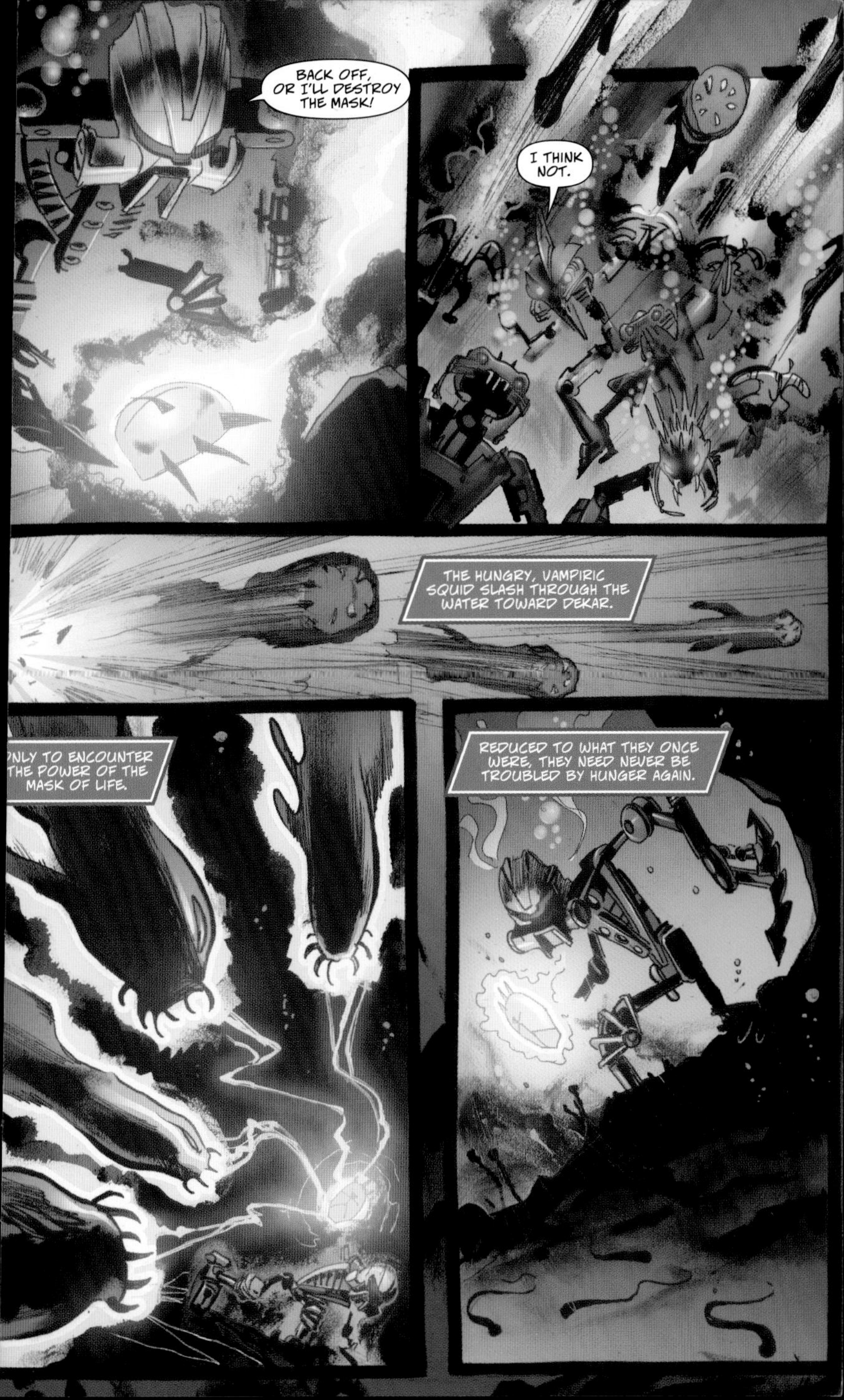
BACK OFF, OR I'LL DESTROY THE MASK!
I THINK NOT.
THE HUNGRY, VAMPIRIC SQUID SLASH THROUGH THE WATER TOWARD DEKAR.
ONLY TO ENCOUNTER THE POWER OF THE MASK OF LIFE.
REDUCED TO WHAT THEY ONCE WERE, THEY NEED NEVER BE TROUBLED BY HUNGER AGAIN.

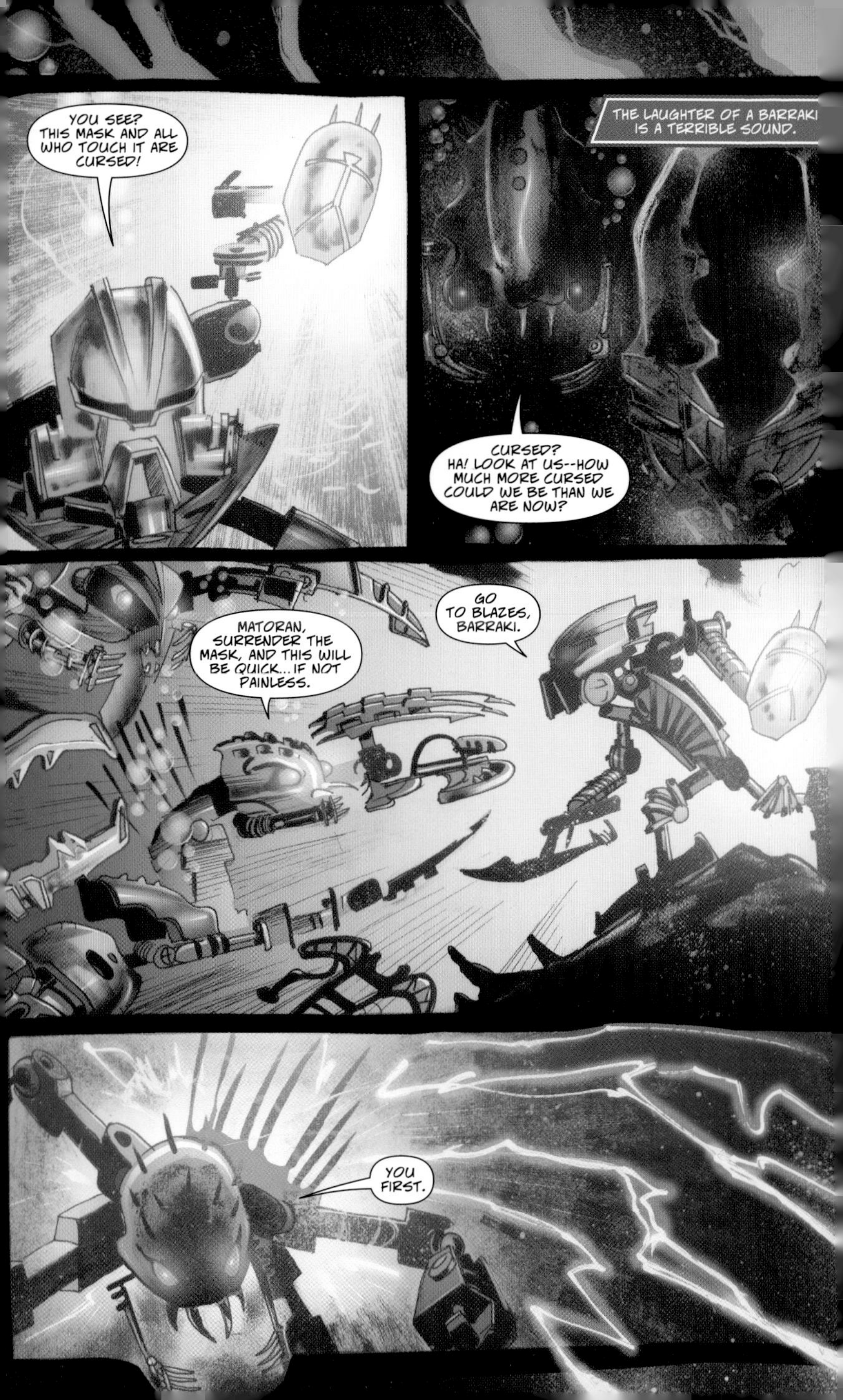
YOU SEE? THIS MASK AND ALL WHO TOUCH IT ARE CURSED!
THE LAUGHTER OF A BARRAKI IS A TERRIBLE SOUND.
CURSED? HA! LOOK AT US--HOW MUCH MORE CURSED COULD WE BE THAN WE ARE NOW?
MATORAN, SURRENDER THE MASK, AND THIS WILL BE QUICK... IF NOT PAINLESS.
GO TO BLAZES, BARRAKI.
YOU FIRST.

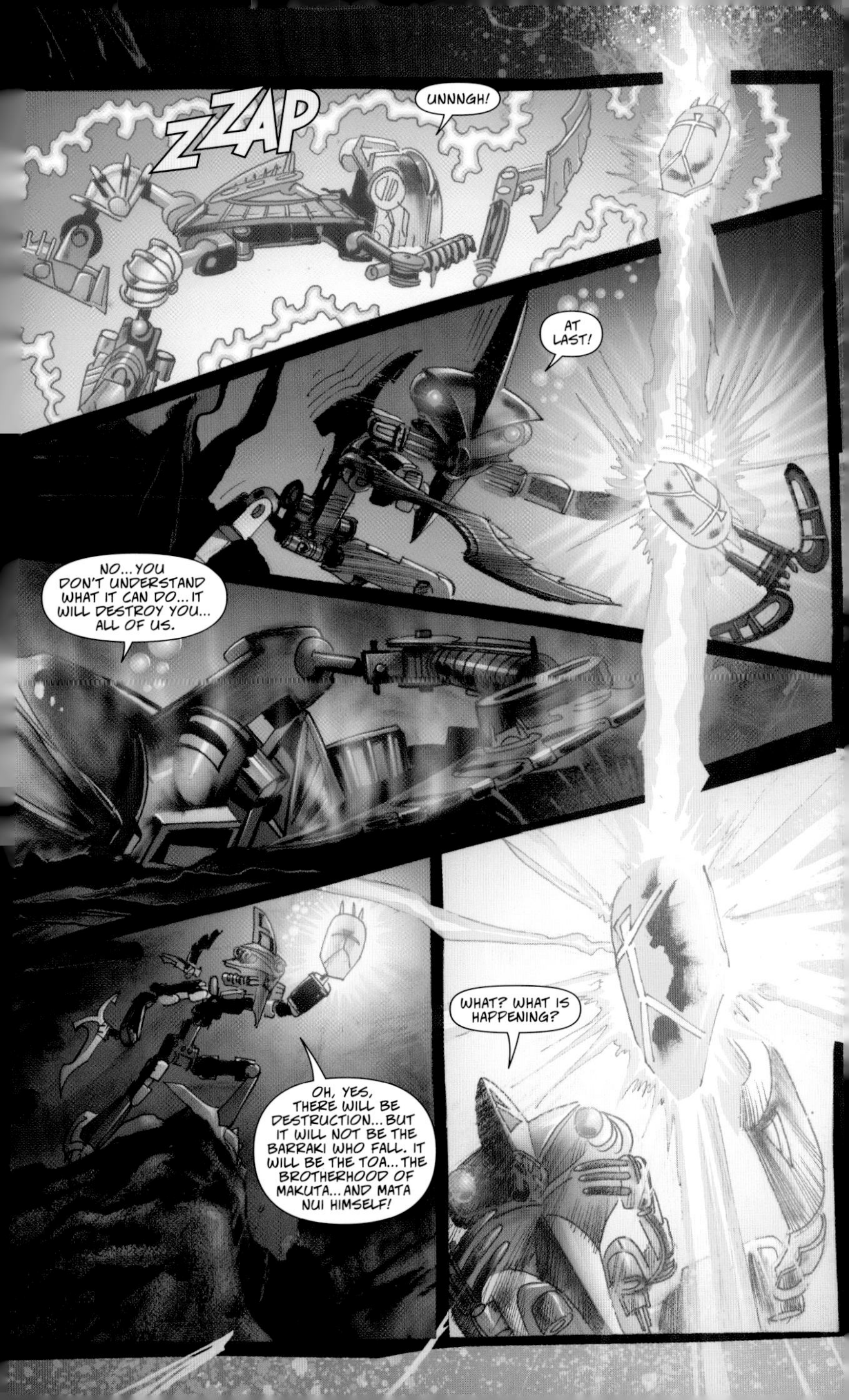
ZZAP
UNNNGH!
AT LAST!
NO... YOU DON'T UNDERSTAND WHAT IT CAN DO... IT WILL DESTROY YOU... ALL OF US.
OH, YES, THERE WILL BE DESTRUCTION... BUT IT WILL NOT BE THE BARRAKI WHO FALL. IT WILL BE THE TOA... THE BROTHERHOOD OF MAKUTA... AND MATA NUI HIMSELF!
WHAT? WHAT IS HAPPENING?

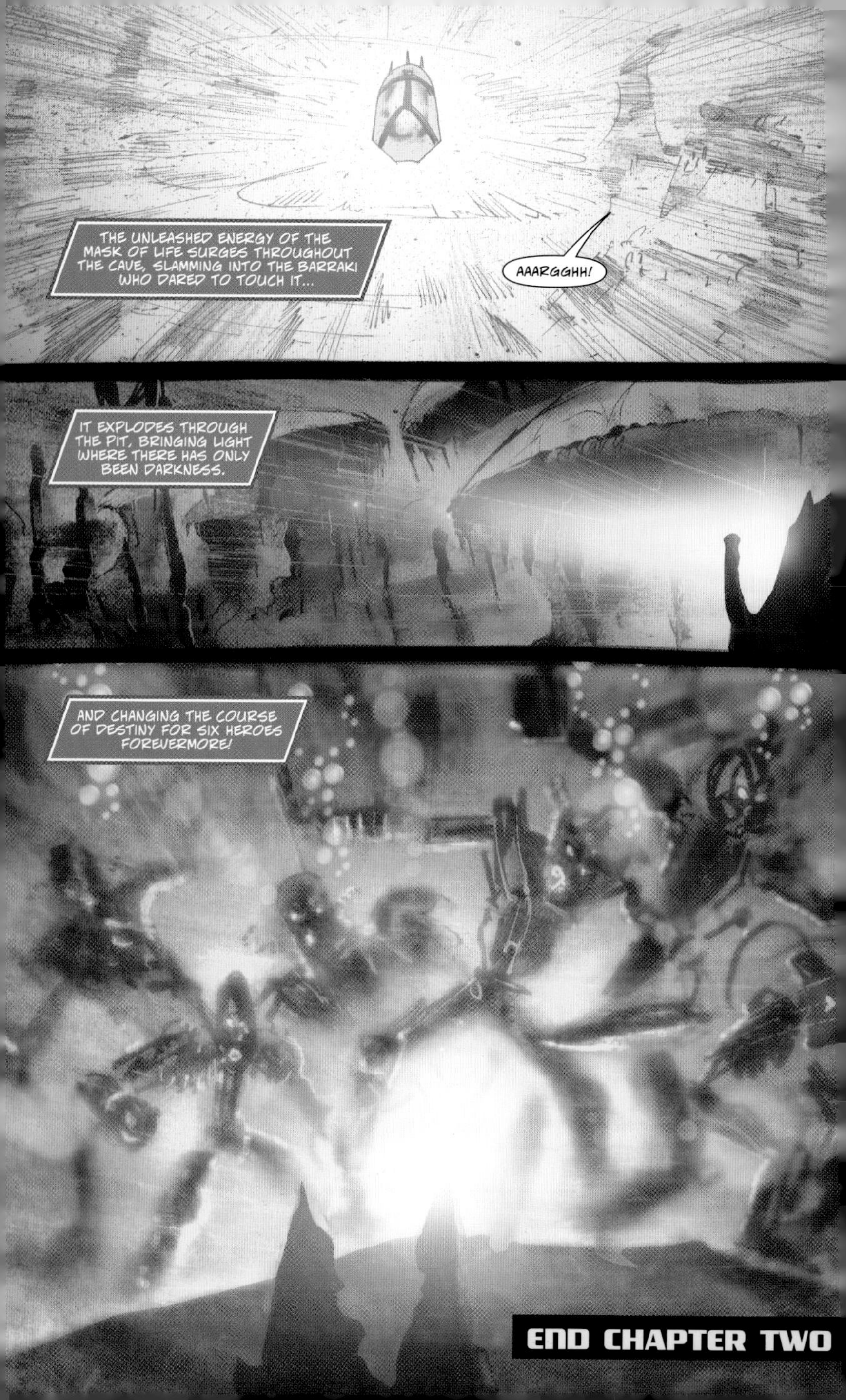
THE UNLEASHED ENERGY OF THE MASK OF LIFE SURGES THROUGHOUT THE CAVE, SLAMMING INTO THE BARRAKI WHO DARED TO TOUCH IT...
AAARGGHH!
IT EXPLODES THROUGH THE PIT, BRINGING LIGHT WHERE THERE HAS ONLY BEEN DARKNESS.
AND CHANGING THE COURSE OF DESTINY FOR SIX HEROES FOREVERMORE!
END CHAPTER TWO

THE UNDERWATER CITY
CHAPTER THREE

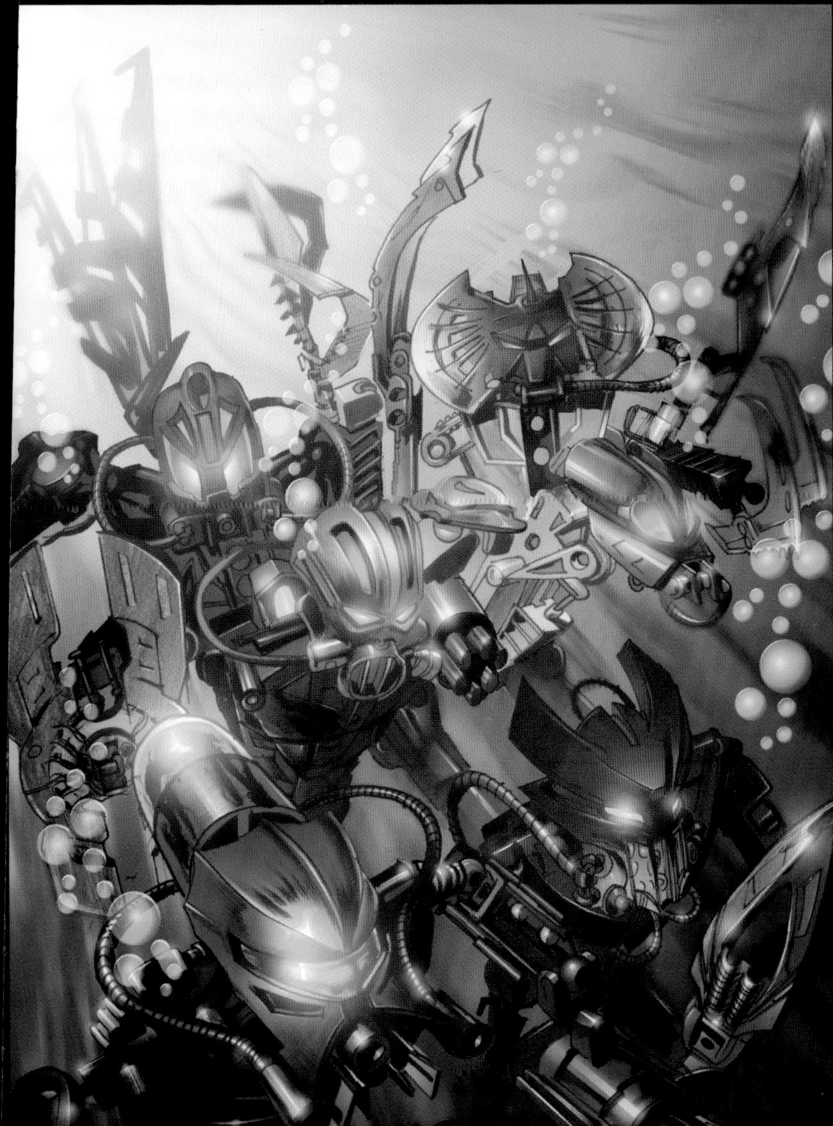

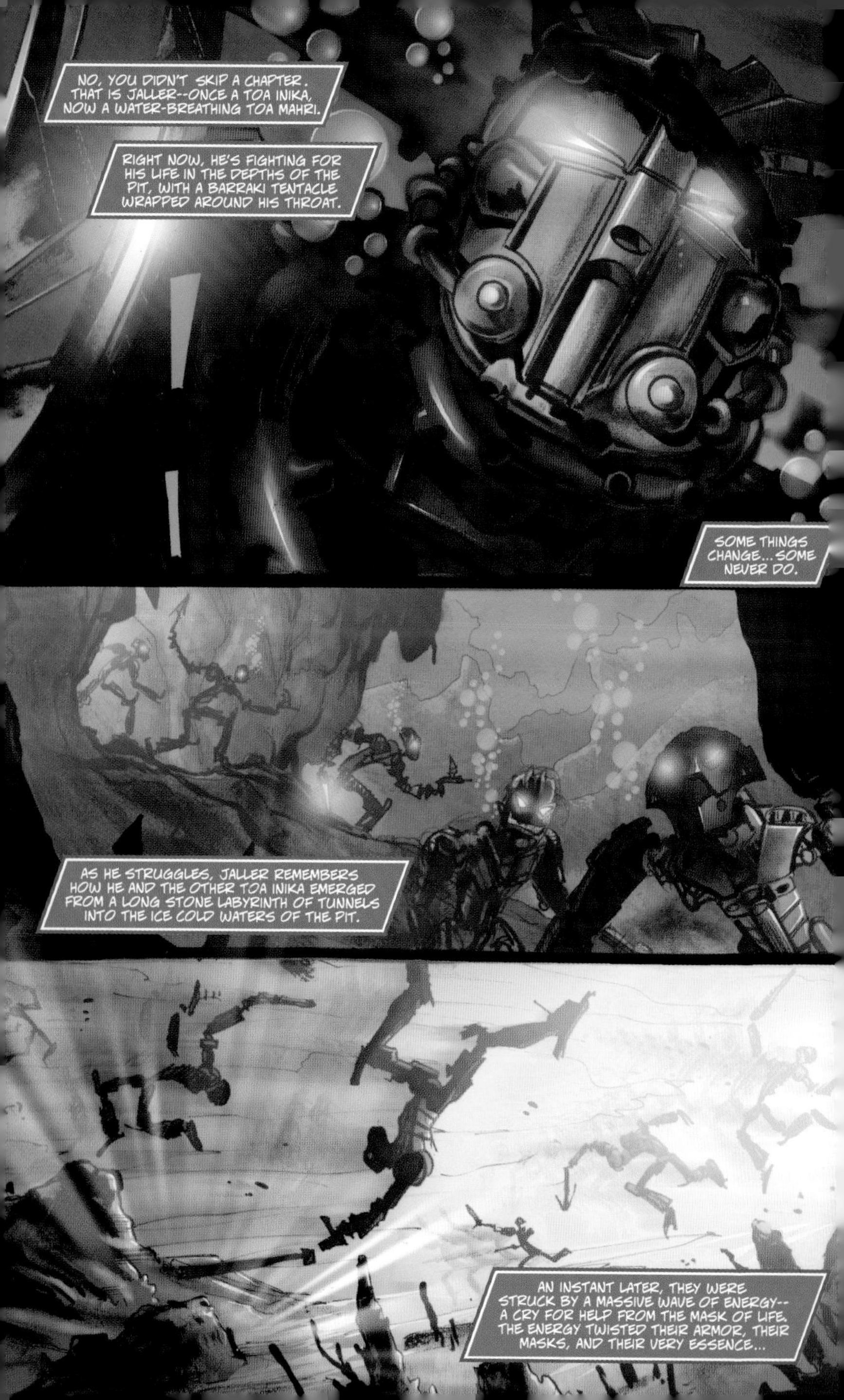
NO, YOU DIDN'T SKIP A CHAPTER. THAT IS JALLER--ONCE A TOA INIKA, NOW A WATER-BREATHING TOA MAHRI.
RIGHT NOW, HE'S FIGHTING FOR HIS LIFE IN THE DEPTHS OF THE PIT, WITH A BARRAKI TENTACLE WRAPPED AROUND HIS THROAT.
SOME THINGS CHANGE... SOME NEVER DO.
AS HE STRUGGLES, JALLER REMEMBERS HOW HE AND THE OTHER TOA INIKA EMERGED FROM A LONG STONE LABYRINTH OF TUNNELS INTO THE ICE COLD WATERS OF THE PIT.
AN INSTANT LATER, THEY WERE STRUCK BY A MASSIVE WAVE OF ENERGY-- A CRY FOR HELP FROM THE MASK OF LIFE. THE ENERGY TWISTED THEIR ARMOR, THEIR MASKS, AND THEIR VERY ESSENCE...

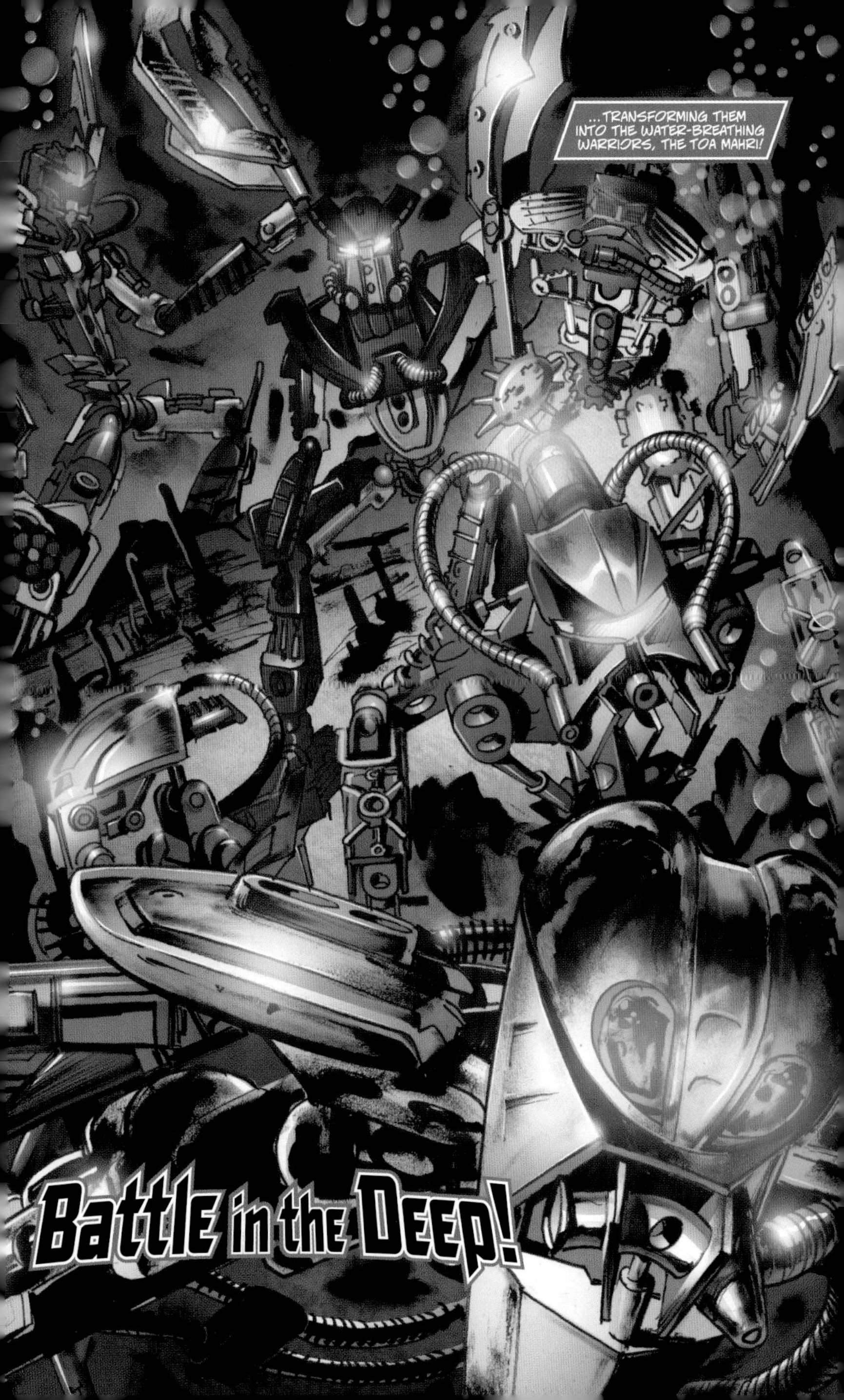
...TRANSFORMING THEM INTO THE WATER-BREATHING WARRIORS, THE TOA MAHRI!
Battle in the Deep!

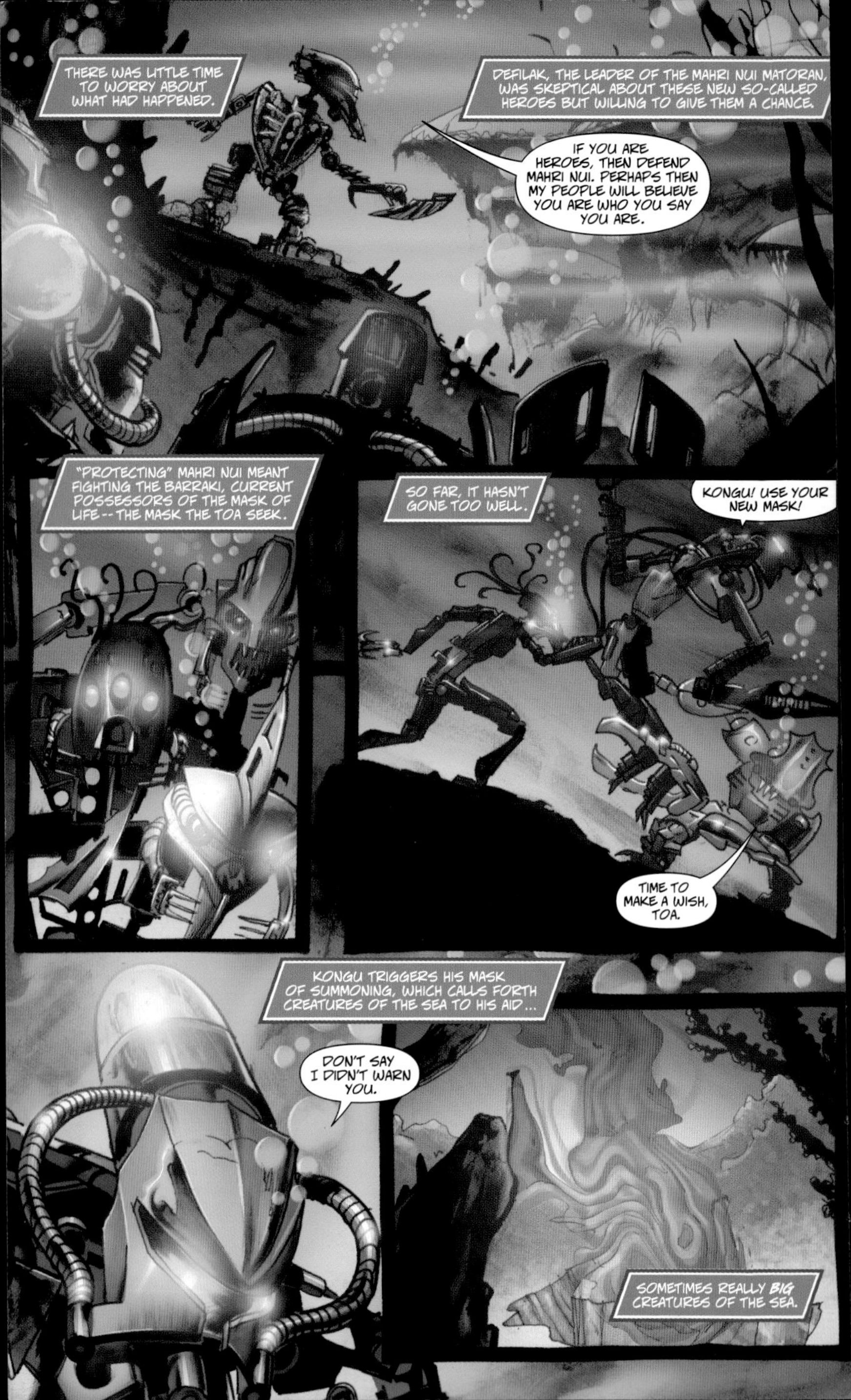
THERE WAS LITTLE TIME TO WORRY ABOUT WHAT HAD HAPPENED.
DEFILAK, THE LEADER OF THE MAHRI NUI MATORAN, WAS SKEPTICAL ABOUT THESE NEW SO-CALLED HEROES BUT WILLING TO GIVE THEM A CHANCE.
IF YOU ARE HEROES, THEN DEFEND MAHRI NUI. PERHAPS THEN MY PEOPLE WILL BELIEVE YOU ARE WHO YOU SAY YOU ARE.
"PROTECTING" MAHRI NUI MEANT FIGHTING THE BARRAKI, CURRENT POSSESSORS OF THE MASK OF LIFE -- THE MASK THE TOA SEEK.
SO FAR, IT HASN'T GONE TOO WELL.
KONGU! USE YOUR NEW MASK!
TIME TO MAKE A WISH, TOA.
KONGU TRIGGERS HIS MASK OF SUMMONING, WHICH CALLS FORTH CREATURES OF THE SEA TO HIS AID...
DON'T SAY I DIDN'T WARN YOU.
SOMETIMES REALLY *BIG* CREATURES OF THE SEA.

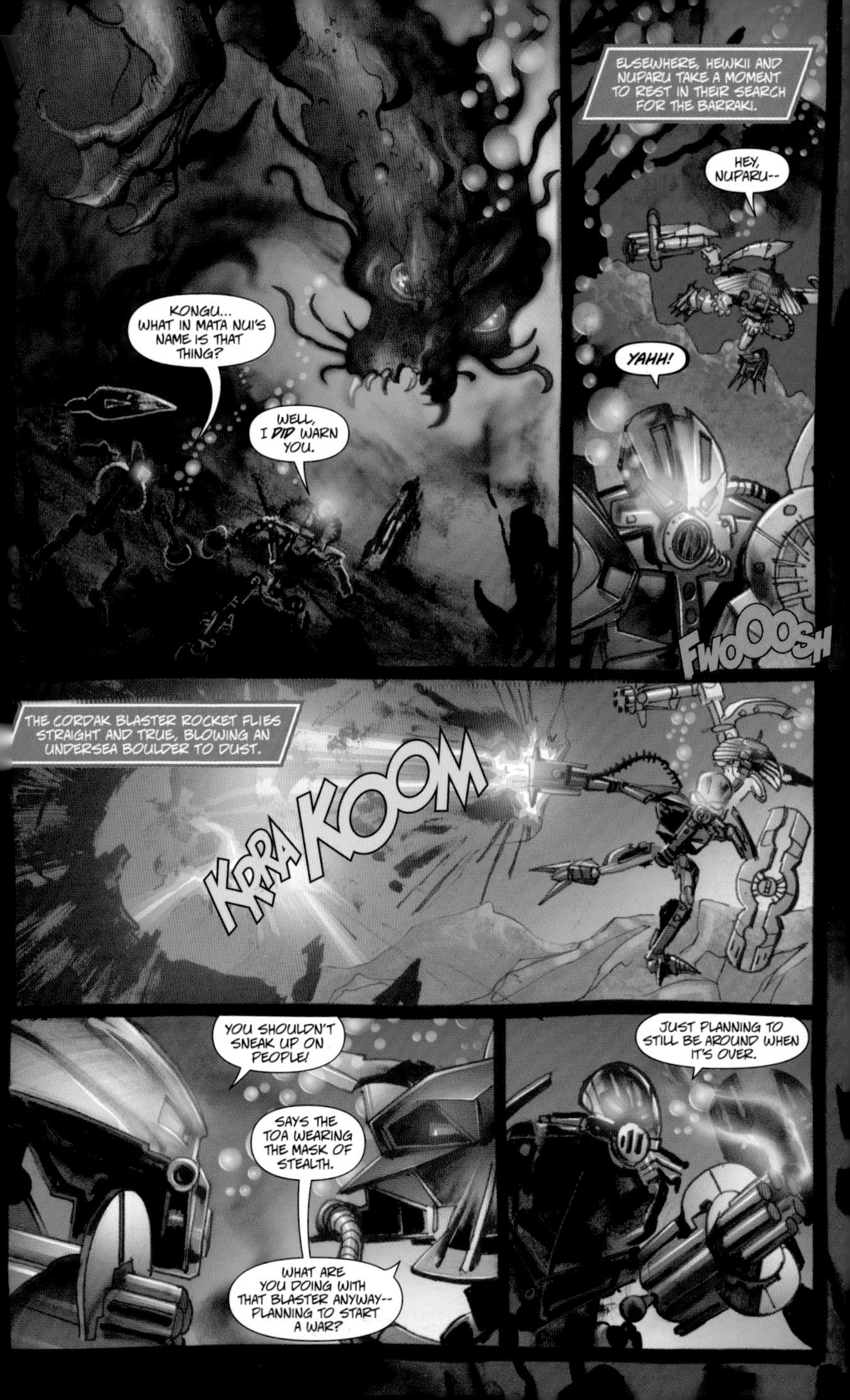
KONGU... WHAT IN MATA NUI'S NAME IS THAT THING?
WELL, I *DID* WARN YOU.
ELSEWHERE, HEWKII AND NUPARU TAKE A MOMENT TO REST IN THEIR SEARCH FOR THE BARRAKI.
HEY, NUPARU--
YAHH!
FWOOOOSH
THE CORDAK BLASTER ROCKET FLIES STRAIGHT AND TRUE, BLOWING AN UNDERSEA BOULDER TO DUST.
KRAKOOM
YOU SHOULDN'T SNEAK UP ON PEOPLE!
SAYS THE TOA WEARING THE MASK OF STEALTH.
WHAT ARE YOU DOING WITH THAT BLASTER ANYWAY-- PLANNING TO START A WAR?
JUST PLANNING TO STILL BE AROUND WHEN IT'S OVER.

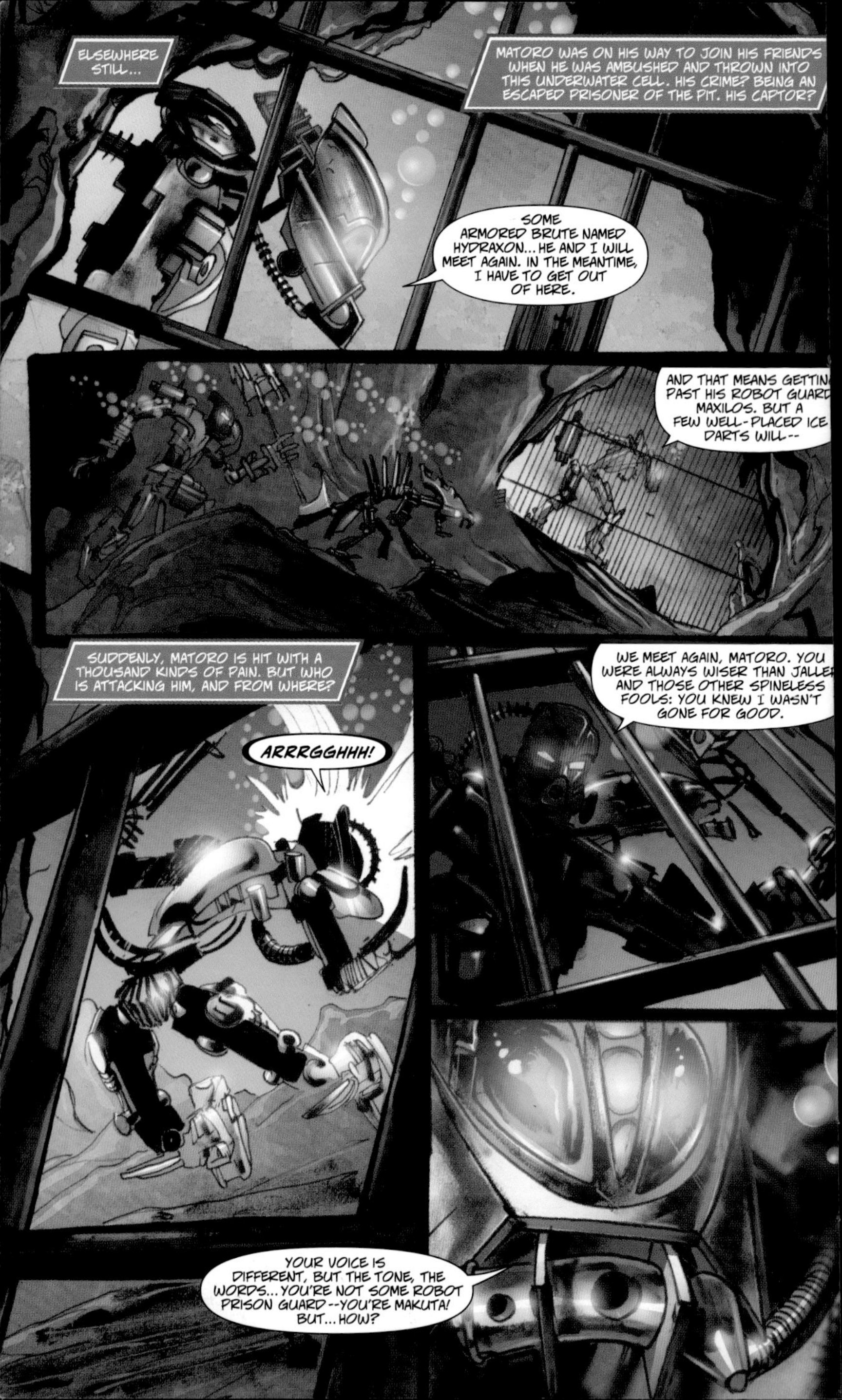

ELSEWHERE STILL...
MATORO WAS ON HIS WAY TO JOIN HIS FRIENDS WHEN HE WAS AMBUSHED AND THROWN INTO THIS UNDERWATER CELL. HIS CRIME? BEING AN ESCAPED PRISONER OF THE PIT. HIS CAPTOR?
SOME ARMORED BRUTE NAMED HYDRAXON... HE AND I WILL MEET AGAIN. IN THE MEANTIME, I HAVE TO GET OUT OF HERE.
AND THAT MEANS GETTIN PAST HIS ROBOT GUARD MAXILOS. BUT A FEW WELL-PLACED ICE DARTS WILL--
SUDDENLY, MATORO IS HIT WITH A THOUSAND KINDS OF PAIN. BUT WHO IS ATTACKING HIM, AND FROM WHERE?
ARRRGGHHH!
WE MEET AGAIN, MATORO. YOU WERE ALWAYS WISER THAN JALLER AND THOSE OTHER SPINELESS FOOLS: YOU KNEW I WASN'T GONE FOR GOOD.
YOUR VOICE IS DIFFERENT, BUT THE TONE, THE WORDS... YOU'RE NOT SOME ROBOT PRISON GUARD--YOU'RE MAKUTA! BUT... HOW?

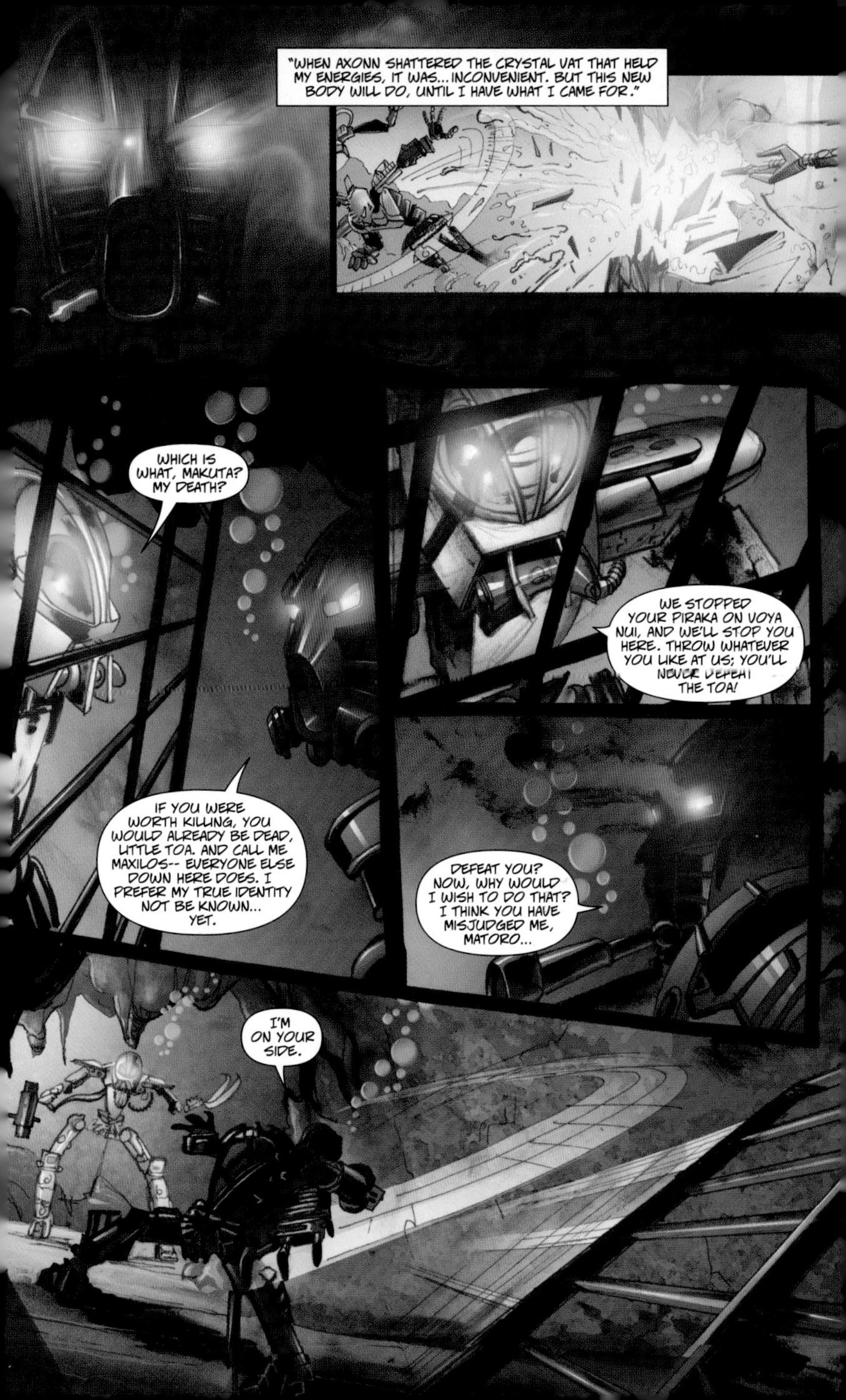
"WHEN AXONN SHATTERED THE CRYSTAL VAT THAT HELD MY ENERGIES, IT WAS... INCONVENIENT. BUT THIS NEW BODY WILL DO, UNTIL I HAVE WHAT I CAME FOR."
WHICH IS WHAT, MAKUTA? MY DEATH?
WE STOPPED YOUR PIRAKA ON VOYA NUI, AND WE'LL STOP YOU HERE. THROW WHATEVER YOU LIKE AT US; YOU'LL NEVER DEFEAT THE TOA!
IF YOU WERE WORTH KILLING, YOU WOULD ALREADY BE DEAD, LITTLE TOA. AND CALL ME MAXILOS-- EVERYONE ELSE DOWN HERE DOES. I PREFER MY TRUE IDENTITY NOT BE KNOWN... YET.
DEFEAT YOU? NOW, WHY WOULD I WISH TO DO THAT? I THINK YOU HAVE MISJUDGED ME, MATORO...
I'M ON YOUR SIDE.

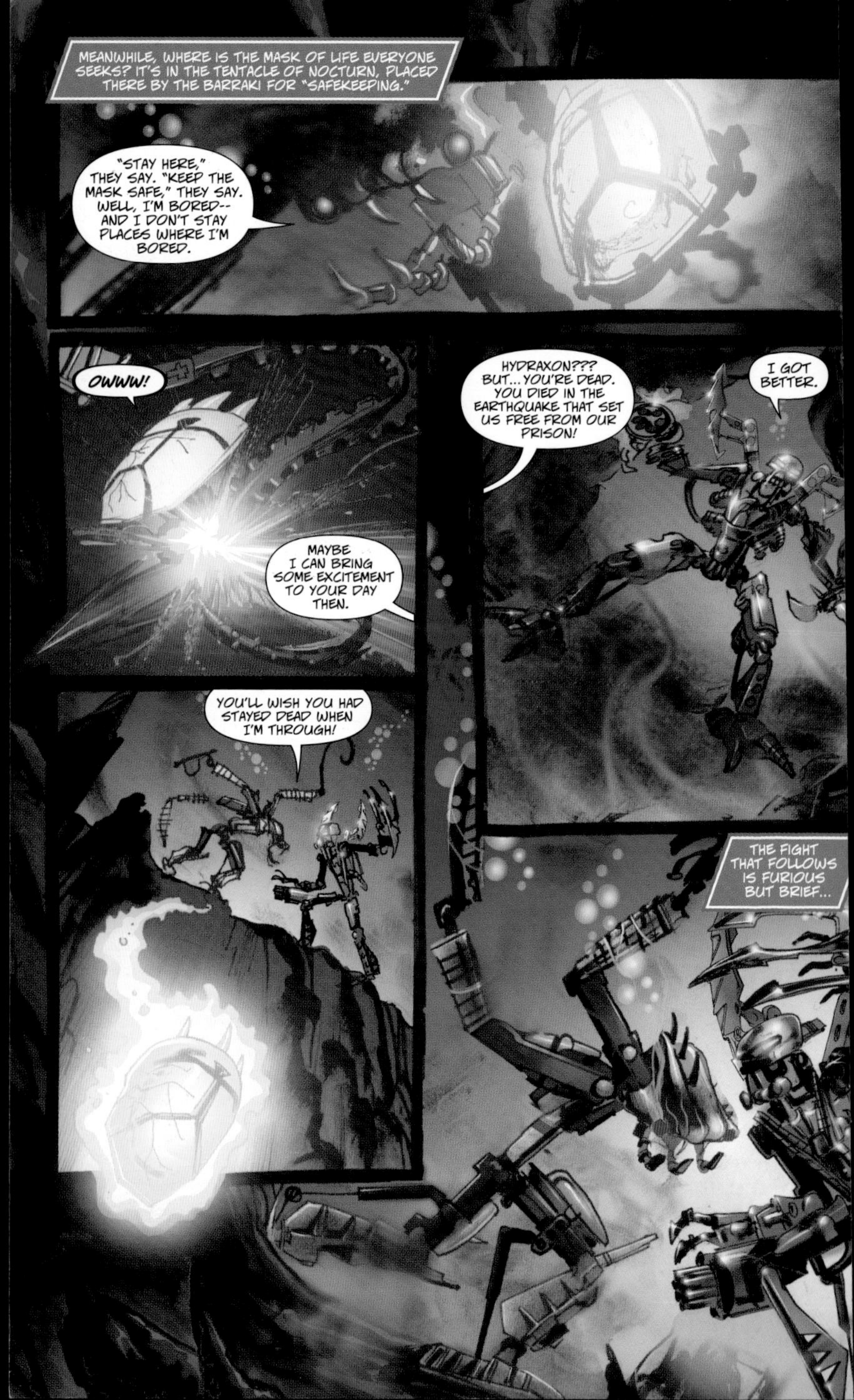
MEANWHILE, WHERE IS THE MASK OF LIFE EVERYONE SEEKS? IT'S IN THE TENTACLE OF NOCTURN, PLACED THERE BY THE BARRAKI FOR "SAFEKEEPING."
"STAY HERE," THEY SAY. "KEEP THE MASK SAFE," THEY SAY. WELL, I'M BORED-- AND I DON'T STAY PLACES WHERE I'M BORED.
OWWW!
MAYBE I CAN BRING SOME EXCITEMENT TO YOUR DAY THEN.
HYDRAXON??? BUT... YOU'RE DEAD. YOU DIED IN THE EARTHQUAKE THAT SET US FREE FROM OUR PRISON!
I GOT BETTER.
YOU'LL WISH YOU HAD STAYED DEAD WHEN I'M THROUGH!
THE FIGHT THAT FOLLOWS IS FURIOUS BUT BRIEF...

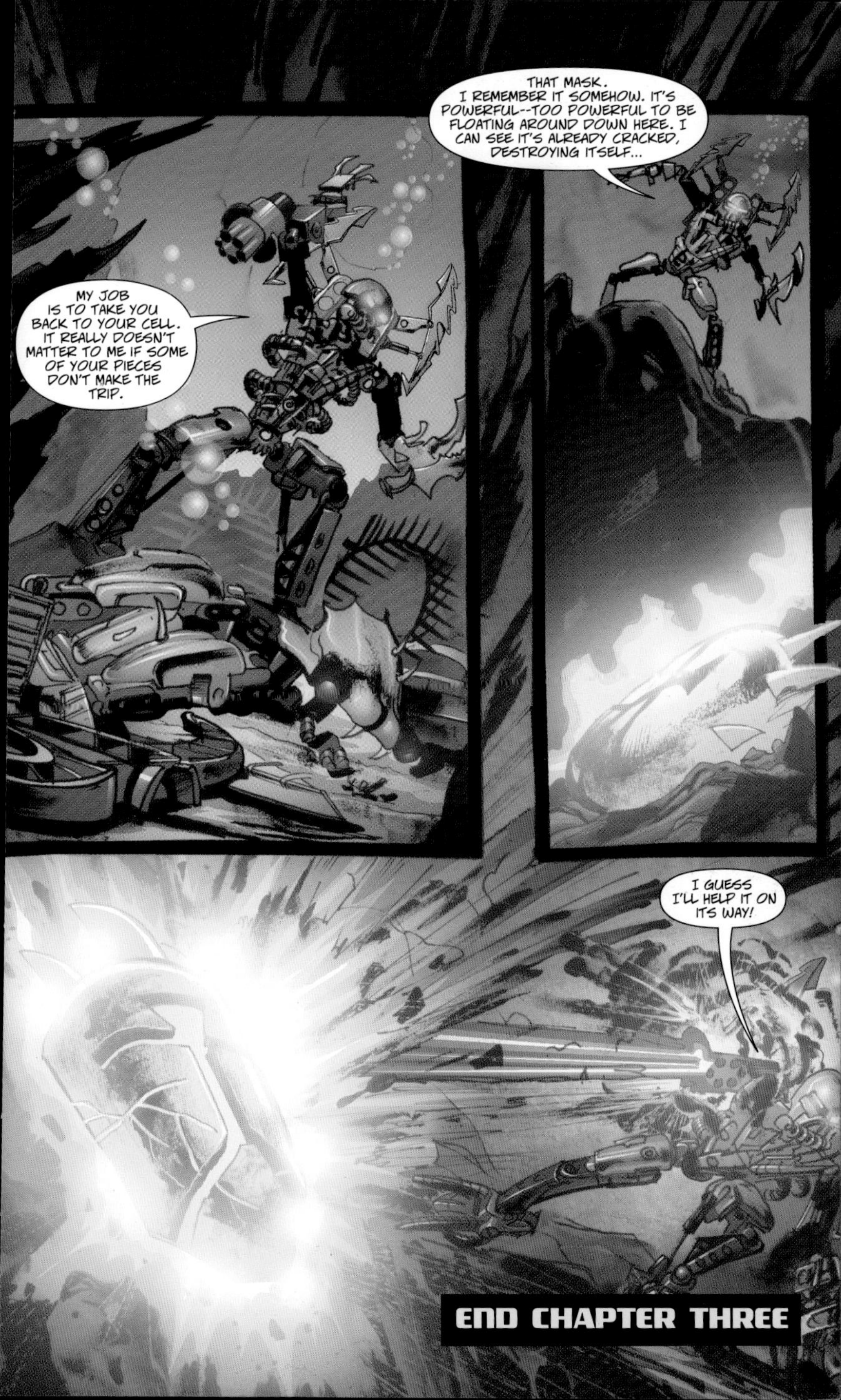
MY JOB IS TO TAKE YOU BACK TO YOUR CELL. IT REALLY DOESN'T MATTER TO ME IF SOME OF YOUR PIECES DON'T MAKE THE TRIP.
THAT MASK. I REMEMBER IT SOMEHOW. IT'S POWERFUL--TOO POWERFUL TO BE FLOATING AROUND DOWN HERE. I CAN SEE IT'S ALREADY CRACKED, DESTROYING ITSELF...
I GUESS I'LL HELP IT ON ITS WAY!
END CHAPTER THREE

THE UNDERWATER CITY
CHAPTER FOUR

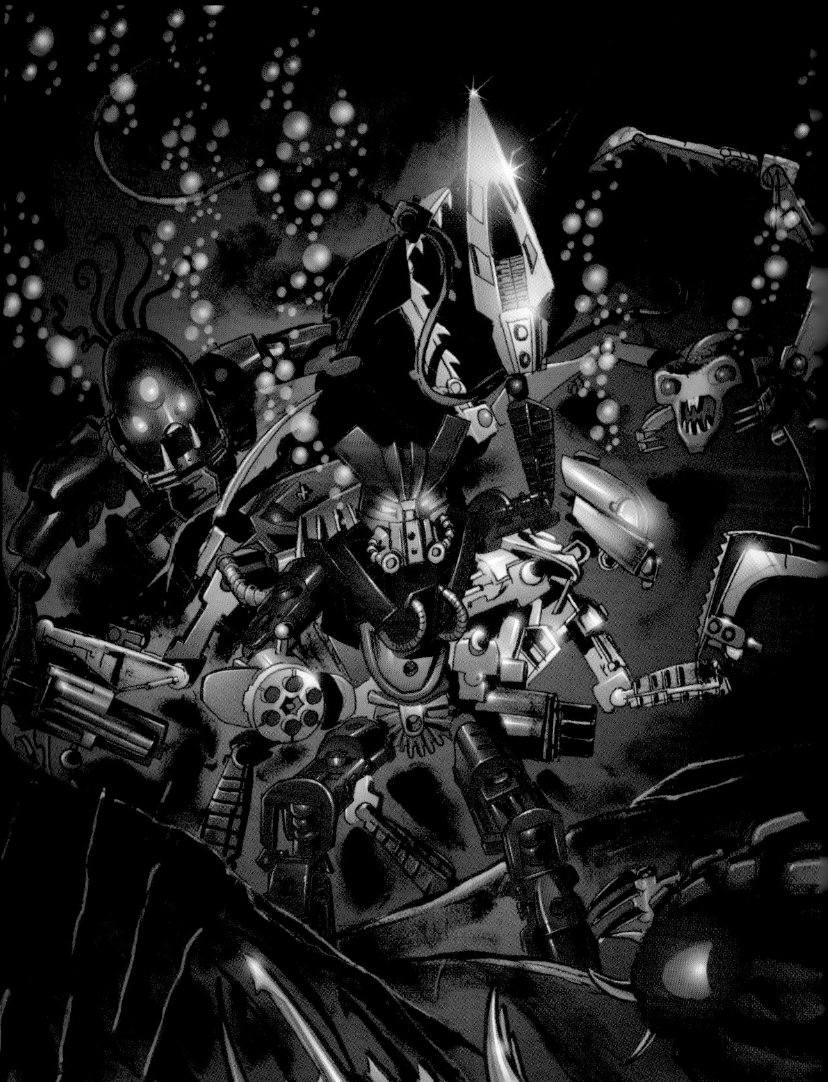

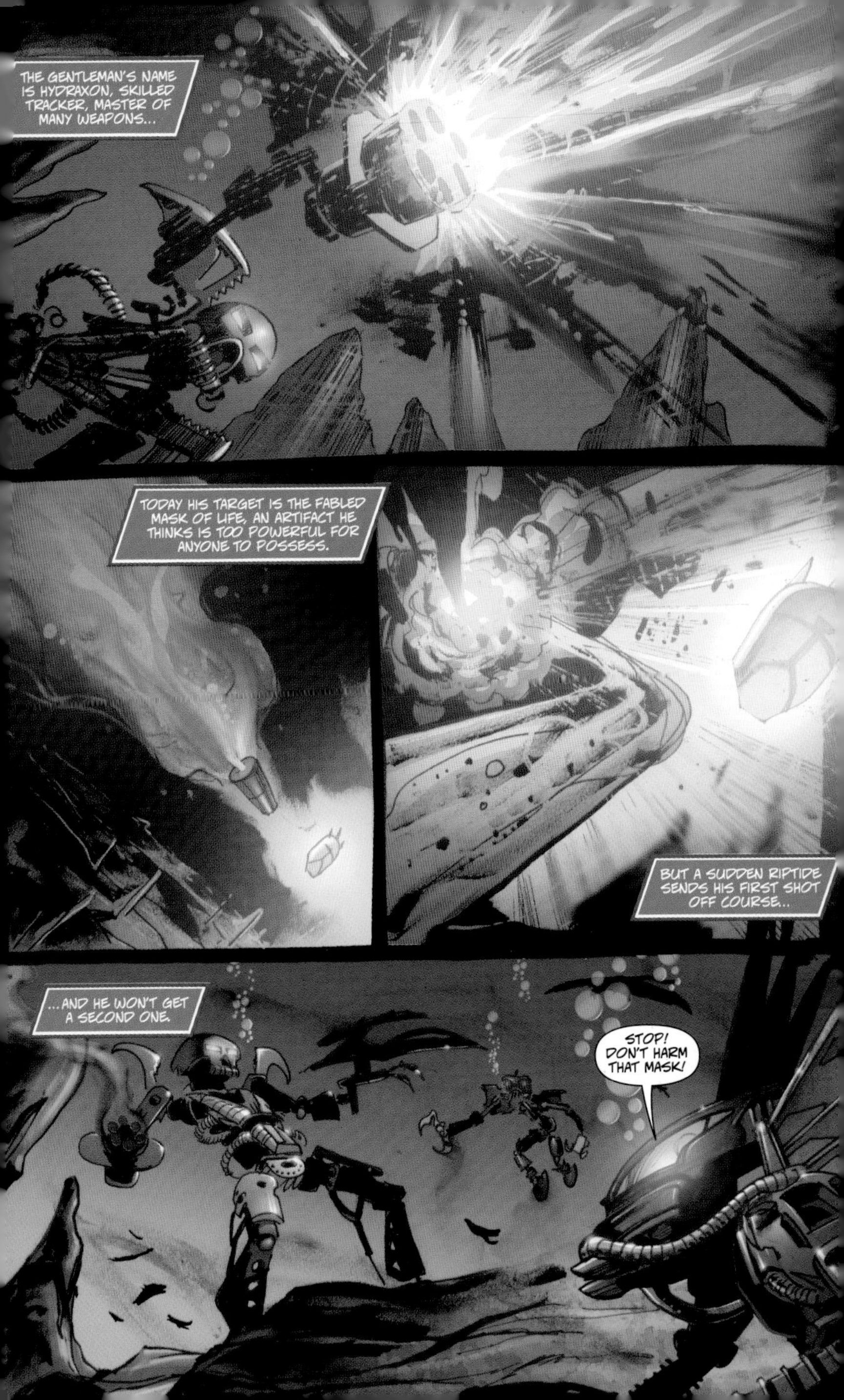
THE GENTLEMAN'S NAME IS HYDRAXON, SKILLED TRACKER, MASTER OF MANY WEAPONS...
TODAY HIS TARGET IS THE FABLED MASK OF LIFE, AN ARTIFACT HE THINKS IS TOO POWERFUL FOR ANYONE TO POSSESS.
BUT A SUDDEN RIPTIDE SENDS HIS FIRST SHOT OFF COURSE...
...AND HE WON'T GET A SECOND ONE.
STOP! DON'T HARM THAT MASK!

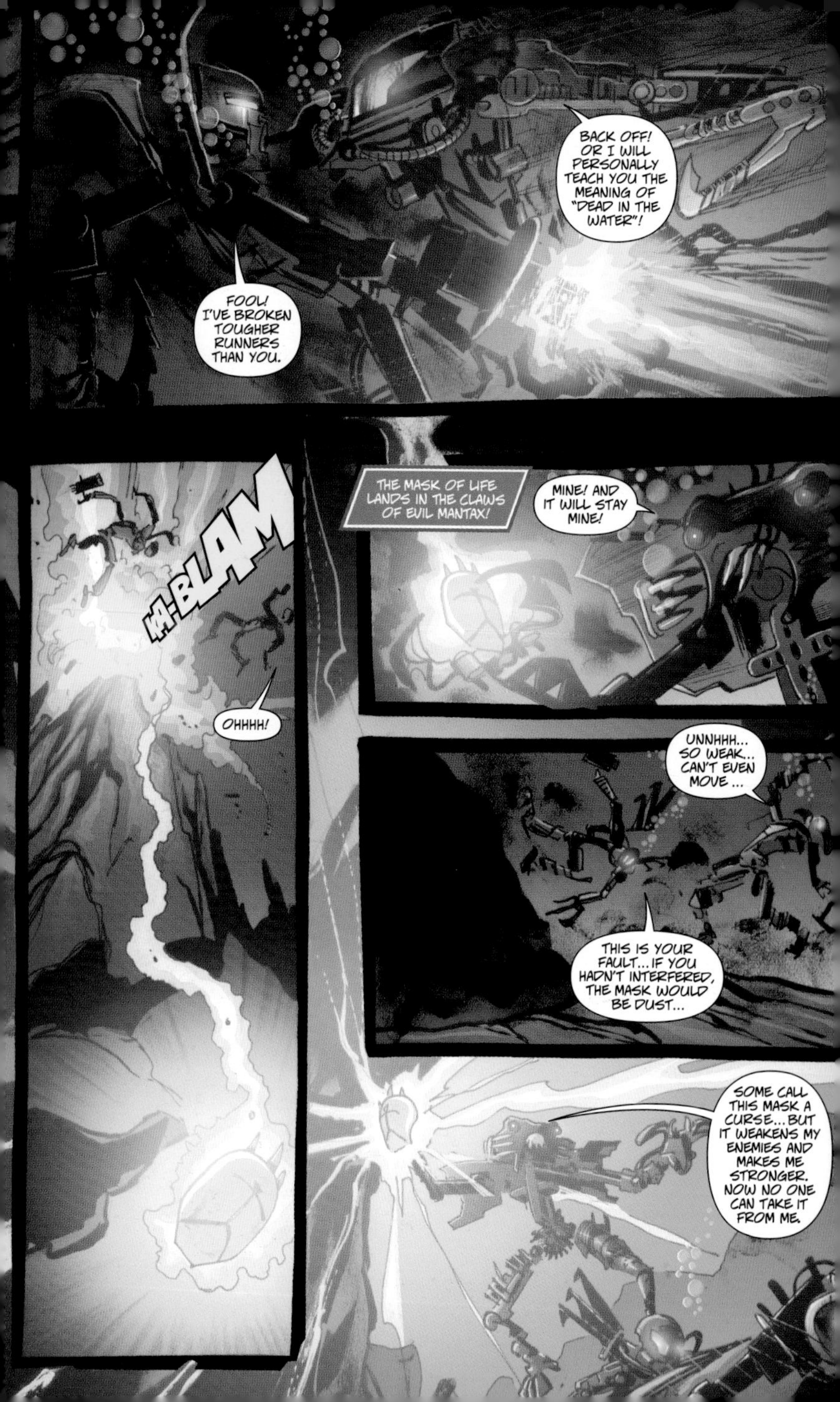
BACK OFF! OR I WILL PERSONALLY TEACH YOU THE MEANING OF "DEAD IN THE WATER"!
FOOL! I'VE BROKEN TOUGHER RUNNERS THAN YOU.
KA-BLAM!
OHHHH!
THE MASK OF LIFE LANDS IN THE CLAWS OF EVIL MANTAX!
MINE! AND IT WILL STAY MINE!
UNNHHH... SO WEAK... CAN'T EVEN MOVE...
THIS IS YOUR FAULT... IF YOU HADN'T INTERFERED, THE MASK WOULD BE DUST...
SOME CALL THIS MASK A CURSE... BUT IT WEAKENS MY ENEMIES AND MAKES ME STRONGER. NOW NO ONE CAN TAKE IT FROM ME.

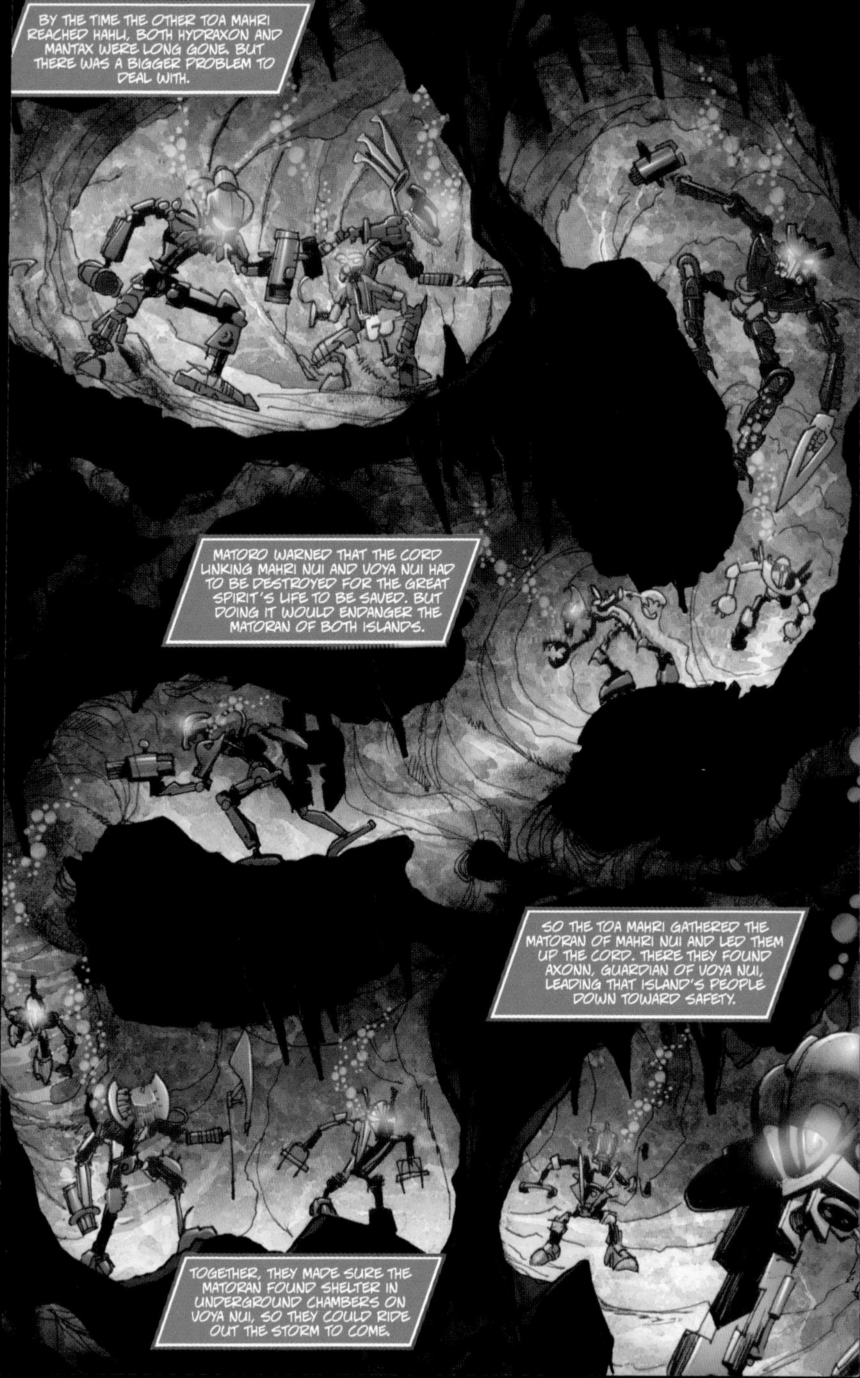
BY THE TIME THE OTHER TOA MAHRI REACHED HAHLI, BOTH HYDRAXON AND MANTAX WERE LONG GONE. BUT THERE WAS A BIGGER PROBLEM TO DEAL WITH.
MATORO WARNED THAT THE CORD LINKING MAHRI NUI AND VOYA NUI HAD TO BE DESTROYED FOR THE GREAT SPIRIT'S LIFE TO BE SAVED. BUT DOING IT WOULD ENDANGER THE MATORAN OF BOTH ISLANDS.
SO THE TOA MAHRI GATHERED THE MATORAN OF MAHRI NUI AND LED THEM UP THE CORD. THERE THEY FOUND AXONN, GUARDIAN OF VOYA NUI, LEADING THAT ISLAND'S PEOPLE DOWN TOWARD SAFETY.
TOGETHER, THEY MADE SURE THE MATORAN FOUND SHELTER IN UNDERGROUND CHAMBERS ON VOYA NUI, SO THEY COULD RIDE OUT THE STORM TO COME.

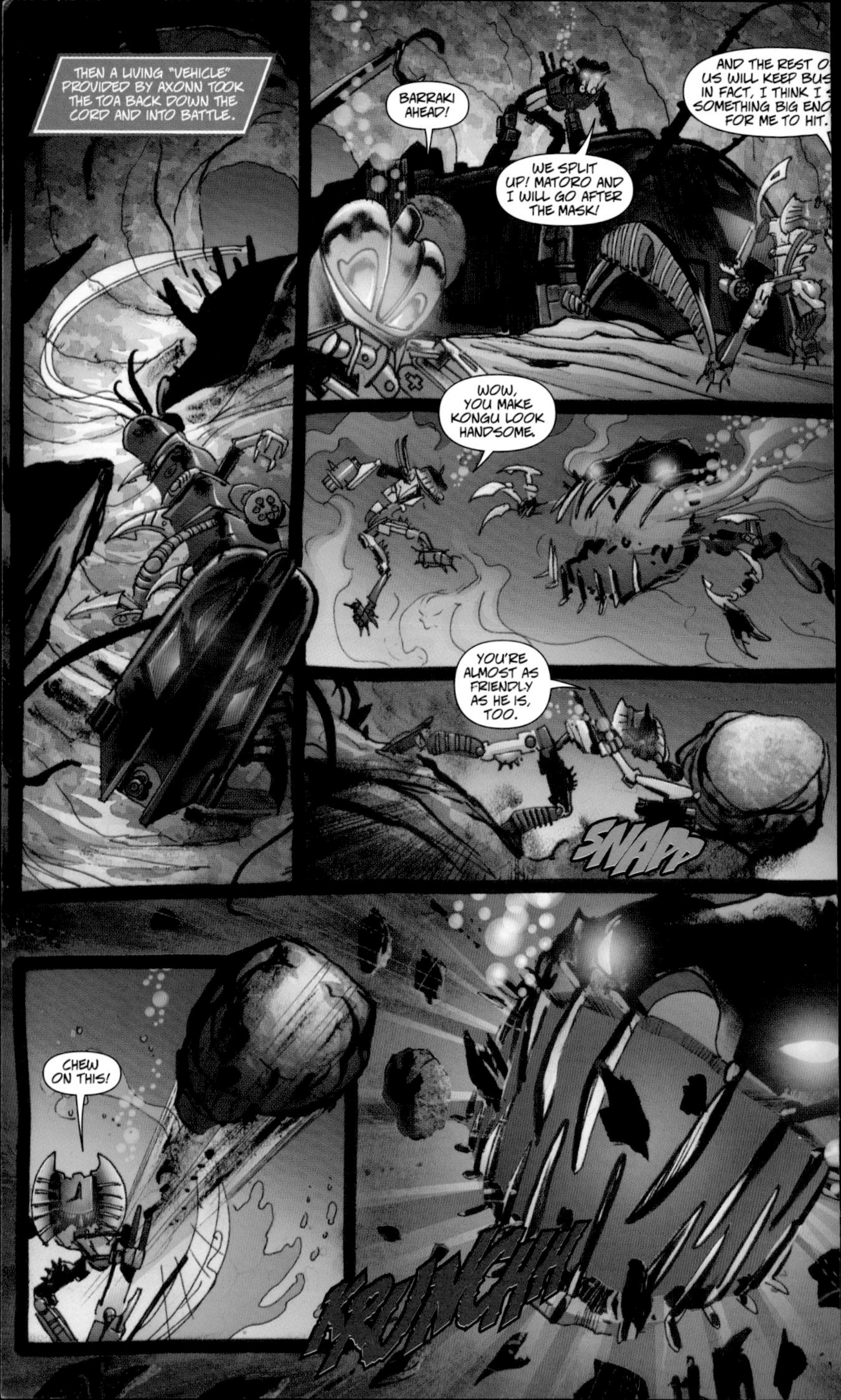
THEN A LIVING "VEHICLE" PROVIDED BY AXONN TOOK THE TOA BACK DOWN THE CORD AND INTO BATTLE.
BARRAKI AHEAD!
WE SPLIT UP! MATORO AND I WILL GO AFTER THE MASK!
AND THE REST O US WILL KEEP BUS IN FACT, I THINK I S SOMETHING BIG ENO FOR ME TO HIT.
WOW, YOU MAKE KONGU LOOK HANDSOME.
YOU'RE ALMOST AS FRIENDLY AS HE IS, TOO.
SNAPP
CHEW ON THIS!
KRUNCHH

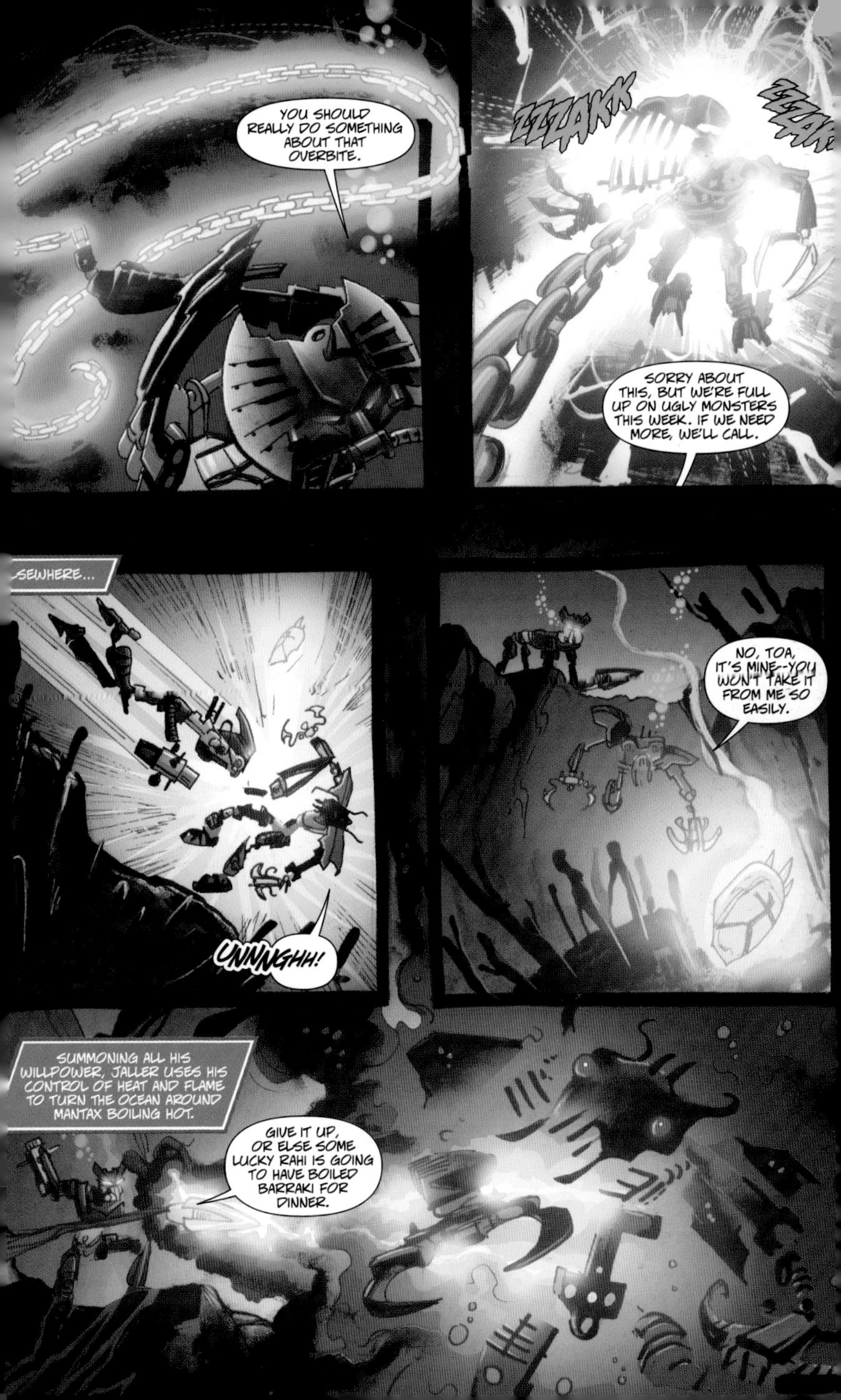

YOU SHOULD REALLY DO SOMETHING ABOUT THAT OVERBITE.
ZZZAKK
SORRY ABOUT THIS, BUT WE'RE FULL UP ON UGLY MONSTERS THIS WEEK. IF WE NEED MORE, WE'LL CALL.
SEWHERE...
UNNNGHH!
NO, TOA, IT'S MINE--YOU WON'T TAKE IT FROM ME SO EASILY.
SUMMONING ALL HIS WILLPOWER, JALLER USES HIS CONTROL OF HEAT AND FLAME TO TURN THE OCEAN AROUND MANTAX BOILING HOT.
GIVE IT UP, OR ELSE SOME LUCKY RAHI IS GOING TO HAVE BOILED BARRAKI FOR DINNER.

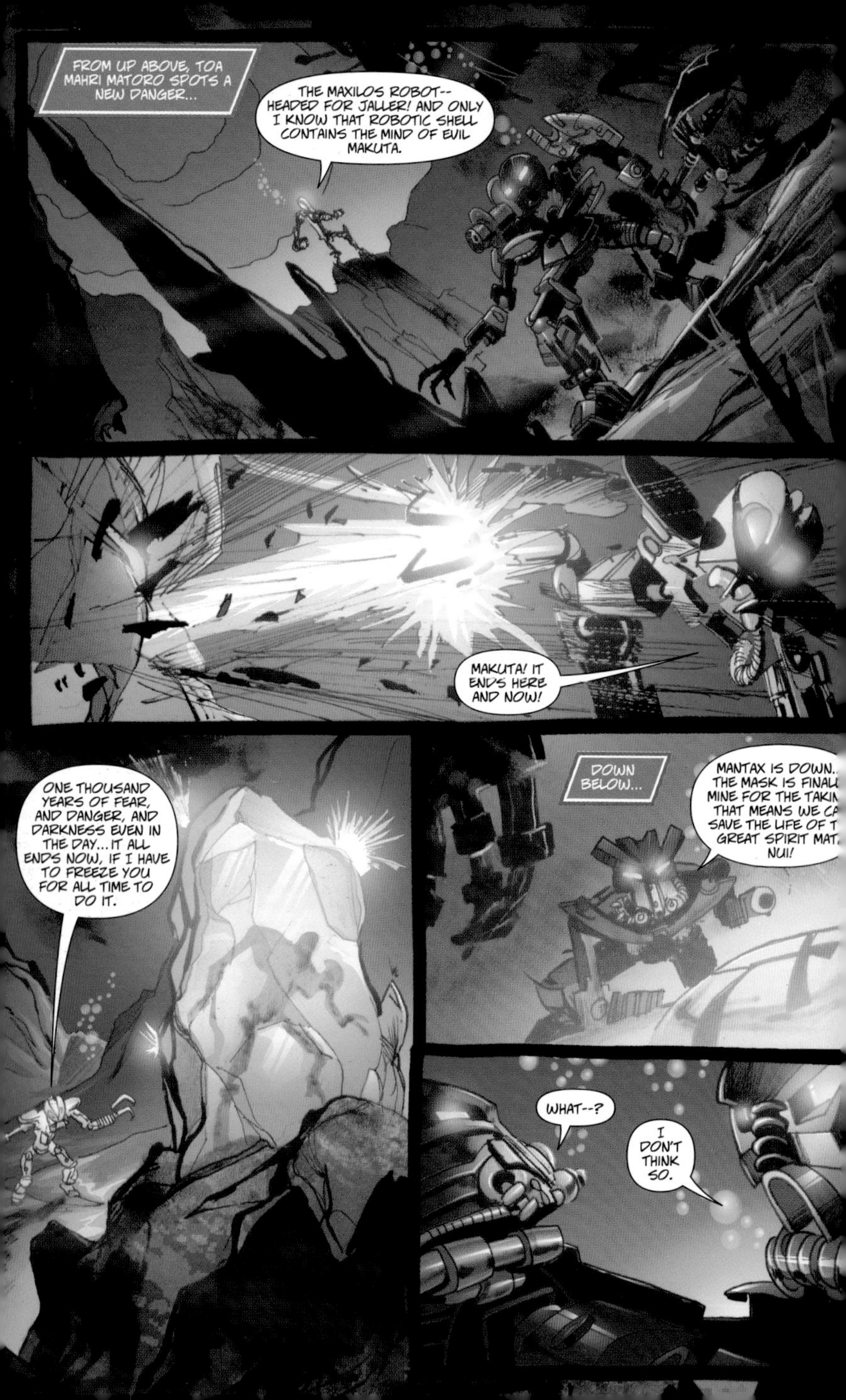
FROM UP ABOVE, TOA MAHRI MATORO SPOTS A NEW DANGER...
THE MAXILOS ROBOT--HEADED FOR JALLER! AND ONLY I KNOW THAT ROBOTIC SHELL CONTAINS THE MIND OF EVIL MAKUTA.
MAKUTA! IT END'S HERE AND NOW!
ONE THOUSAND YEARS OF FEAR, AND DANGER, AND DARKNESS EVEN IN THE DAY... IT ALL ENDS NOW, IF I HAVE TO FREEZE YOU FOR ALL TIME TO DO IT.
DOWN BELOW...
MANTAX IS DOWN.. THE MASK IS FINAL MINE FOR THE TAKIN THAT MEANS WE CA SAVE THE LIFE OF T GREAT SPIRIT MAT NUI!
WHAT--?
I DON'T THINK SO.

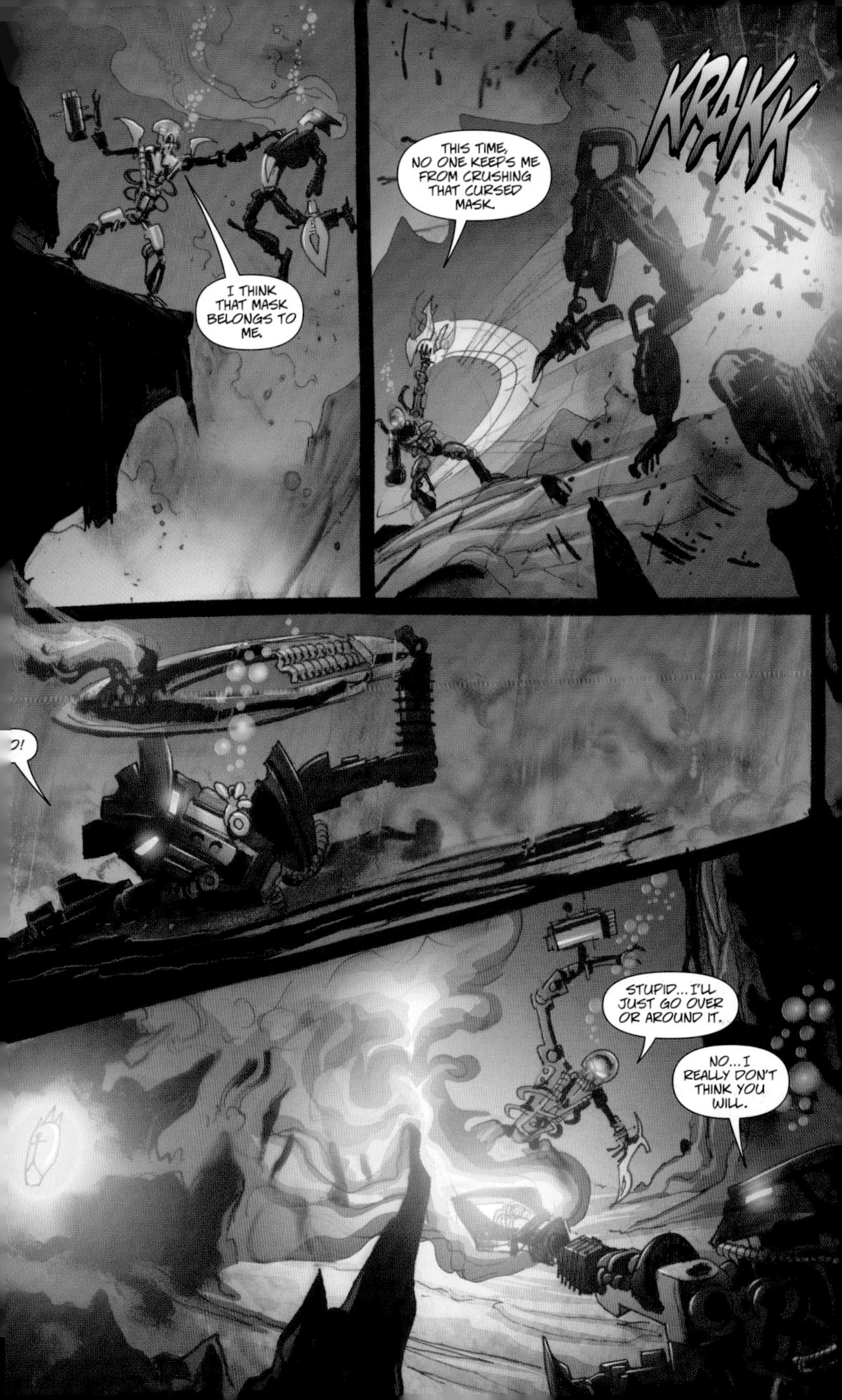
I THINK THAT MASK BELONGS TO ME.
THIS TIME, NO ONE KEEPS ME FROM CRUSHING THAT CURSED MASK.
KRAKK
STUPID... I'LL JUST GO OVER OR AROUND IT.
NO... I REALLY DON'T THINK YOU WILL.

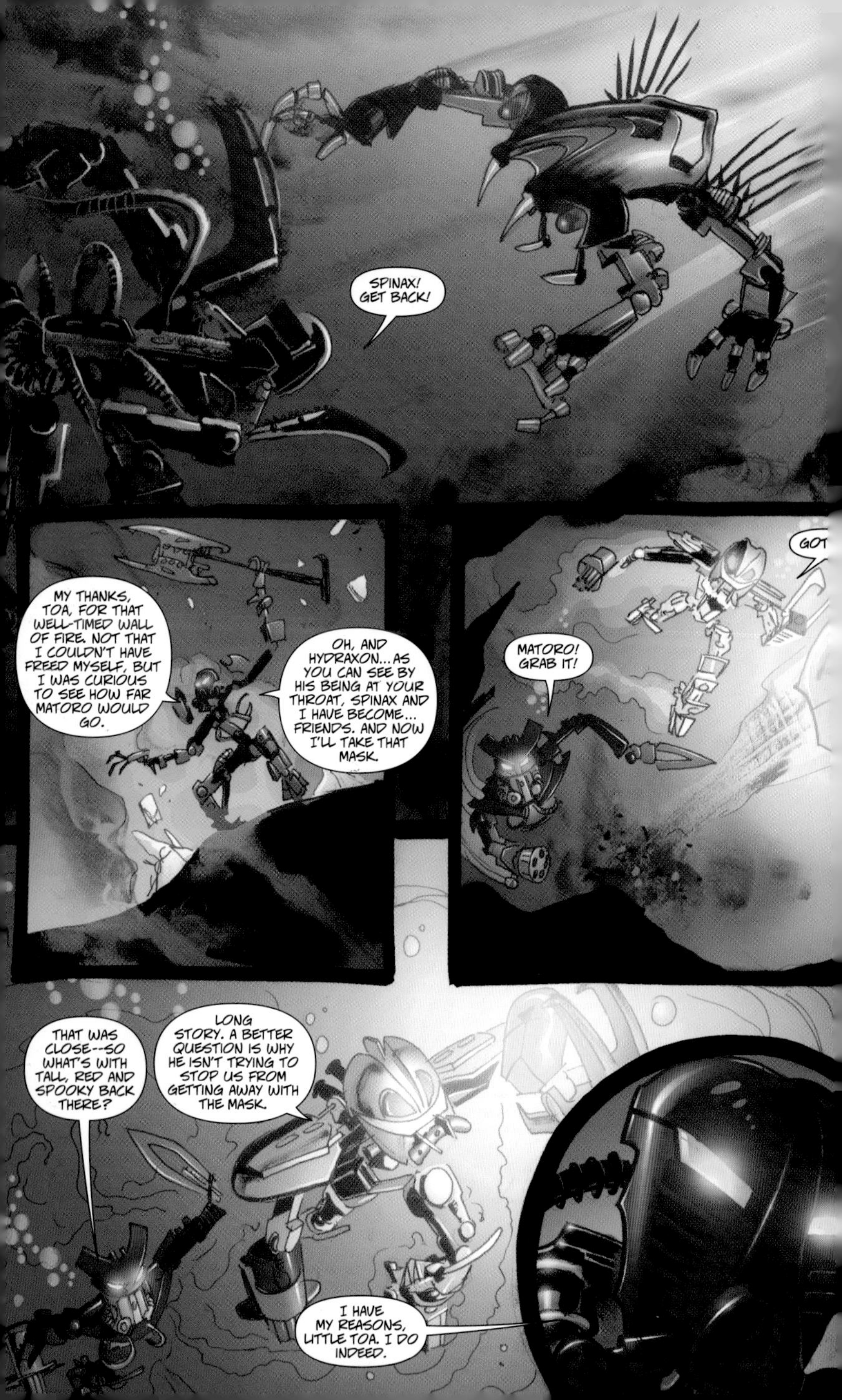
SPINAX! GET BACK!
MY THANKS, TOA, FOR THAT WELL-TIMED WALL OF FIRE. NOT THAT I COULDN'T HAVE FREED MYSELF, BUT I WAS CURIOUS TO SEE HOW FAR MATORO WOULD GO.
OH, AND HYDRAXON... AS YOU CAN SEE BY HIS BEING AT YOUR THROAT, SPINAX AND I HAVE BECOME... FRIENDS. AND NOW I'LL TAKE THAT MASK.
GOT
MATORO! GRAB IT!
THAT WAS CLOSE--SO WHAT'S WITH TALL, RED AND SPOOKY BACK THERE?
LONG STORY. A BETTER QUESTION IS WHY HE ISN'T TRYING TO STOP US FROM GETTING AWAY WITH THE MASK.
I HAVE MY REASONS, LITTLE TOA. I DO INDEED.

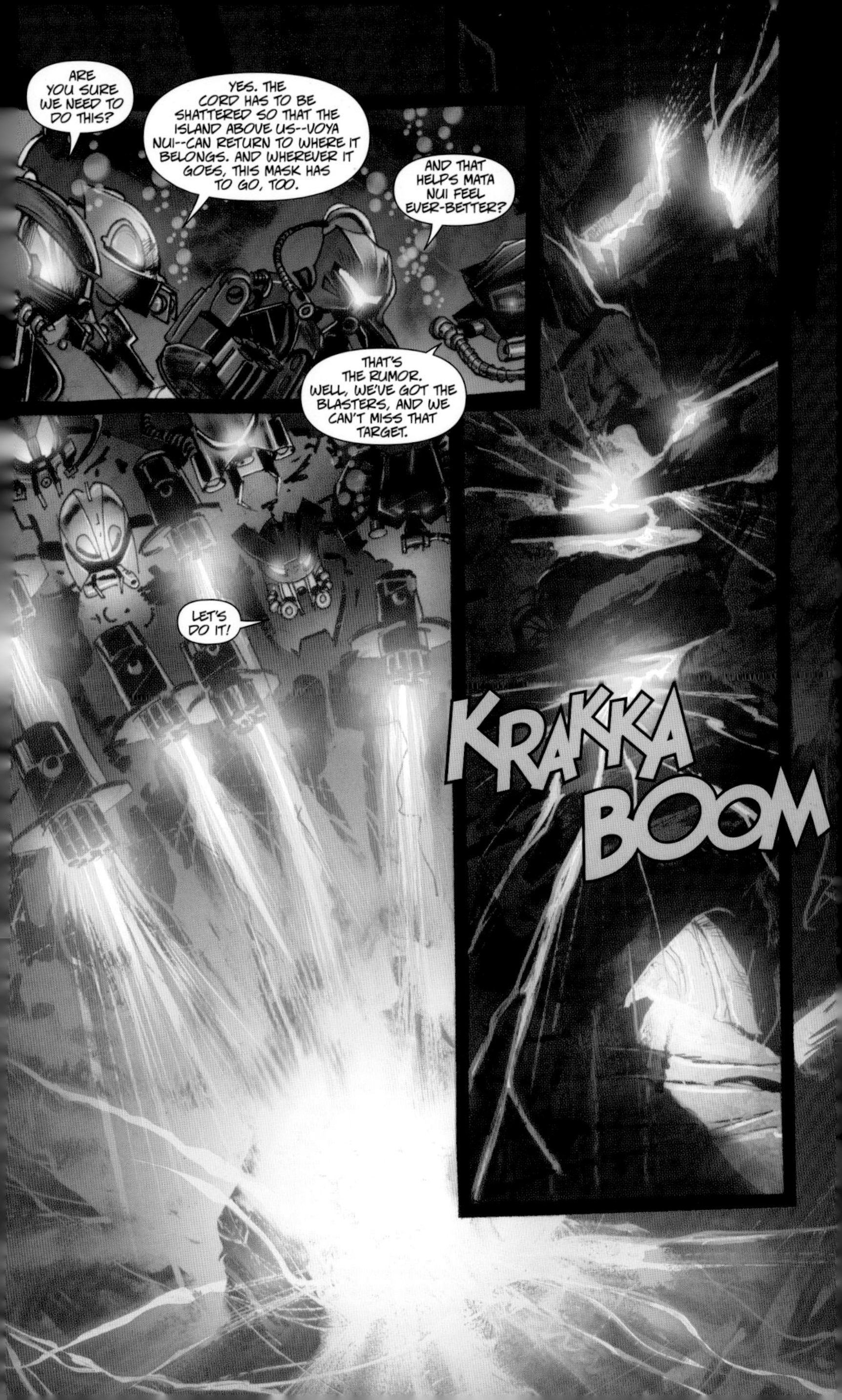

ARE YOU SURE WE NEED TO DO THIS?
YES. THE CORD HAS TO BE SHATTERED SO THAT THE ISLAND ABOVE US--VOYA NUI--CAN RETURN TO WHERE IT BELONGS. AND WHEREVER IT GOES, THIS MASK HAS TO GO, TOO.
AND THAT HELPS MATA NUI FEEL EVER-BETTER?
THAT'S THE RUMOR. WELL, WE'VE GOT THE BLASTERS, AND WE CAN'T MISS THAT TARGET.
LET'S DO IT!
KRAKKA
BOOM

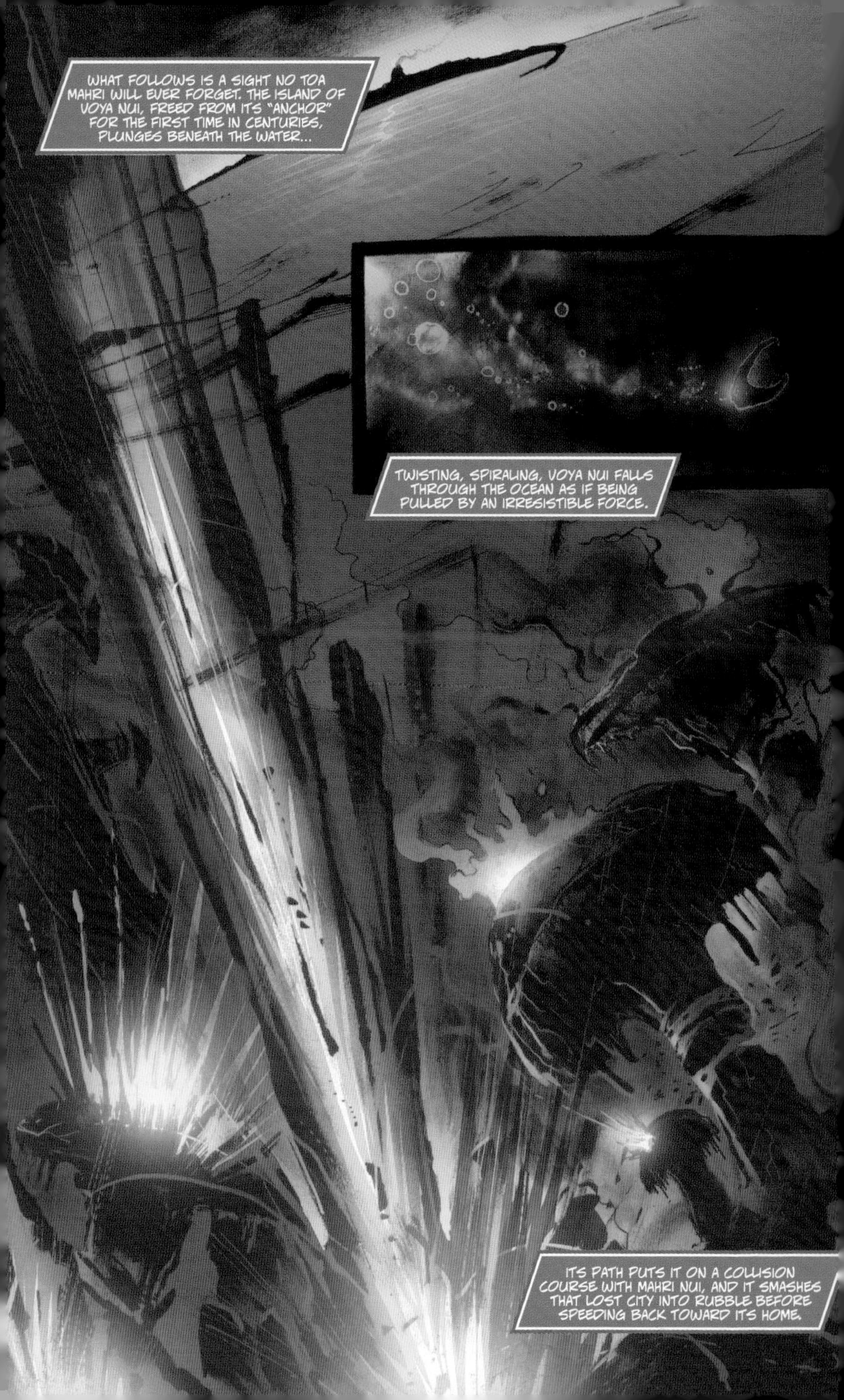
WHAT FOLLOWS IS A SIGHT NO TOA MAHRI WILL EVER FORGET. THE ISLAND OF VOYA NUI, FREED FROM ITS "ANCHOR" FOR THE FIRST TIME IN CENTURIES, PLUNGES BENEATH THE WATER...
TWISTING, SPIRALING, VOYA NUI FALLS THROUGH THE OCEAN AS IF BEING PULLED BY AN IRRESISTIBLE FORCE.
ITS PATH PUTS IT ON A COLLISION COURSE WITH MAHRI NUI, AND IT SMASHES THAT LOST CITY INTO RUBBLE BEFORE SPEEDING BACK TOWARD ITS HOME.

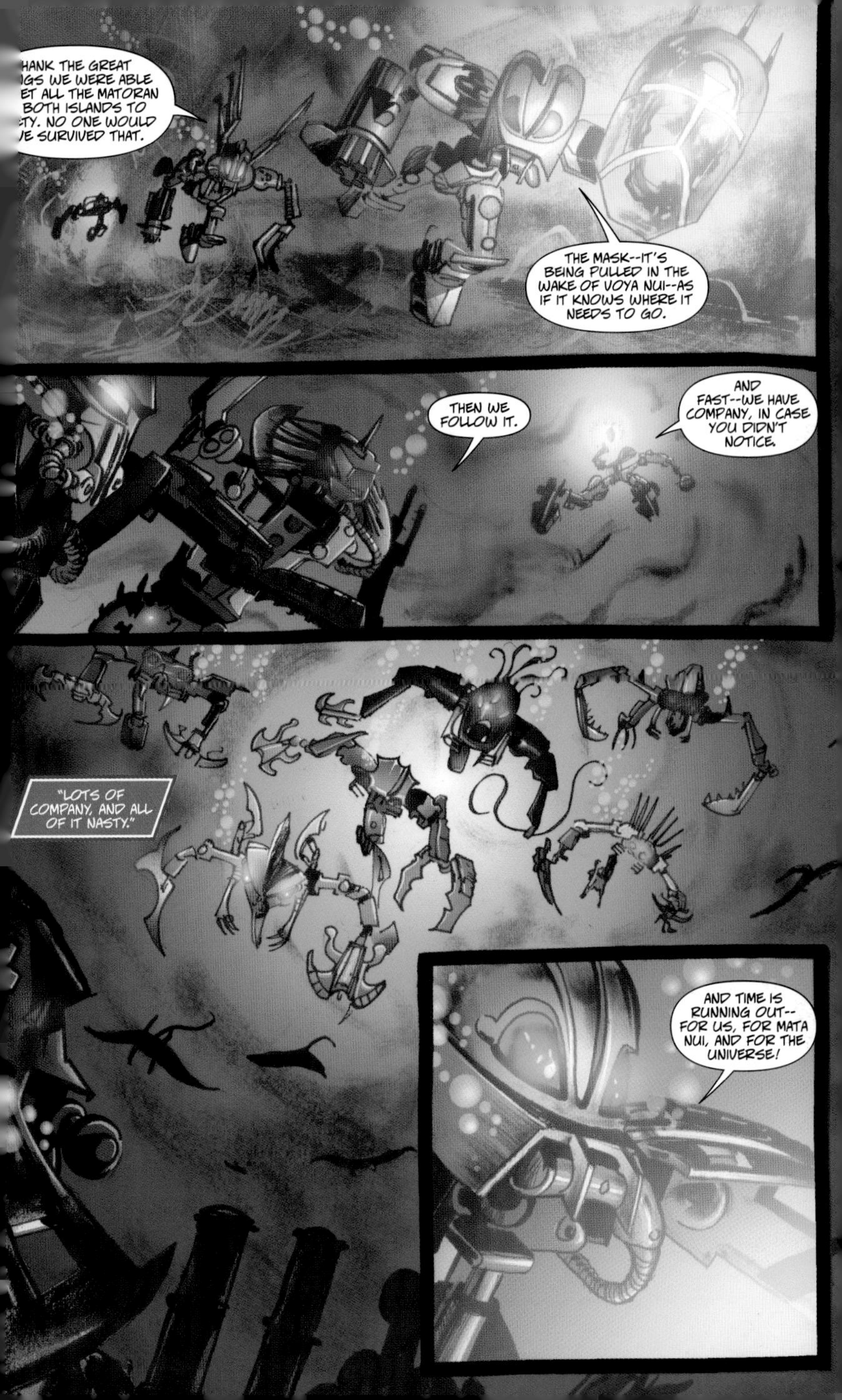
HANK THE GREAT NGS WE WERE ABLE ET ALL THE MATORAN BOTH ISLANDS TO CTY. NO ONE WOULD VE SURVIVED THAT.
THE MASK--IT'S BEING PULLED IN THE WAKE OF VOYA NUI--AS IF IT KNOWS WHERE IT NEEDS TO GO.
THEN WE FOLLOW IT.
AND FAST--WE HAVE COMPANY, IN CASE YOU DIDN'T NOTICE.
"LOTS OF COMPANY, AND ALL OF IT NASTY."
AND TIME IS RUNNING OUT--FOR US, FOR MATA NUI, AND FOR THE UNIVERSE!

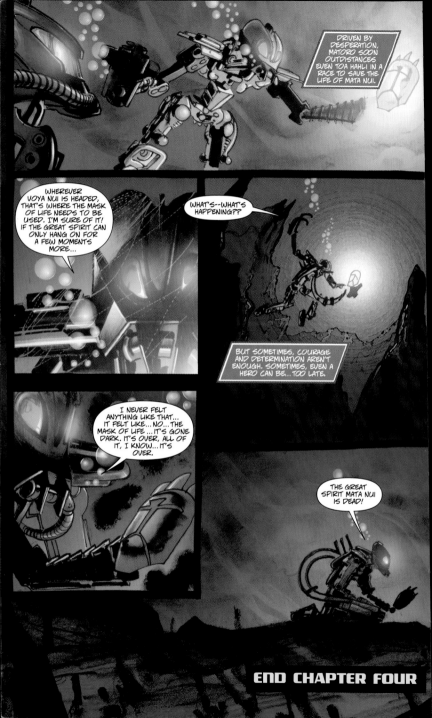

DRIVEN BY DESPERATION, MATORO SOON OUTDISTANCES EVEN TOA HAHLI IN A RACE TO SAVE THE LIFE OF MATA NUI.

WHEREVER VOYA NUI IS HEADED, THAT'S WHERE THE MASK OF LIFE NEEDS TO BE USED. I'M SURE OF IT! IF THE GREAT SPIRIT CAN ONLY HANG ON FOR A FEW MOMENTS MORE...

WHAT'S--WHAT'S HAPPENING??

BUT SOMETIMES, COURAGE AND DETERMINATION AREN'T ENOUGH. SOMETIMES, EVEN A HERO CAN BE...TOO LATE.

I NEVER FELT ANYTHING LIKE THAT... IT FELT LIKE...NO...THE MASK OF LIFE...IT'S GONE DARK. IT'S OVER, ALL OF IT, I KNOW...IT'S OVER.

THE GREAT SPIRIT MATA NUI IS DEAD!

END CHAPTER FOUR

THE UNDERWATER CITY
CHAPTER FIVE

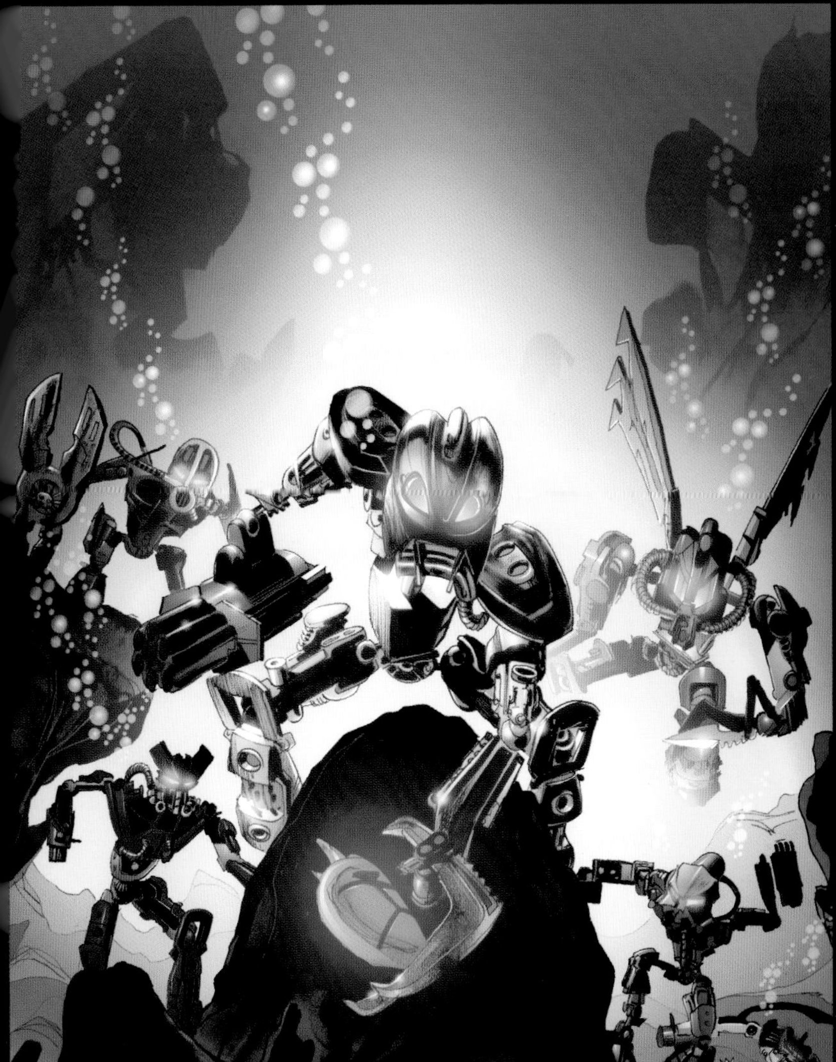

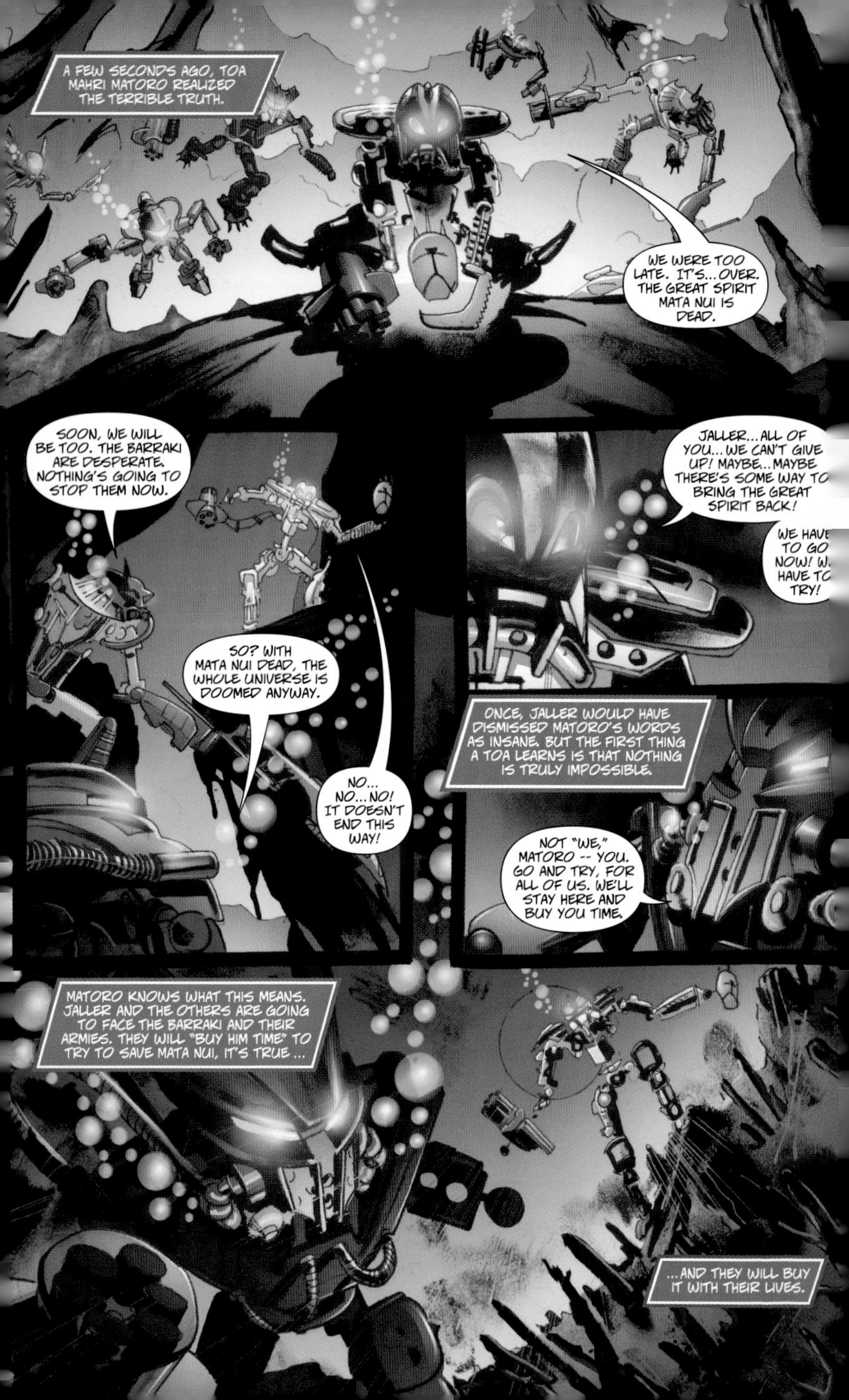
A FEW SECONDS AGO, TOA MAHRI MATORO REALIZED THE TERRIBLE TRUTH.
WE WERE TOO LATE. IT'S...OVER. THE GREAT SPIRIT MATA NUI IS DEAD.
SOON, WE WILL BE TOO. THE BARRAKI ARE DESPERATE. NOTHING'S GOING TO STOP THEM NOW.
SO? WITH MATA NUI DEAD, THE WHOLE UNIVERSE IS DOOMED ANYWAY.
NO... NO...NO! IT DOESN'T END THIS WAY!
JALLER...ALL OF YOU...WE CAN'T GIVE UP! MAYBE...MAYBE THERE'S SOME WAY TO BRING THE GREAT SPIRIT BACK!
WE HAVE TO GO NOW! WE HAVE TO TRY!
ONCE, JALLER WOULD HAVE DISMISSED MATORO'S WORDS AS INSANE. BUT THE FIRST THING A TOA LEARNS IS THAT NOTHING IS TRULY IMPOSSIBLE.
NOT "WE," MATORO -- YOU. GO AND TRY, FOR ALL OF US. WE'LL STAY HERE AND BUY YOU TIME.
MATORO KNOWS WHAT THIS MEANS. JALLER AND THE OTHERS ARE GOING TO FACE THE BARRAKI AND THEIR ARMIES. THEY WILL "BUY HIM TIME" TO TRY TO SAVE MATA NUI, IT'S TRUE ...
...AND THEY WILL BUY IT WITH THEIR LIVES.

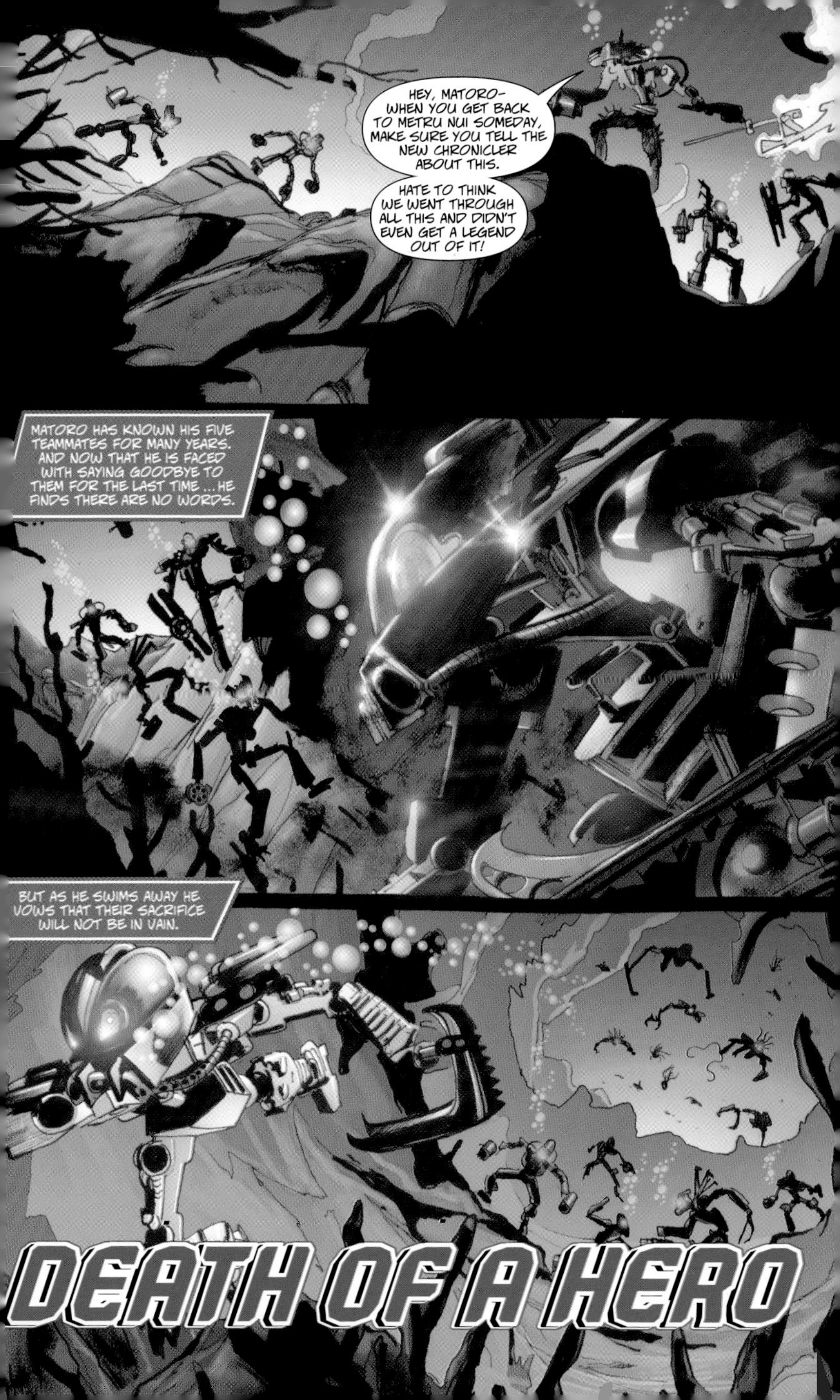
HEY, MATORO- WHEN YOU GET BACK TO METRU NUI SOMEDAY, MAKE SURE YOU TELL THE NEW CHRONICLER ABOUT THIS.
HATE TO THINK WE WENT THROUGH ALL THIS AND DIDN'T EVEN GET A LEGEND OUT OF IT!
MATORO HAS KNOWN HIS FIVE TEAMMATES FOR MANY YEARS. AND NOW THAT HE IS FACED WITH SAYING GOODBYE TO THEM FOR THE LAST TIME ... HE FINDS THERE ARE NO WORDS.
BUT AS HE SWIMS AWAY HE VOWS THAT THEIR SACRIFICE WILL NOT BE IN VAIN.
DEATH OF A HERO

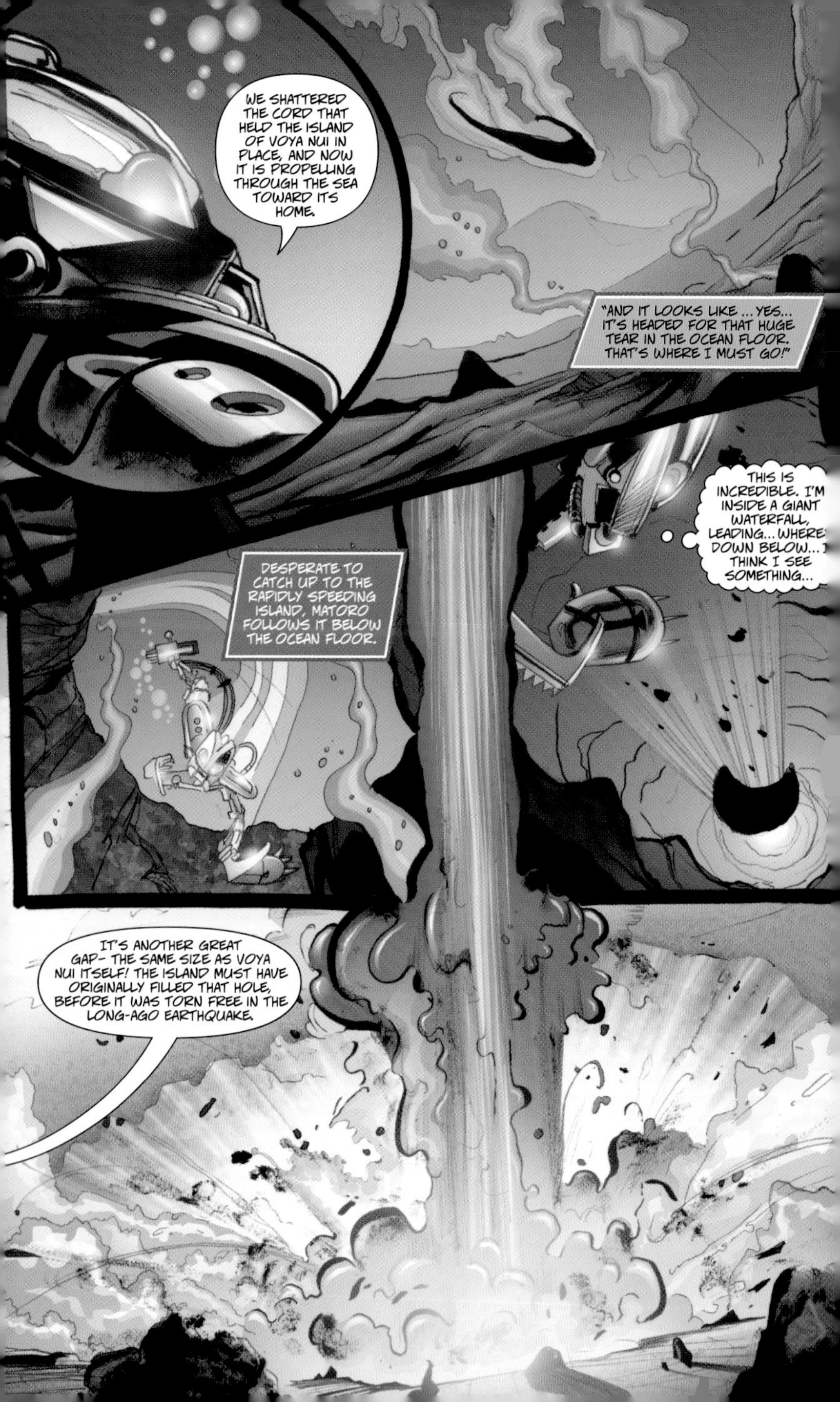
WE SHATTERED THE CORD THAT HELD THE ISLAND OF VOYA NUI IN PLACE, AND NOW IT IS PROPELLING THROUGH THE SEA TOWARD ITS HOME.
"AND IT LOOKS LIKE ... YES... IT'S HEADED FOR THAT HUGE TEAR IN THE OCEAN FLOOR. THAT'S WHERE I MUST GO!"
DESPERATE TO CATCH UP TO THE RAPIDLY SPEEDING ISLAND, MATORO FOLLOWS IT BELOW THE OCEAN FLOOR.
THIS IS INCREDIBLE. I'M INSIDE A GIANT WATERFALL, LEADING... WHERE
DOWN BELOW...
THINK I SEE SOMETHING...
IT'S ANOTHER GREAT GAP- THE SAME SIZE AS VOYA NUI ITSELF! THE ISLAND MUST HAVE ORIGINALLY FILLED THAT HOLE, BEFORE IT WAS TORN FREE IN THE LONG-AGO EARTHQUAKE.

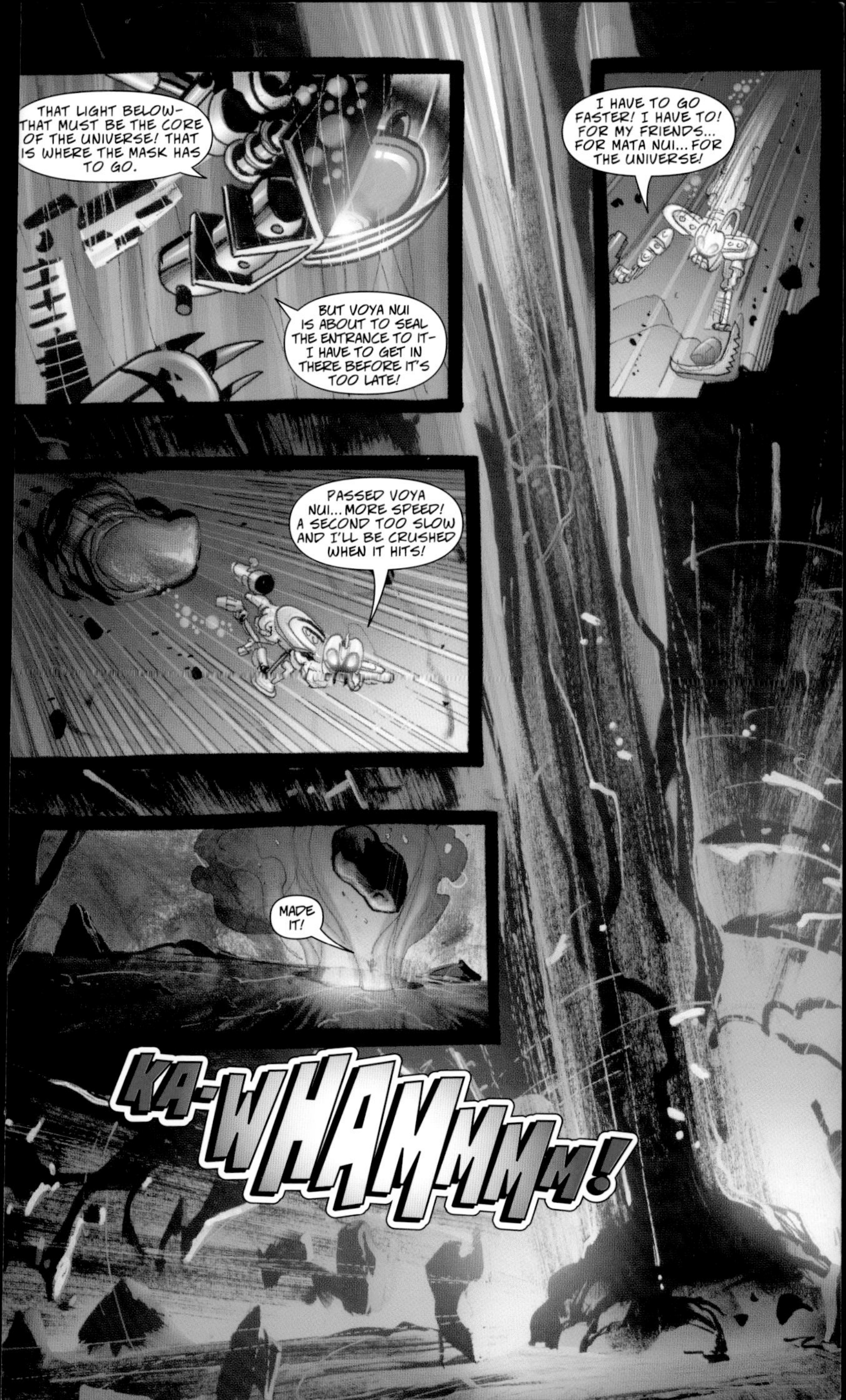
THAT LIGHT BELOW-THAT MUST BE THE CORE OF THE UNIVERSE! THAT IS WHERE THE MASK HAS TO GO.
BUT VOYA NUI IS ABOUT TO SEAL THE ENTRANCE TO IT-I HAVE TO GET IN THERE BEFORE IT'S TOO LATE!
I HAVE TO GO FASTER! I HAVE TO! FOR MY FRIENDS... FOR MATA NUI... FOR THE UNIVERSE!
PASSED VOYA NUI... MORE SPEED! A SECOND TOO SLOW AND I'LL BE CRUSHED WHEN IT HITS!
MADE IT!
KA-WHAMMMMM!

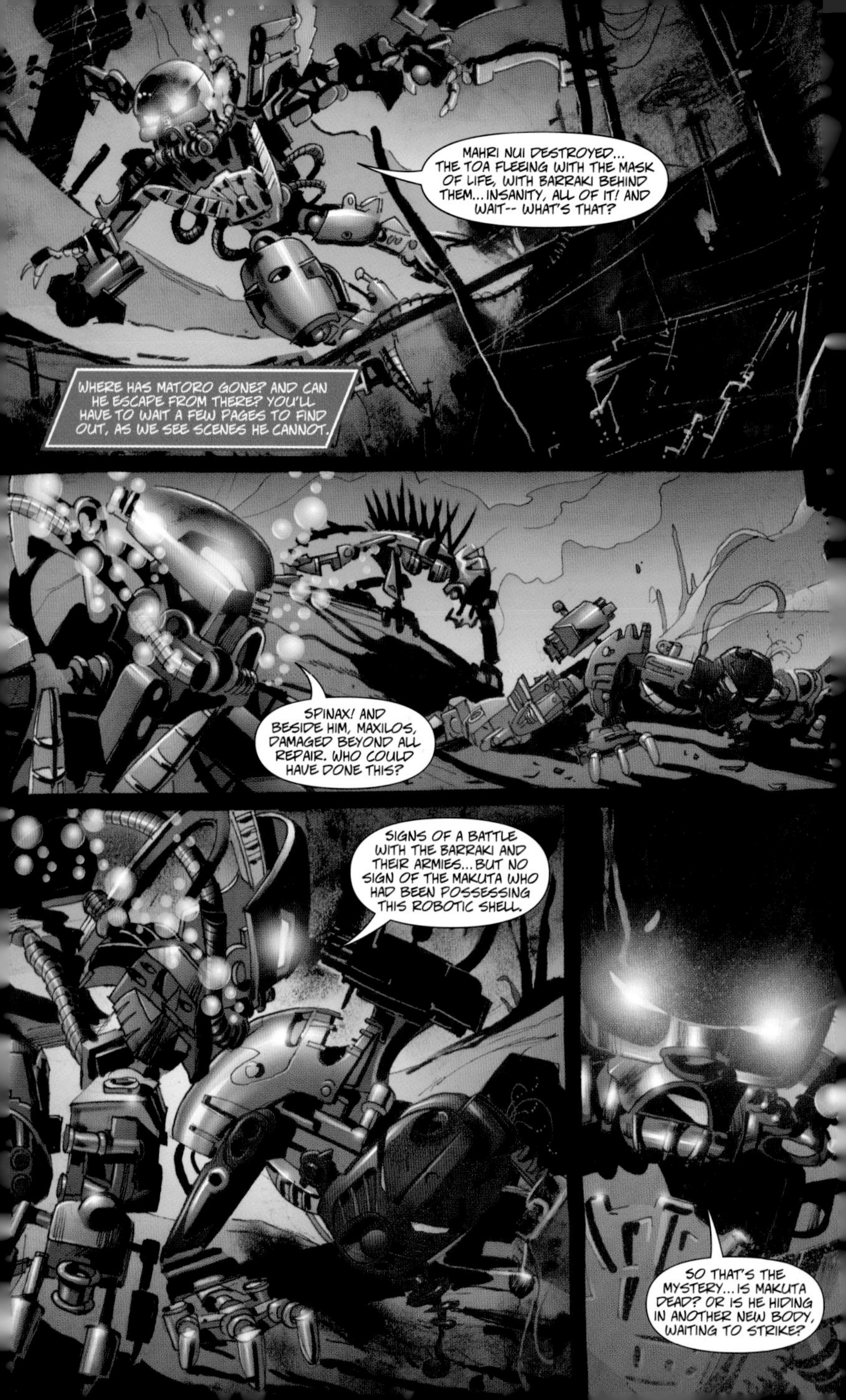
MAHRI NUI DESTROYED... THE TOA FLEEING WITH THE MASK OF LIFE, WITH BARRAKI BEHIND THEM... INSANITY, ALL OF IT! AND WAIT-- WHAT'S THAT?
WHERE HAS MATORO GONE? AND CAN HE ESCAPE FROM THERE? YOU'LL HAVE TO WAIT A FEW PAGES TO FIND OUT, AS WE SEE SCENES HE CANNOT.
SPINAX! AND BESIDE HIM, MAXILOS, DAMAGED BEYOND ALL REPAIR. WHO COULD HAVE DONE THIS?
SIGNS OF A BATTLE WITH THE BARRAKI AND THEIR ARMIES... BUT NO SIGN OF THE MAKUTA WHO HAD BEEN POSSESSING THIS ROBOTIC SHELL.
SO THAT'S THE MYSTERY... IS MAKUTA DEAD? OR IS HE HIDING IN ANOTHER NEW BODY, WAITING TO STRIKE?

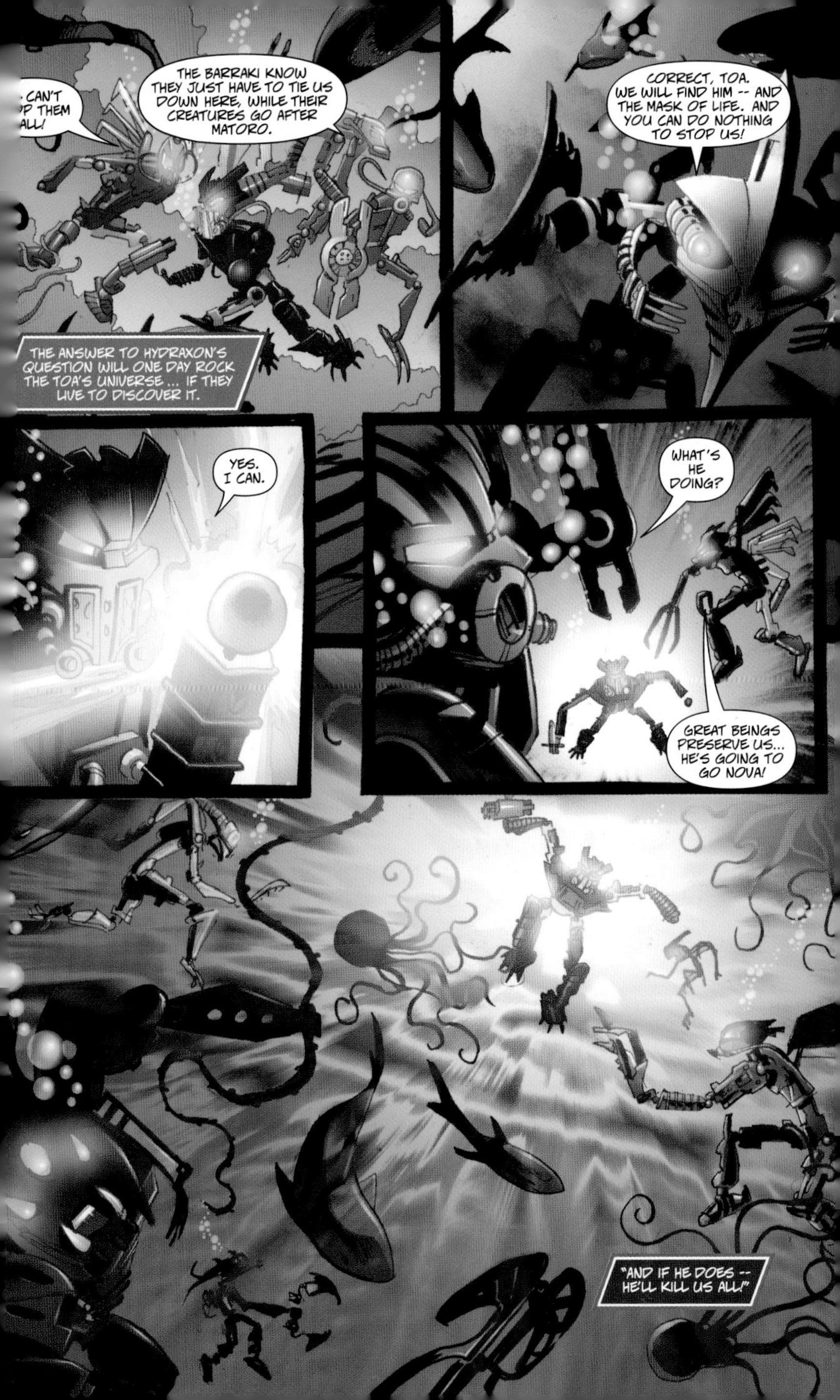
CAN'T P THEM ALL!
THE BARRAKI KNOW THEY JUST HAVE TO TIE US DOWN HERE, WHILE THEIR CREATURES GO AFTER MATORO.
CORRECT, TOA. WE WILL FIND HIM -- AND THE MASK OF LIFE. AND YOU CAN DO NOTHING TO STOP US!
THE ANSWER TO HYDRAXON'S QUESTION WILL ONE DAY ROCK THE TOA'S UNIVERSE ... IF THEY LIVE TO DISCOVER IT.
YES. I CAN.
WHAT'S HE DOING?
GREAT BEINGS PRESERVE US... HE'S GOING TO GO NOVA!
"AND IF HE DOES -- HE'LL KILL US ALL!"

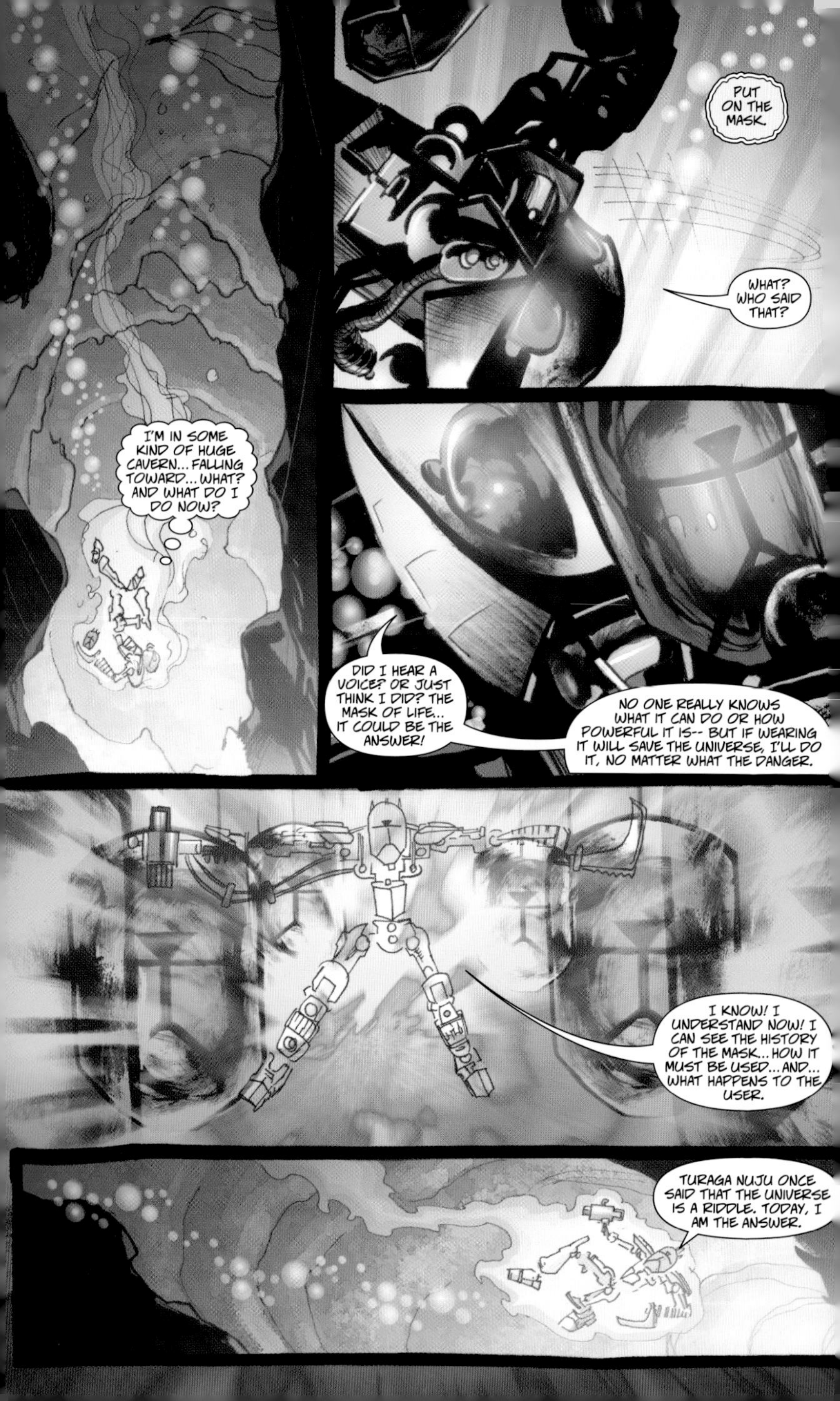
PUT ON THE MASK.
WHAT? WHO SAID THAT?
I'M IN SOME KIND OF HUGE CAVERN... FALLING TOWARD... WHAT? AND WHAT DO I DO NOW?
DID I HEAR A VOICE? OR JUST THINK I DID? THE MASK OF LIFE... IT COULD BE THE ANSWER!
NO ONE REALLY KNOWS WHAT IT CAN DO OR HOW POWERFUL IT IS-- BUT IF WEARING IT WILL SAVE THE UNIVERSE, I'LL DO IT, NO MATTER WHAT THE DANGER.
I KNOW! I UNDERSTAND NOW! I CAN SEE THE HISTORY OF THE MASK... HOW IT MUST BE USED... AND... WHAT HAPPENS TO THE USER.
TURAGA NUJU ONCE SAID THAT THE UNIVERSE IS A RIDDLE. TODAY, I AM THE ANSWER.

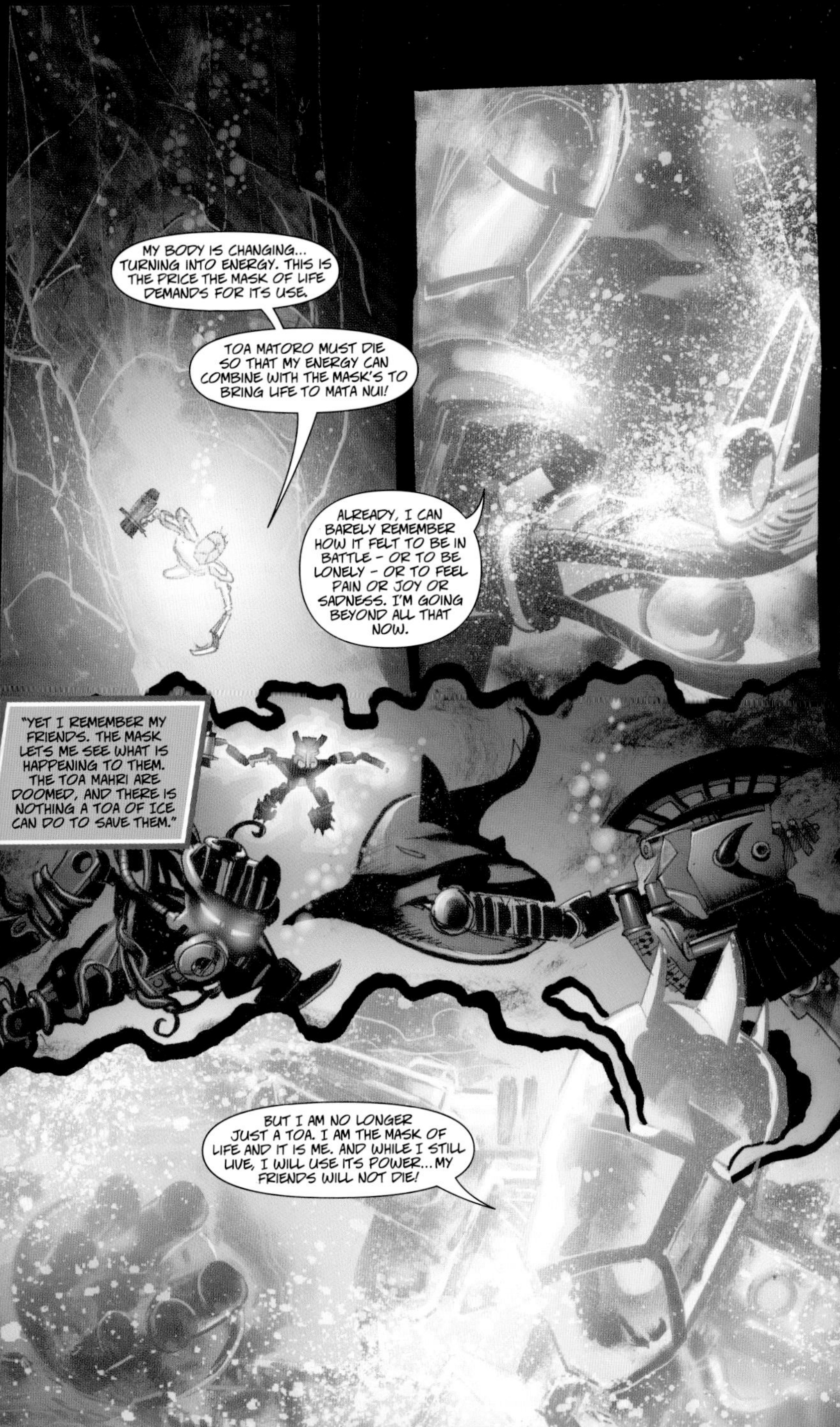
MY BODY IS CHANGING... TURNING INTO ENERGY. THIS IS THE PRICE THE MASK OF LIFE DEMANDS FOR ITS USE.
TOA MATORO MUST DIE SO THAT MY ENERGY CAN COMBINE WITH THE MASK'S TO BRING LIFE TO MATA NUI!
ALREADY, I CAN BARELY REMEMBER HOW IT FELT TO BE IN BATTLE - OR TO BE LONELY - OR TO FEEL PAIN OR JOY OR SADNESS. I'M GOING BEYOND ALL THAT NOW.
"YET I REMEMBER MY FRIENDS. THE MASK LETS ME SEE WHAT IS HAPPENING TO THEM. THE TOA MAHRI ARE DOOMED, AND THERE IS NOTHING A TOA OF ICE CAN DO TO SAVE THEM."
BUT I AM NO LONGER JUST A TOA. I AM THE MASK OF LIFE AND IT IS ME. AND WHILE I STILL LIVE, I WILL USE ITS POWER... MY FRIENDS WILL NOT DIE!

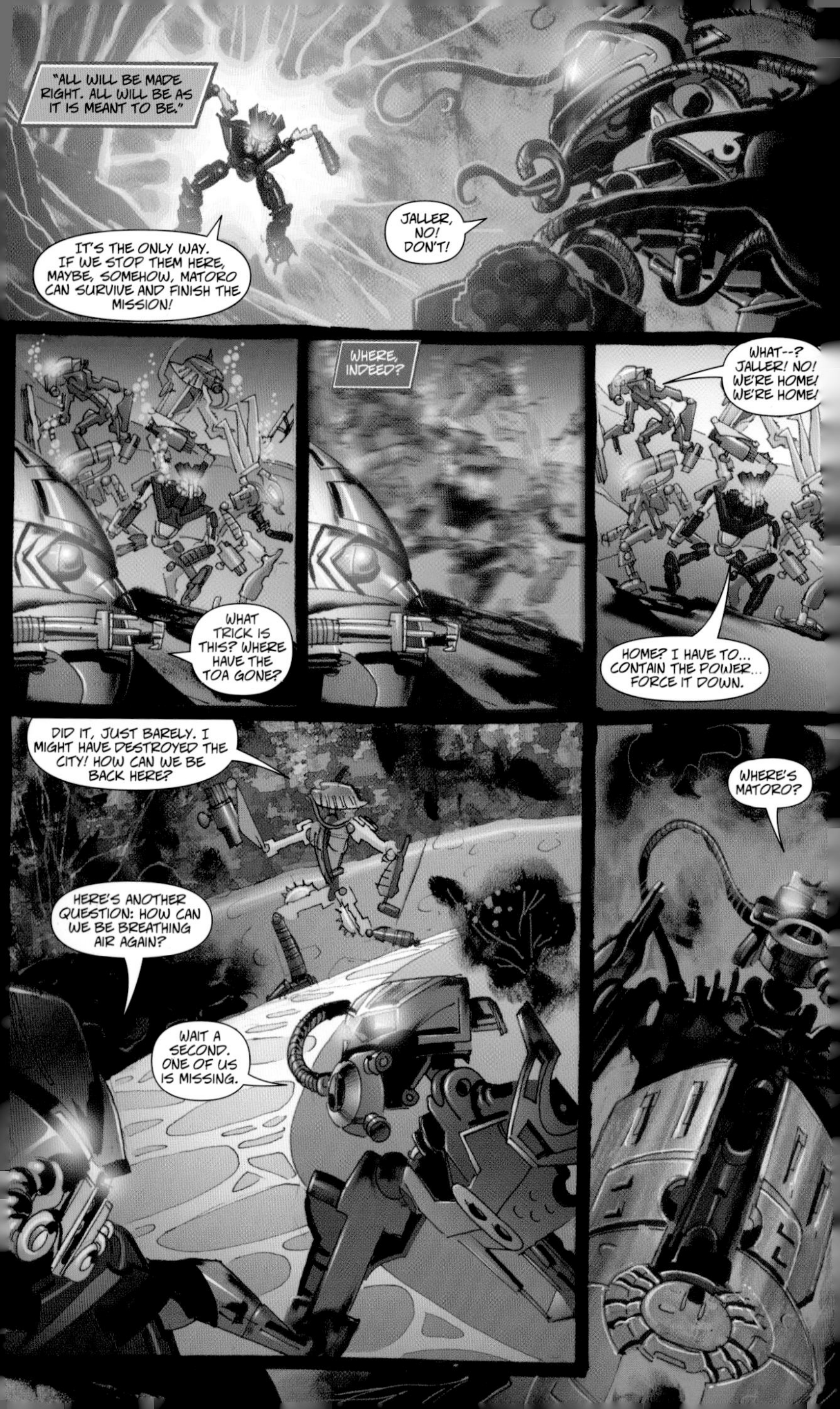
"ALL WILL BE MADE RIGHT. ALL WILL BE AS IT IS MEANT TO BE."
IT'S THE ONLY WAY. IF WE STOP THEM HERE, MAYBE, SOMEHOW, MATORO CAN SURVIVE AND FINISH THE MISSION!
JALLER, NO! DON'T!
WHAT TRICK IS THIS? WHERE HAVE THE TOA GONE?
WHERE, INDEED?
WHAT--? JALLER! NO! WE'RE HOME! WE'RE HOME!
HOME? I HAVE TO... CONTAIN THE POWER... FORCE IT DOWN.
DID IT, JUST BARELY. I MIGHT HAVE DESTROYED THE CITY! HOW CAN WE BE BACK HERE?
HERE'S ANOTHER QUESTION: HOW CAN WE BE BREATHING AIR AGAIN?
WAIT A SECOND. ONE OF US IS MISSING.
WHERE'S MATORO?

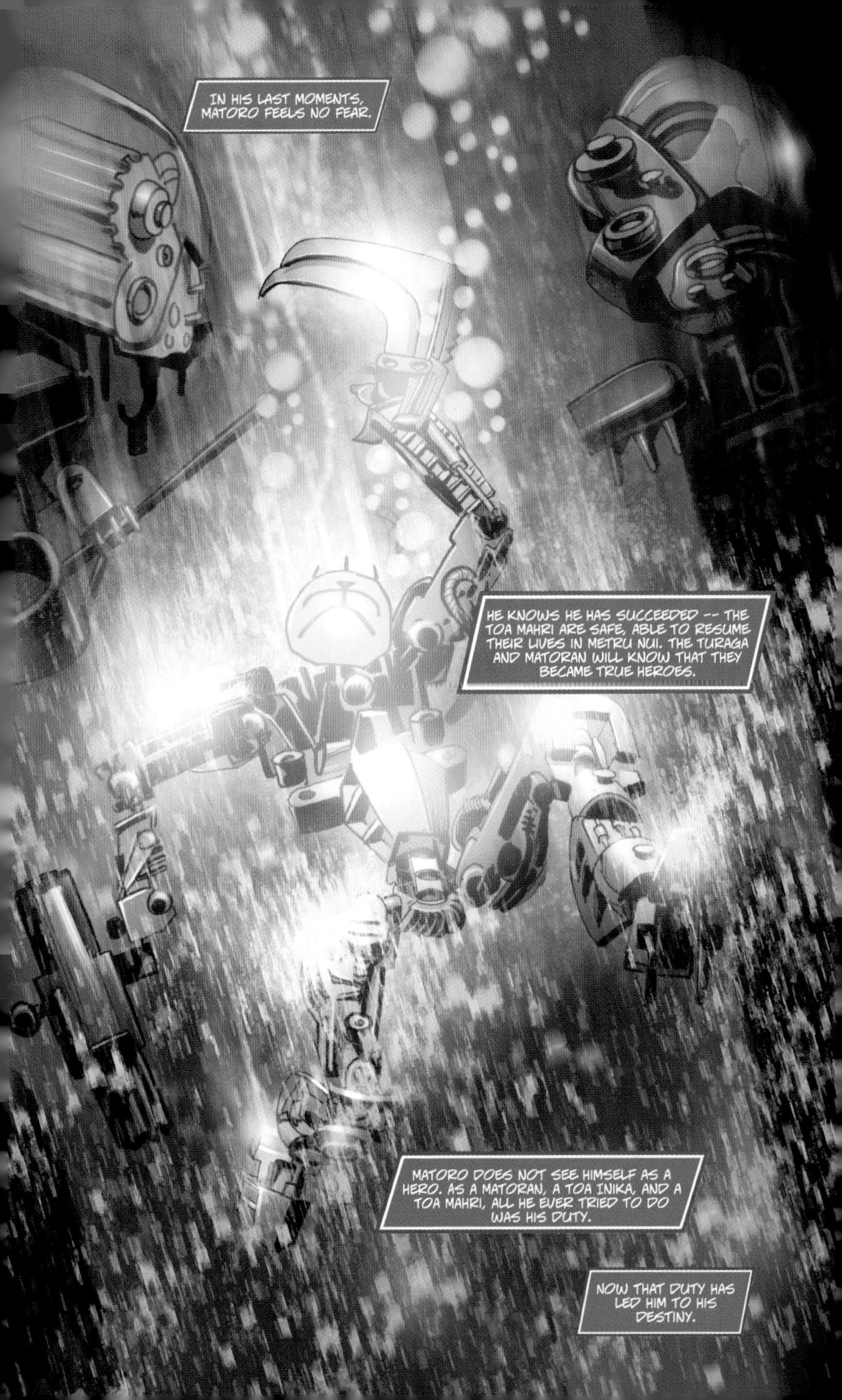
IN HIS LAST MOMENTS, MATORO FEELS NO FEAR.
HE KNOWS HE HAS SUCCEEDED -- THE TOA MAHRI ARE SAFE, ABLE TO RESUME THEIR LIVES IN METRU NUI. THE TURAGA AND MATORAN WILL KNOW THAT THEY BECAME TRUE HEROES.
MATORO DOES NOT SEE HIMSELF AS A HERO. AS A MATORAN, A TOA INIKA, AND A TOA MAHRI, ALL HE EVER TRIED TO DO WAS HIS DUTY.
NOW THAT DUTY HAS LED HIM TO HIS DESTINY.

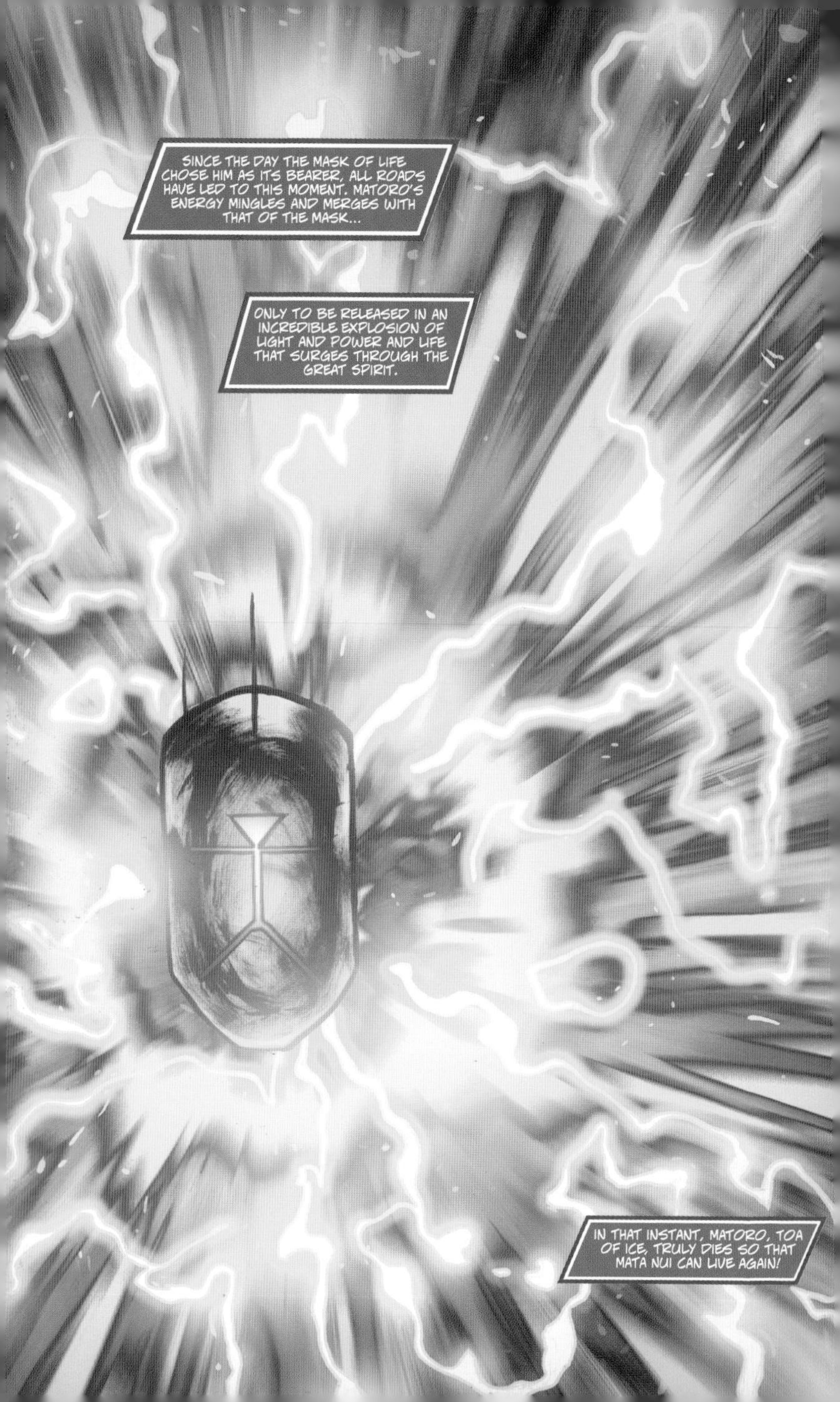
SINCE THE DAY THE MASK OF LIFE CHOSE HIM AS ITS BEARER, ALL ROADS HAVE LED TO THIS MOMENT. MATORO'S ENERGY MINGLES AND MERGES WITH THAT OF THE MASK...
ONLY TO BE RELEASED IN AN INCREDIBLE EXPLOSION OF LIGHT AND POWER AND LIFE THAT SURGES THROUGH THE GREAT SPIRIT.
IN THAT INSTANT, MATORO, TOA OF ICE, TRULY DIES SO THAT MATA NUI CAN LIVE AGAIN!

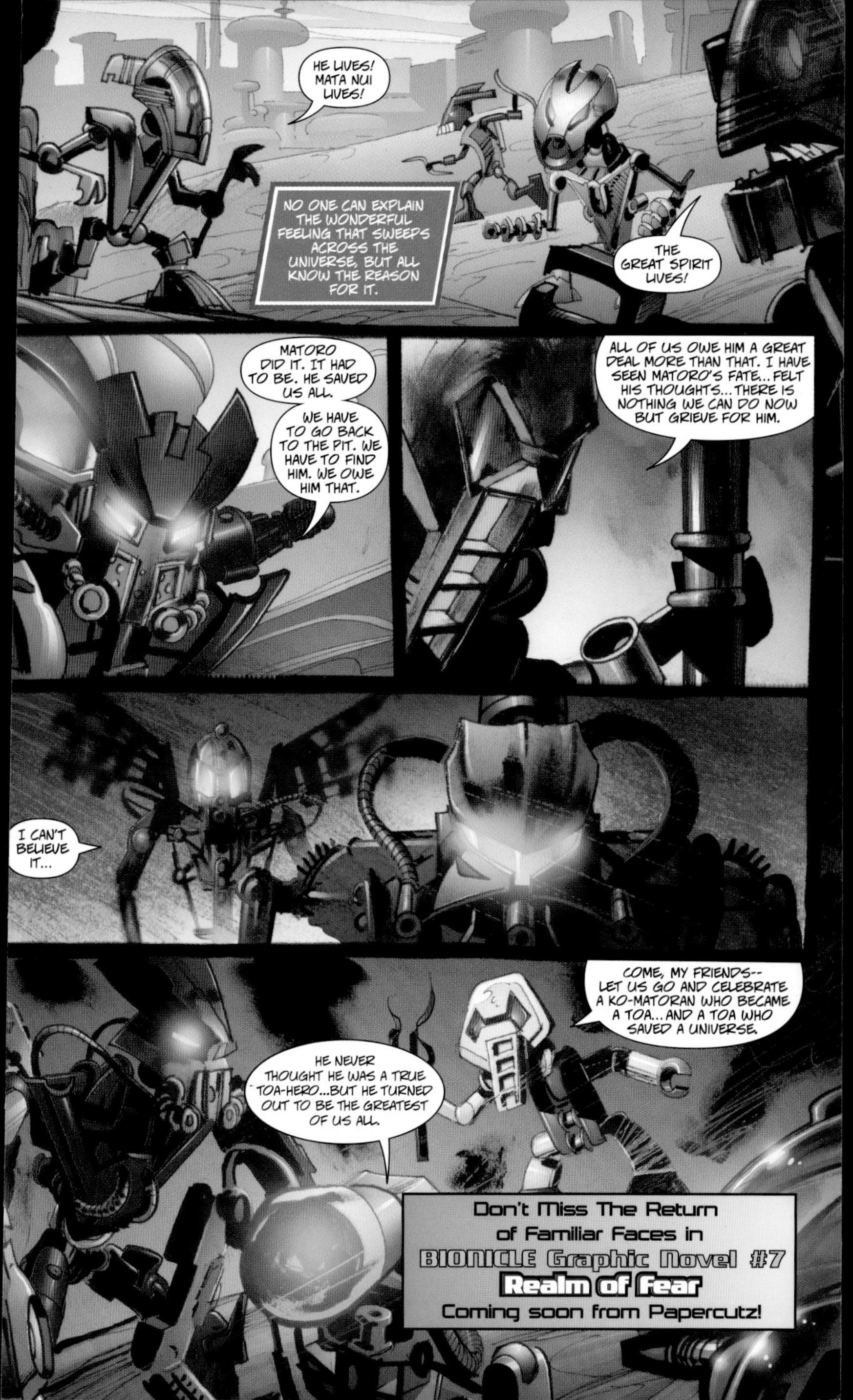
HE LIVES! MATA NUI LIVES!
NO ONE CAN EXPLAIN THE WONDERFUL FEELING THAT SWEEPS ACROSS THE UNIVERSE, BUT ALL KNOW THE REASON FOR IT.
THE GREAT SPIRIT LIVES!
MATORO DID IT. IT HAD TO BE. HE SAVED US ALL.
WE HAVE TO GO BACK TO THE PIT. WE HAVE TO FIND HIM. WE OWE HIM THAT.
ALL OF US OWE HIM A GREAT DEAL MORE THAN THAT. I HAVE SEEN MATORO'S FATE...FELT HIS THOUGHTS...THERE IS NOTHING WE CAN DO NOW BUT GRIEVE FOR HIM.
I CAN'T BELIEVE IT...
HE NEVER THOUGHT HE WAS A TRUE TOA-HERO...BUT HE TURNED OUT TO BE THE GREATEST OF US ALL.
COME, MY FRIENDS-- LET US GO AND CELEBRATE A KO-MATORAN WHO BECAME A TOA...AND A TOA WHO SAVED A UNIVERSE.
Don't Miss The Return of Familiar Faces in
BIONICLE Graphic Novel #7
Realm of Fear
Coming soon from Papercutz!

PAPERCUTZ™ AND

PROUDLY PRESENT:
AN EXCLUSIVE

ALL-NEW

BIONICLE®

STORY

BY
GREG FARSHTEY
AND
CHRISTIAN ZANIER

YESTERDAY, THE TOA MAHRI SAVED THE UNIVERSE, THEN ABRUPTLY DISAPPEARED FROM THE PIT.
THEY LEFT BEHIND A SHATTERED MAHRI NUI, SIX VERY ANGRY BARRAKI ... AND ONE HERO WHO HAS TO CLEAN UP THE MESS.
I HAVE SIX CELLS READY AND WAITING ... NOW I JUST NEED BARRAKI TO FILL THEM.
Hydraxon's Tale

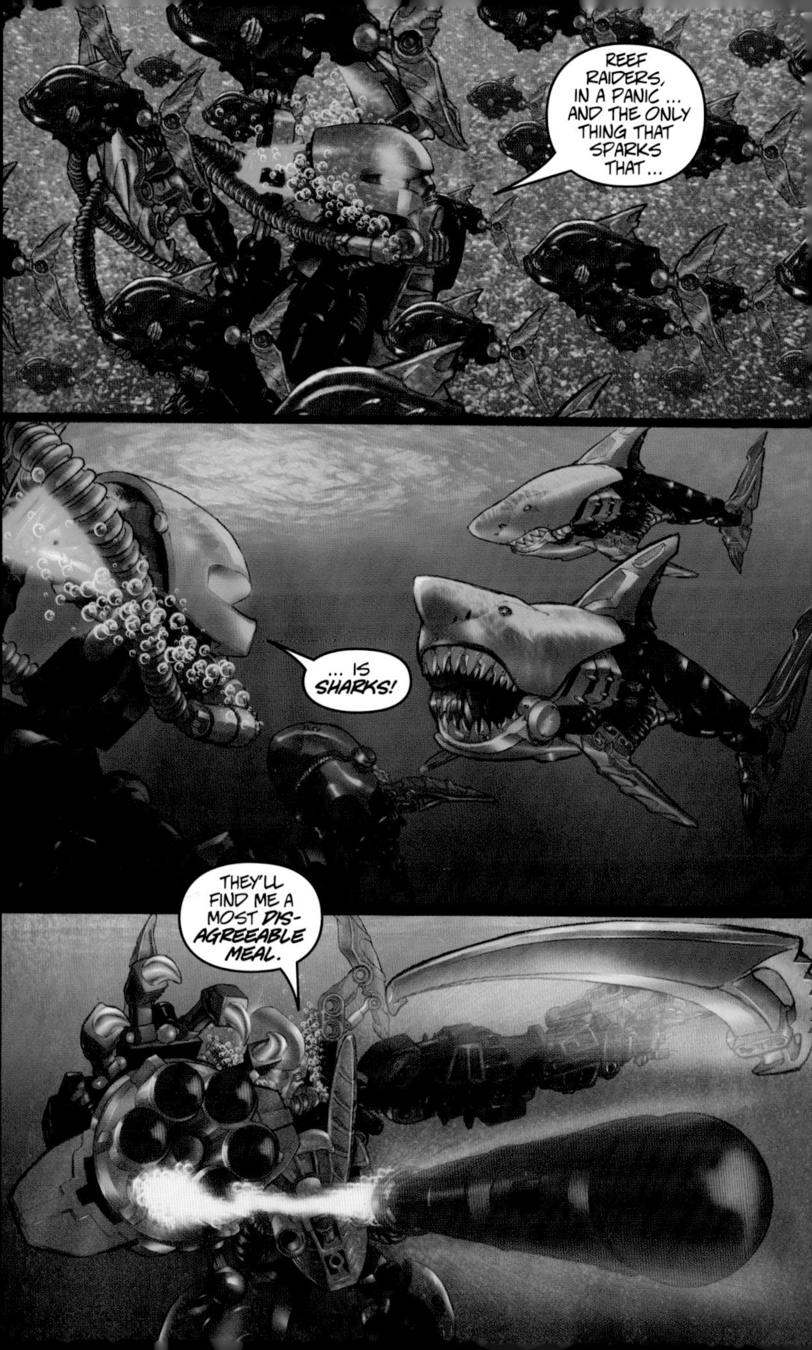
REEF RAIDERS, IN A PANIC ... AND THE ONLY THING THAT SPARKS THAT ...
... IS SHARKS!
THEY'LL FIND ME A MOST DIS-AGREEABLE MEAL.

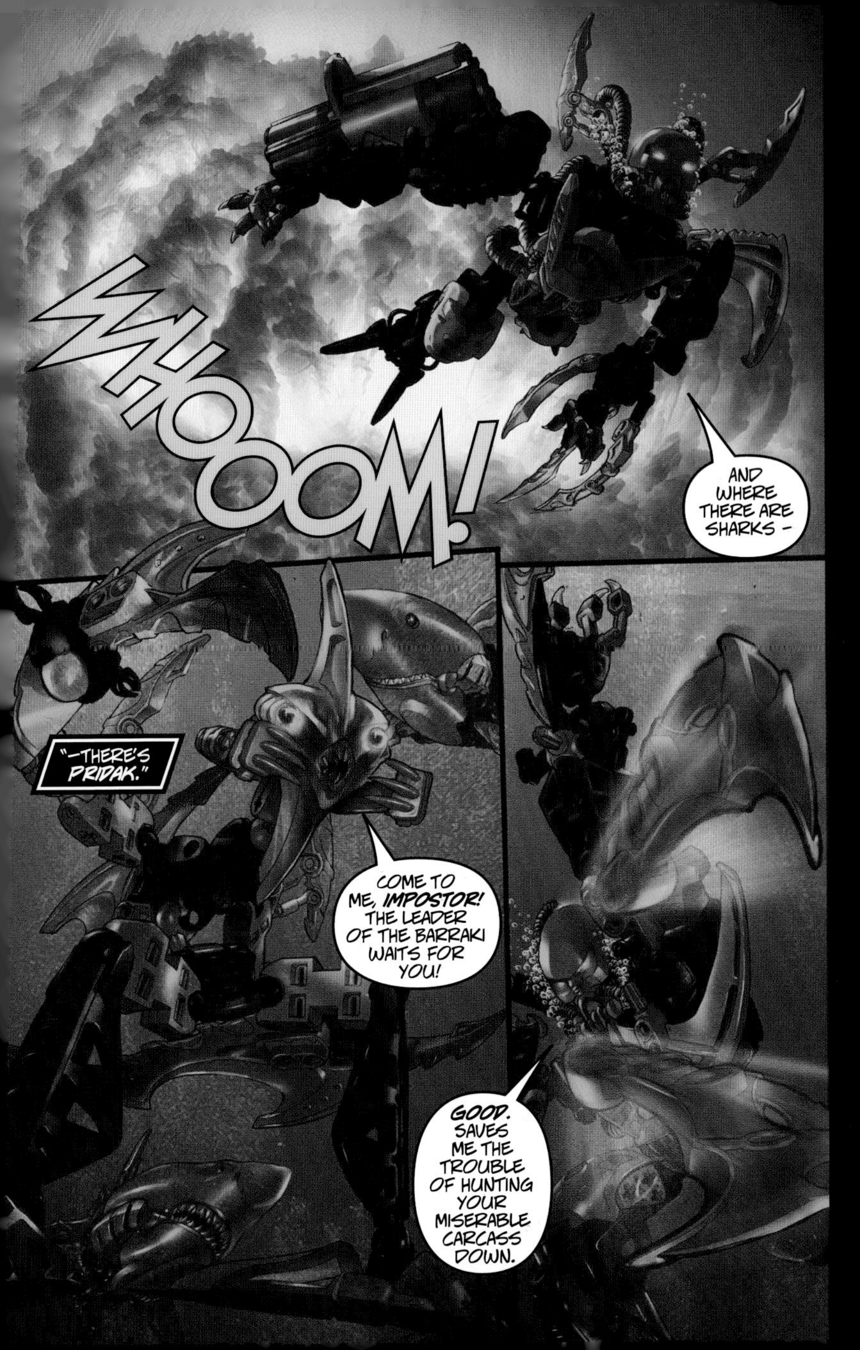
WHOOOOM!
AND WHERE THERE ARE SHARKS –
"–THERE'S PRIDAK."
COME TO ME, IMPOSTOR! THE LEADER OF THE BARRAKI WAITS FOR YOU!
GOOD. SAVES ME THE TROUBLE OF HUNTING YOUR MISERABLE CARCASS DOWN.

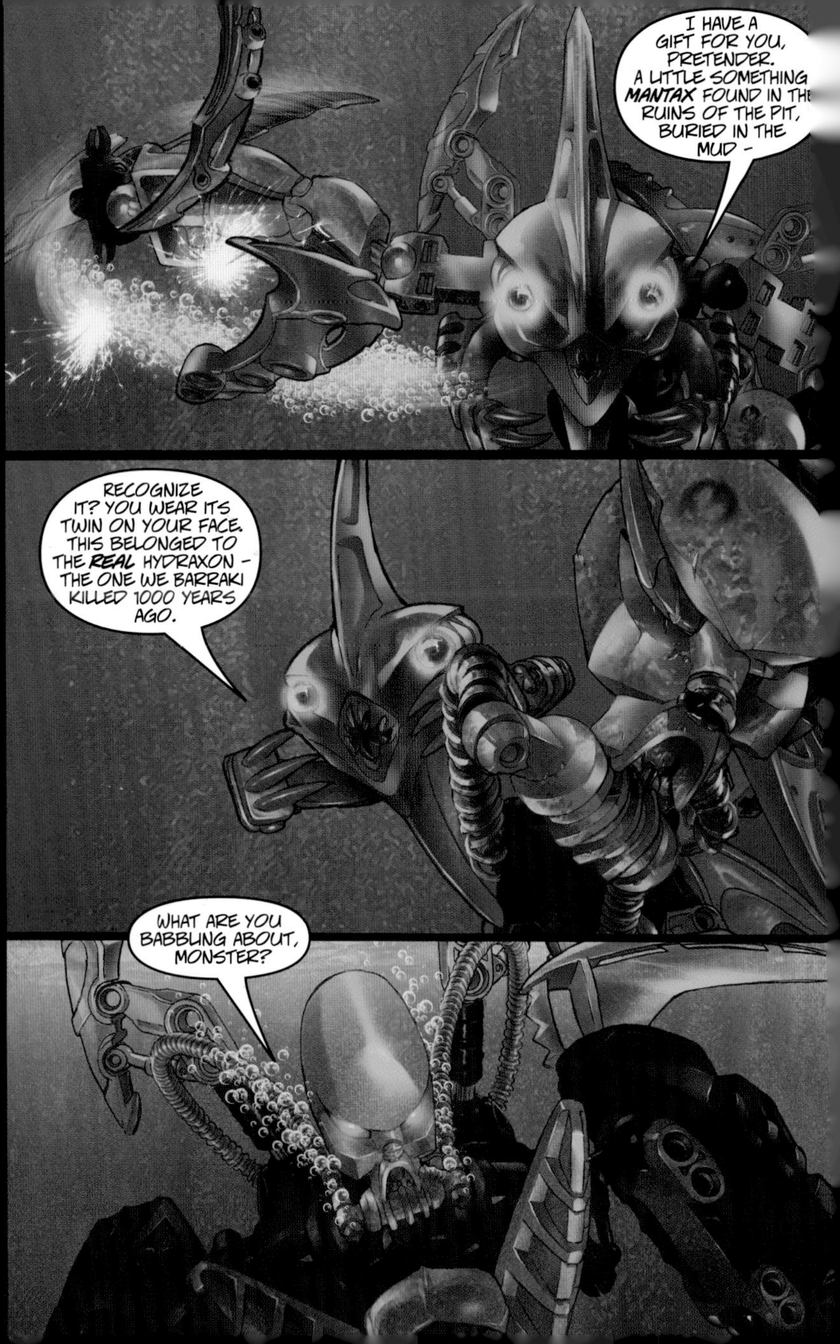
I HAVE A GIFT FOR YOU, PRETENDER. A LITTLE SOMETHING **MANTAX** FOUND IN THE RUINS OF THE PIT, BURIED IN THE MUD -
RECOGNIZE IT? YOU WEAR ITS TWIN ON YOUR FACE. THIS BELONGED TO THE **REAL** HYDRAXON - THE ONE WE BARRAKI KILLED 1000 YEARS AGO.
WHAT ARE YOU BABBLING ABOUT, MONSTER?

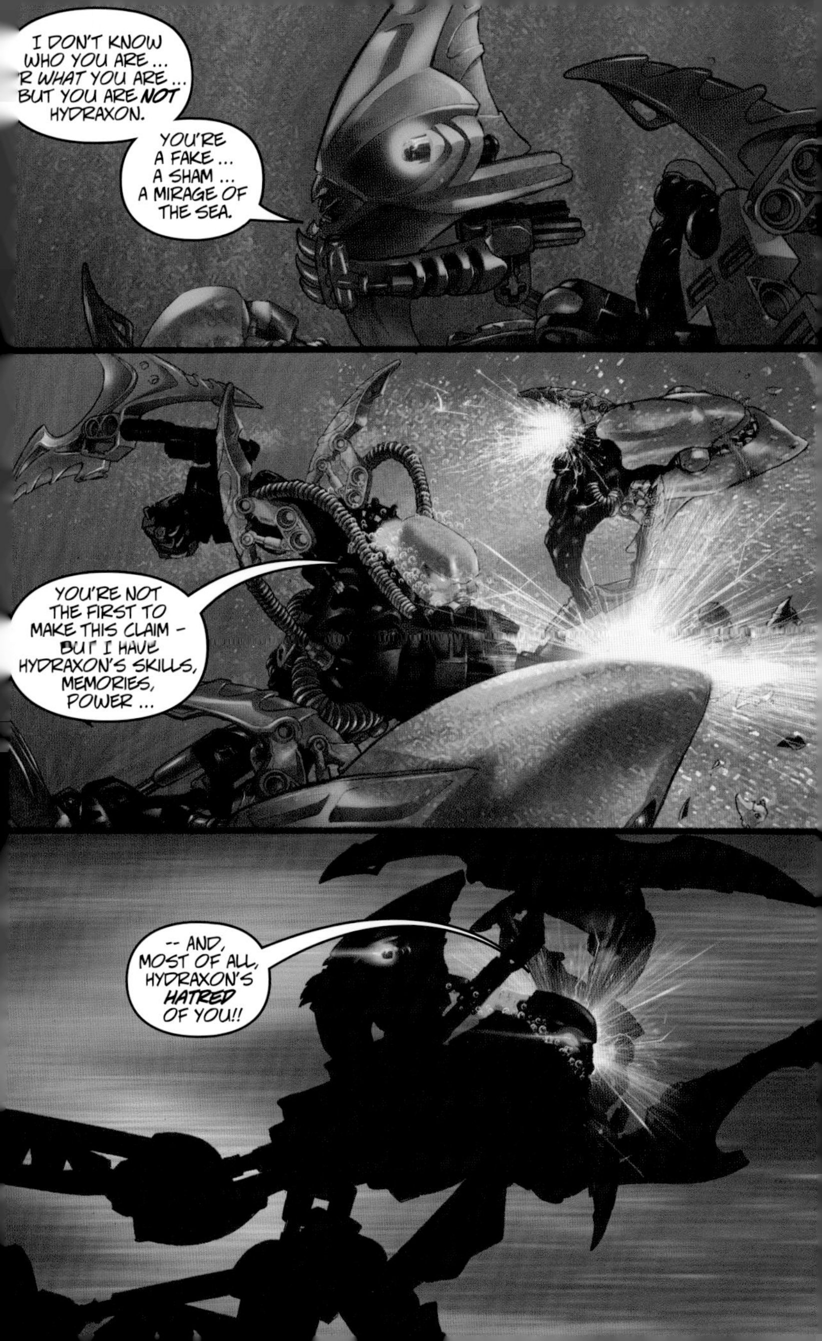
I DON'T KNOW WHO YOU ARE ... 'R WHAT YOU ARE ... BUT YOU ARE **NOT** HYDRAXON.
YOU'RE A FAKE ... A SHAM ... A MIRAGE OF THE SEA.
YOU'RE NOT THE FIRST TO MAKE THIS CLAIM – BUT I HAVE HYDRAXON'S SKILLS, MEMORIES, POWER ...
-- AND, MOST OF ALL, HYDRAXON'S **HATRED** OF YOU!!

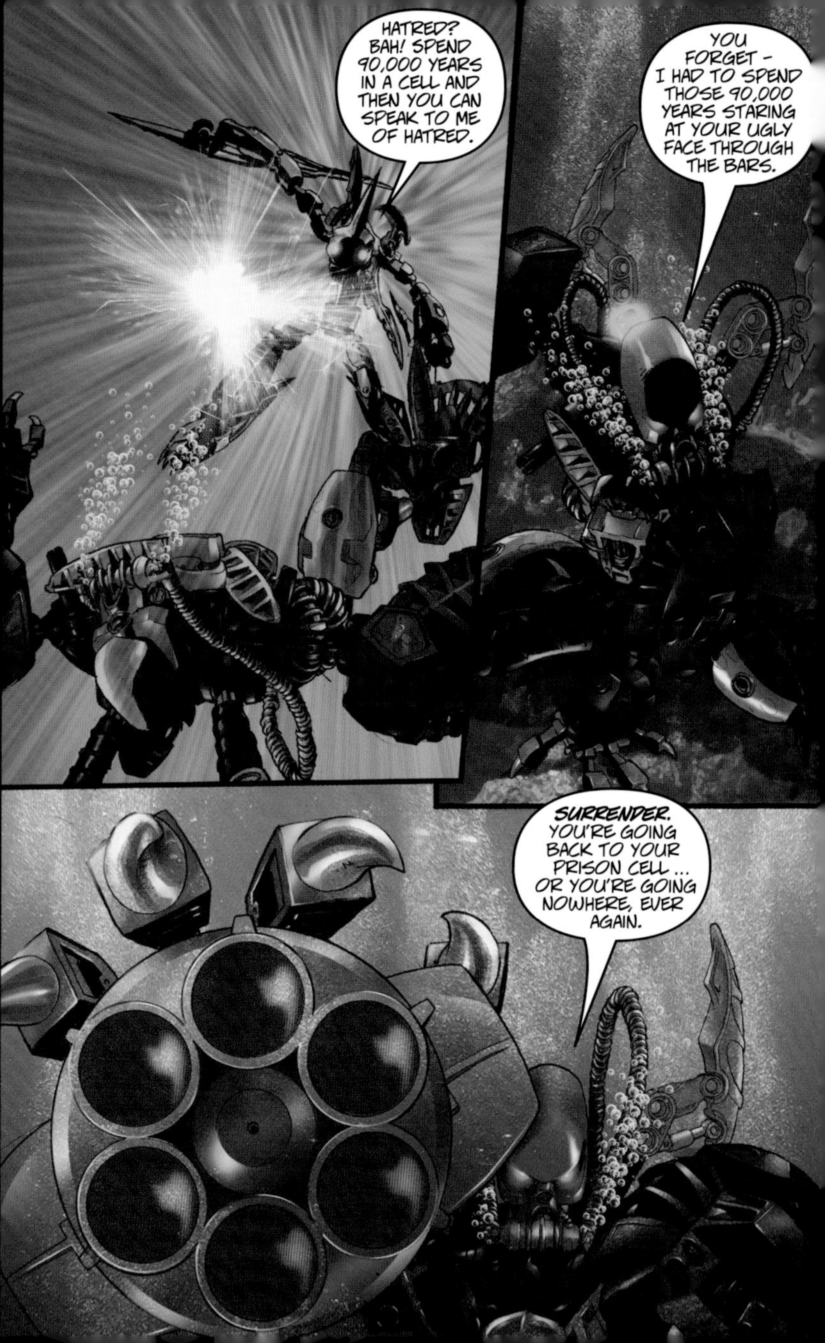

HATRED? BAH! SPEND 90,000 YEARS IN A CELL AND THEN YOU CAN SPEAK TO ME OF HATRED.
YOU FORGET - I HAD TO SPEND THOSE 90,000 YEARS STARING AT YOUR UGLY FACE THROUGH THE BARS.
SURRENDER. YOU'RE GOING BACK TO YOUR PRISON CELL ... OR YOU'RE GOING NOWHERE, EVER AGAIN.

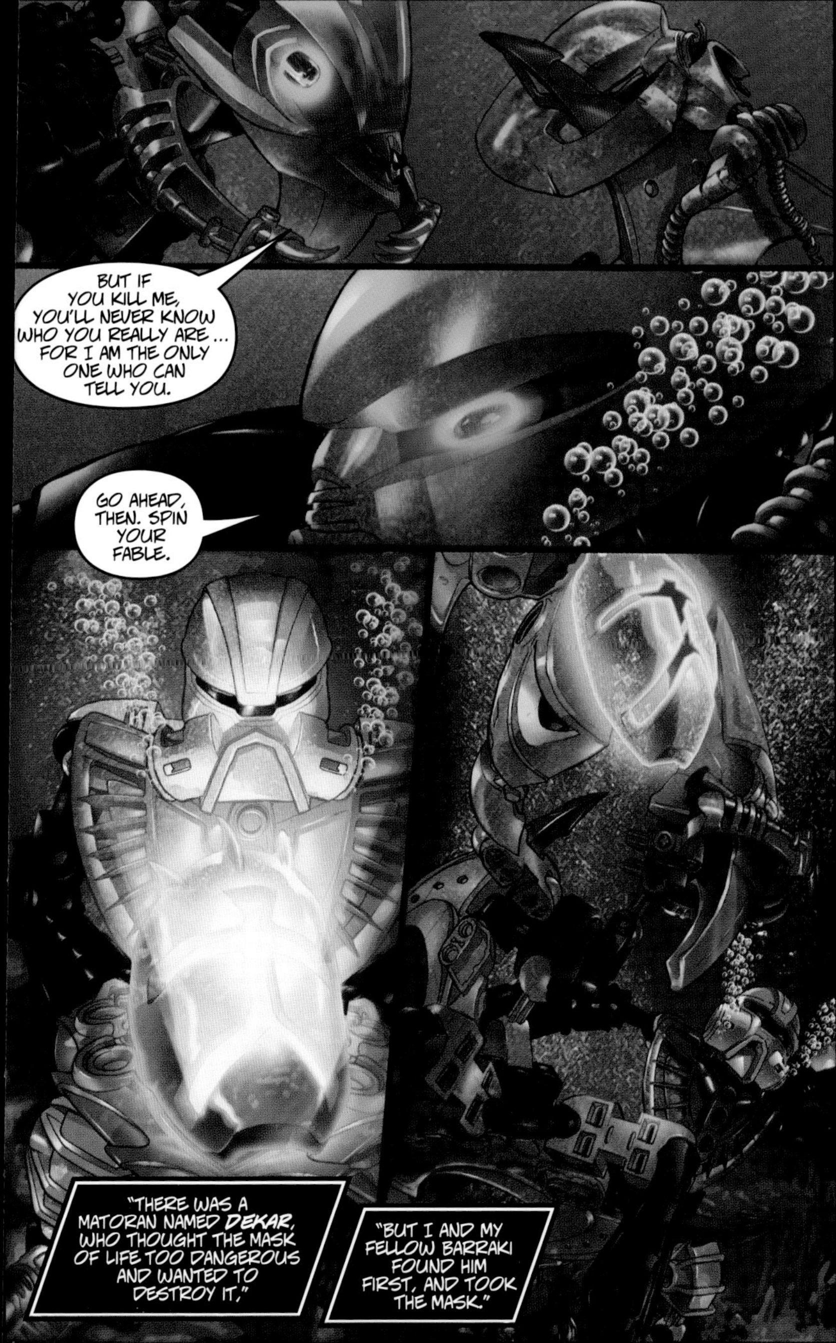
BUT IF YOU KILL ME, YOU'LL NEVER KNOW WHO YOU REALLY ARE ... FOR I AM THE ONLY ONE WHO CAN TELL YOU.
GO AHEAD, THEN. SPIN YOUR FABLE.
"THERE WAS A MATORAN NAMED **DEKAR**, WHO THOUGHT THE MASK OF LIFE TOO DANGEROUS AND WANTED TO DESTROY IT,"
"BUT I AND MY FELLOW BARRAKI FOUND HIM FIRST, AND TOOK THE MASK."

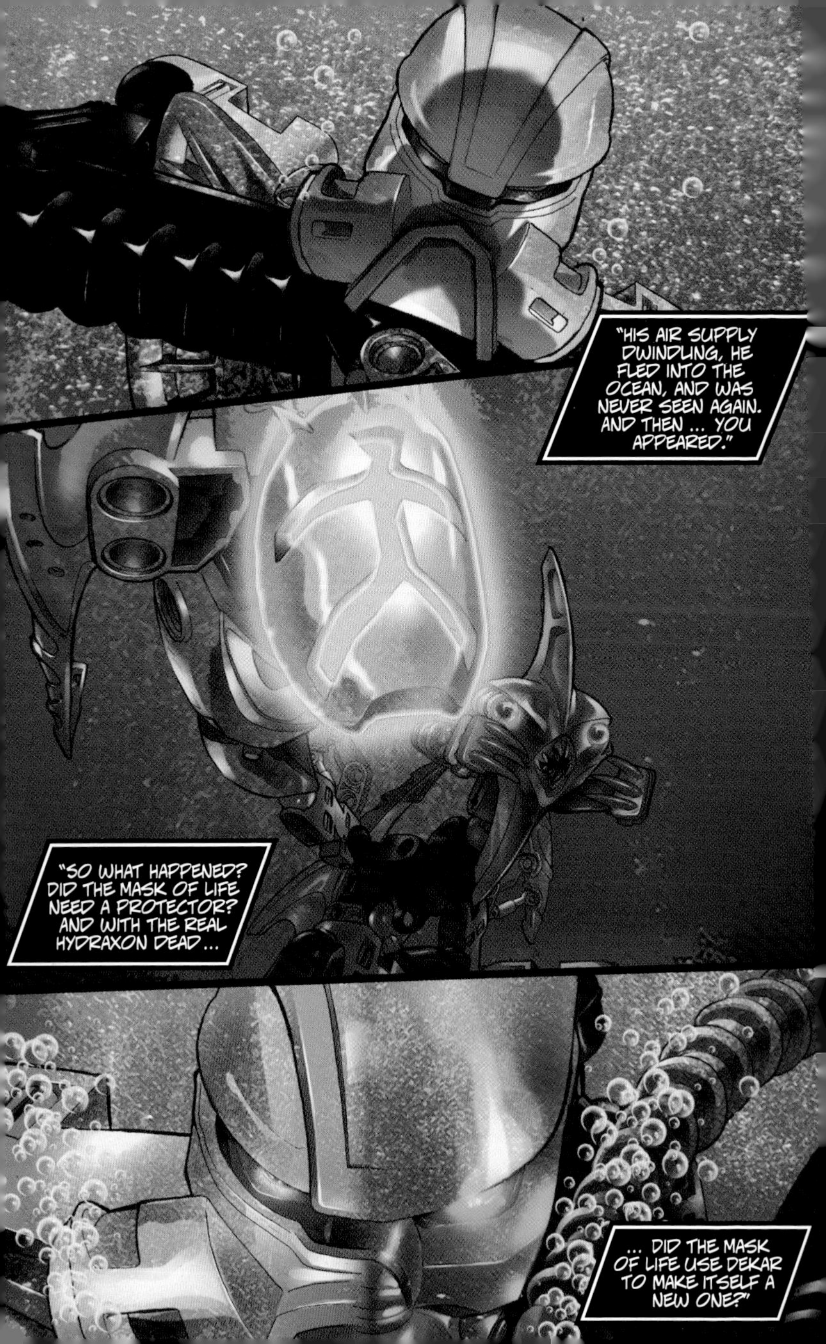
"HIS AIR SUPPLY DWINDLING, HE FLED INTO THE OCEAN, AND WAS NEVER SEEN AGAIN. AND THEN ... YOU APPEARED."
"SO WHAT HAPPENED? DID THE MASK OF LIFE NEED A PROTECTOR? AND WITH THE REAL HYDRAXON DEAD ...
... DID THE MASK OF LIFE USE DEKAR TO MAKE ITSELF A NEW ONE?"

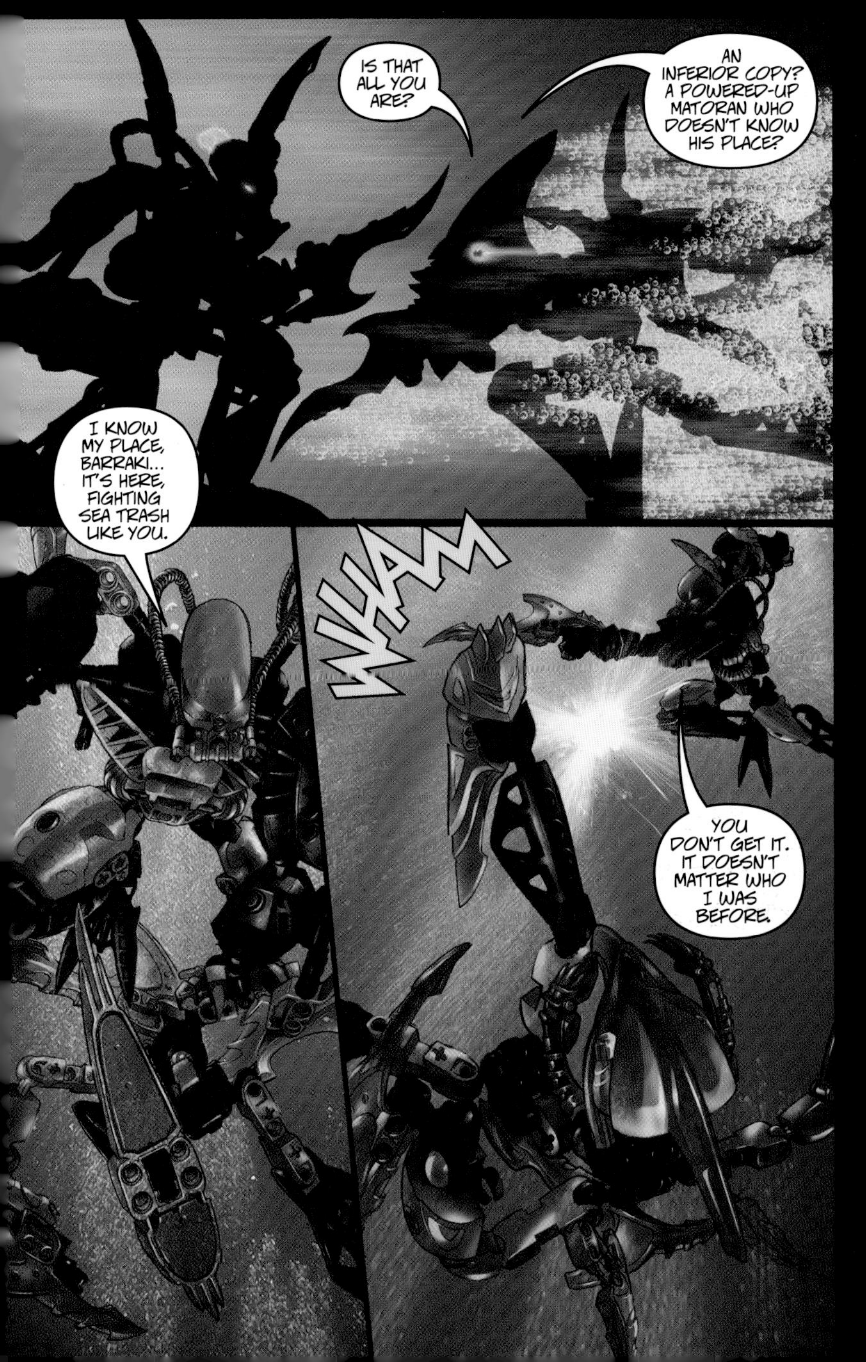
IS THAT ALL YOU ARE?
AN INFERIOR COPY? A POWERED-UP MATORAN WHO DOESN'T KNOW HIS PLACE?
I KNOW MY PLACE, BARRAKI... IT'S HERE, FIGHTING SEA TRASH LIKE YOU.
WHAM
YOU DON'T GET IT. IT DOESN'T MATTER WHO I WAS BEFORE.

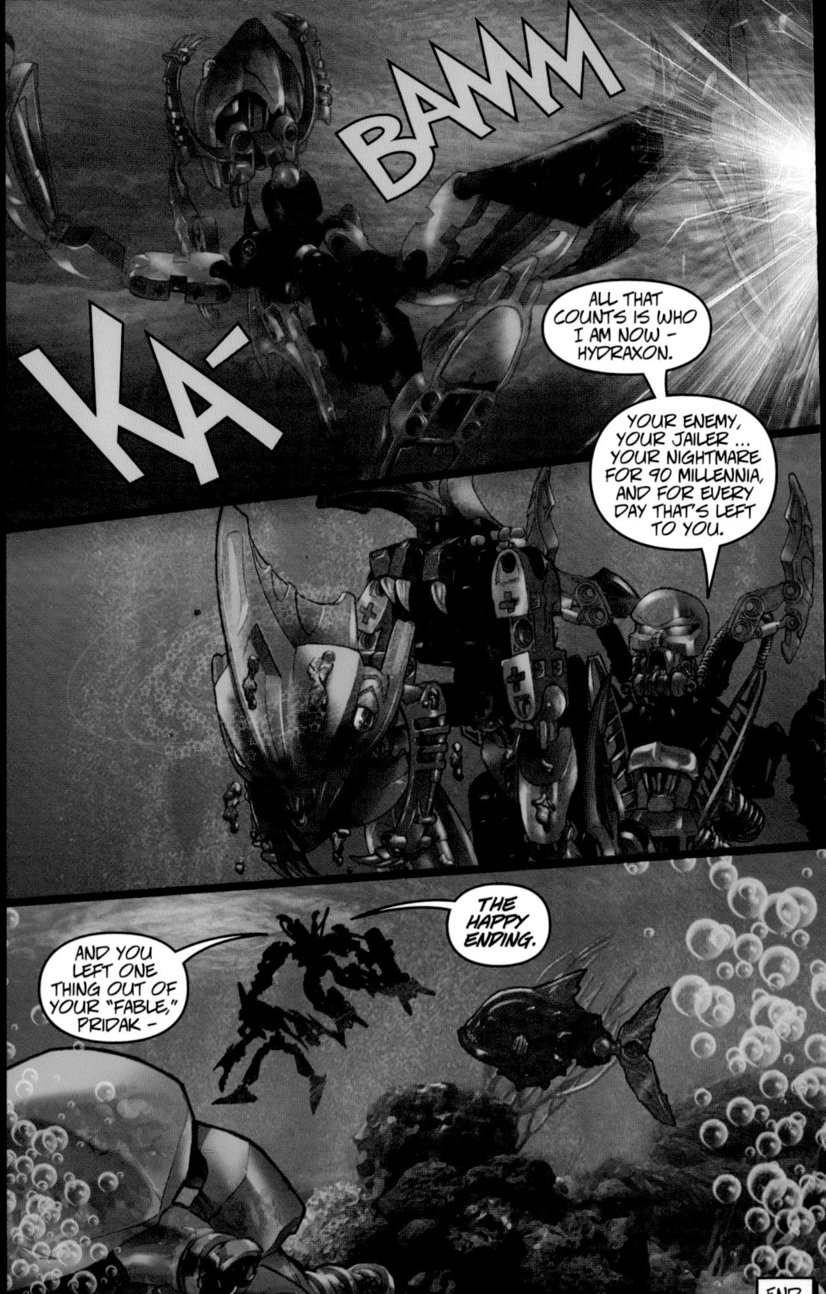
KA-BAMM
ALL THAT COUNTS IS WHO I AM NOW - HYDRAXON.
YOUR ENEMY, YOUR JAILER ... YOUR NIGHTMARE FOR 90 MILLENNIA, AND FOR EVERY DAY THAT'S LEFT TO YOU.
AND YOU LEFT ONE THING OUT OF YOUR "FABLE," PRIDAK -
THE HAPPY ENDING.
END.

THE HARDY BOYS

NEW GRAPHIC NOVEL
VERY 3 MONTHS!

13 “The Deadliest Stunt”
BN - 978-1-59707-102-4
14 “Haley Danielle's Top Eight!”
BN – 978-1-59707-113-0
15 “Live Free, Die Hardy!”
BN – 978-1-59707-123-9
16 “SHHHHHH!”
BN – 978-1-59707-138-3
EW! #17 “Word Up!”
BN – 978-1-59707-147-5
lso available – Hardy Boys #1-12
ll: Pocket sized, 96-112 pp., full-color, $7.95
lso available in hardcover! $12.95

NEW!

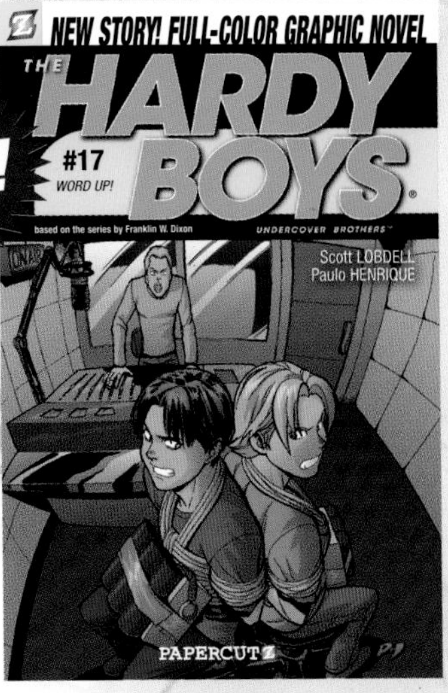
NEW STORY! FULL-COLOR GRAPHIC NOVEL
THE HARDY BOYS
#17
WORD UP!
based on the series by Franklin W. Dixon
UNDERCOVER BROTHERS
Scott LOBDELL
Paulo HENRIQUE
PAPERCUTZ

HE HARDY BOYS BOXED SETS
1-4 ISBN – 978-1-59707-040-9
5-8 ISBN – 978-1-59707-075-1
9-12 ISBN – 978-1-59707-125-3
All: Full-color, $29.95

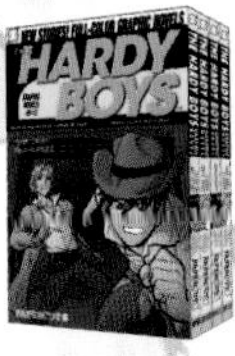
HARDY BOYS

CLASSICS *Illustrated*
Featuring Stories by the World's Greatest Authors

#1 “Great Expectations”
ISBN - 978-1-59707-097-3
#2 “The Invisible Man”
ISBN - 978-1-59707-106-2
#3 “Through the Looking-Glass”
ISBN - 978-1-59707-115-4
#4 “The Raven and Other Poems”
ISBN - 978-1-59707-140-6
NEW! #5 “Hamlet”
ISBN - 978-1-59707-149-9
All: 6 1/2 x 9, 56 pp., full-color, $9.95, hardcover

NEW!

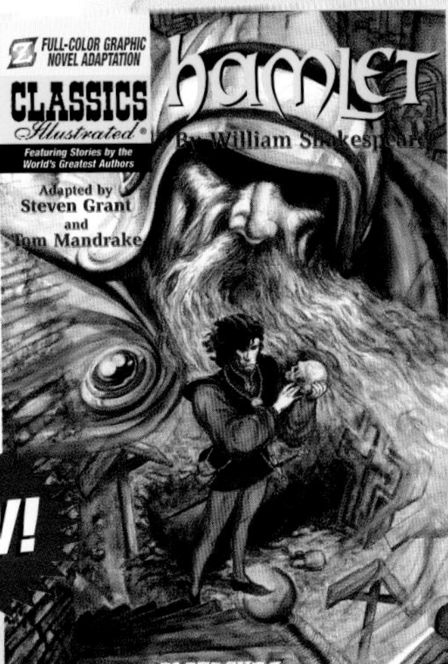
FULL-COLOR GRAPHIC NOVEL ADAPTATION
CLASSICS Illustrated
Featuring Stories by the World's Greatest Authors
Hamlet
William
Adapted by
Steven Grant
and
Mandrake
PAPERCUTZ

Please add $4.00 postage and handling. Add $1.00 for each additional item.
Make check payable to NBM publishing. Send To:
Papercutz, 40 Exchange Place, Suite 1308,
New York, New York 10005, 1-800-886-1223
www.papercutz.com

E.C. FANS!

COLLECTING STORIES BY BILGREY, CABRAL, MR.EXES, GNIEWEK, HUDSO[N], KAPLAN, KLEID, LANSDALE, LOBDELL, MANNION, MARTINEZ, McGREGOR, MURASE, NOETH, PETRUCHA, ROMBERGER, SIMMONS, SMITH 3, TODD, VELILLA AND VOLLMAR!

#1 GHOULS GONE WILD!

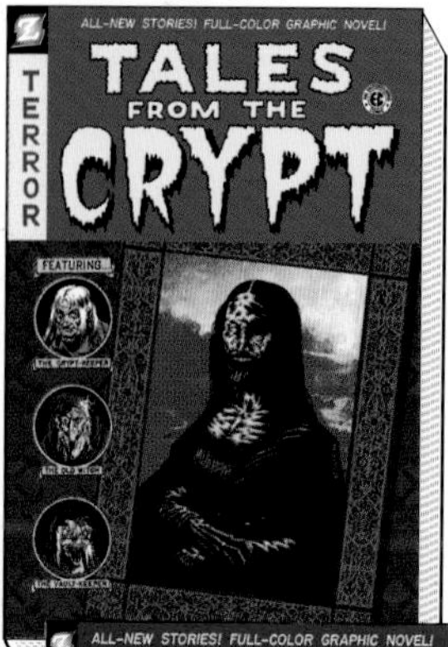
ALL-NEW STORIES! FULL-COLOR GRAPHIC NOVEL!
TERROR
TALES FROM THE CRYPT
FEATURING...

#2 CAN YOU FEAR ME NOW?

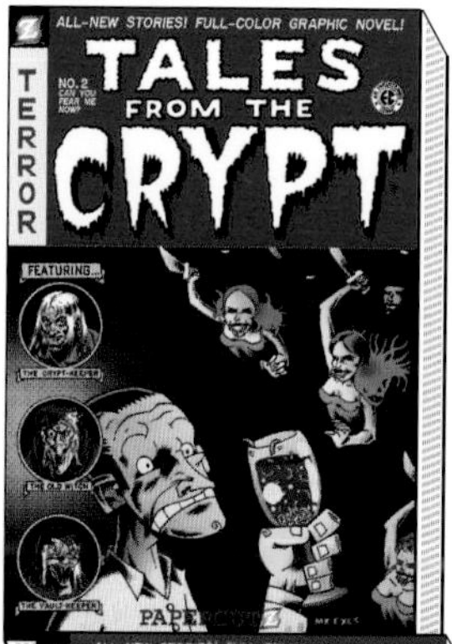
ALL-NEW STORIES! FULL-COLOR GRAPHIC NOVEL!
TERROR
NO. 2
TALES FROM THE CRYPT
FEATURING...
PAPERCUTZ

#3 ZOMBIELICIOUS

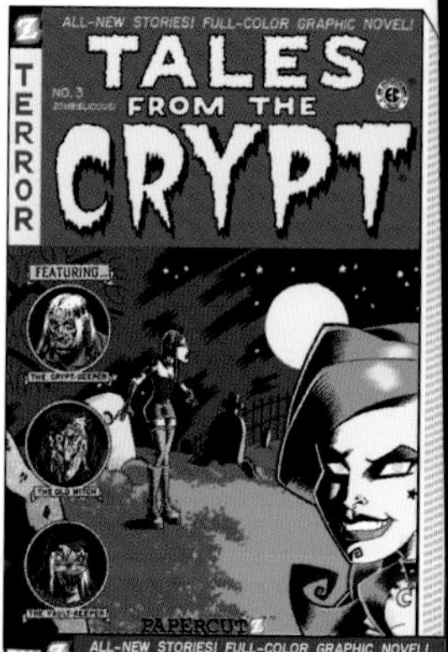
ALL-NEW STORIES! FULL-COLOR GRAPHIC NOVEL!
TERROR
NO. 3
TALES FROM THE CRYPT
FEATURING...
PAPERCUTZ

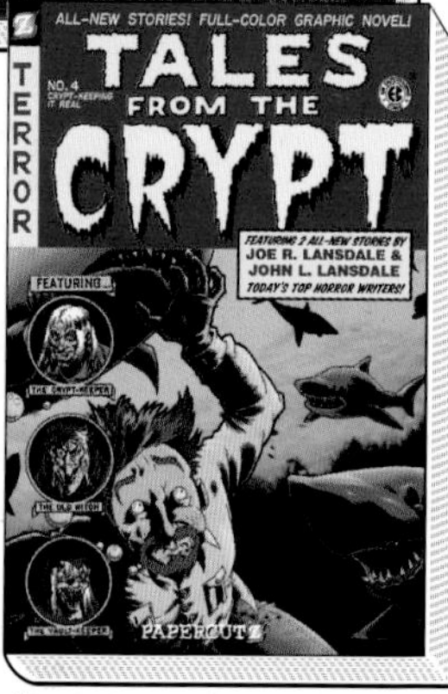
ALL-NEW STORIES! FULL-COLOR GRAPHIC NOVEL!
TERROR
NO. 4
TALES FROM THE CRYPT
FEATURING 2 ALL-NEW STORIES BY JOE R. LANSDALE & JOHN L. LANSDALE TODAY'S TOP HORROR WRITERS!
FEATURING...
PAPERCUTZ

#4 CRYPT-KEEPING IT REAL

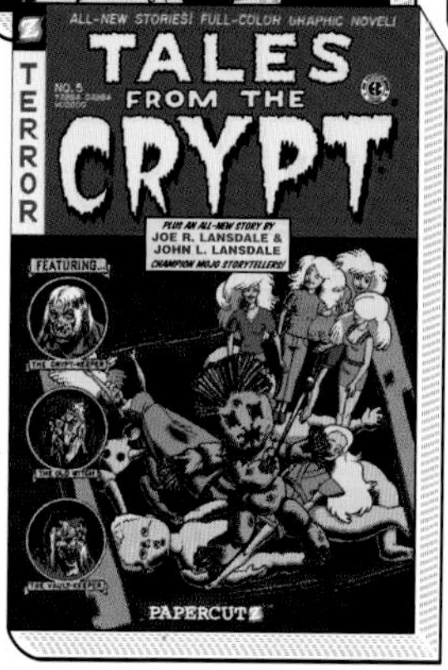
ALL-NEW STORIES! FULL-COLOR GRAPHIC NOVEL!
TERROR
NO. 5
TALES FROM THE CRYPT
PLUS AN ALL-NEW STORY BY JOE R. LANSDALE & JOHN L. LANSDALE CHAMPION MOJO STORYTELLERS!
FEATURING...
PAPERCUTZ

#5 YABBA DABBA VOODOO

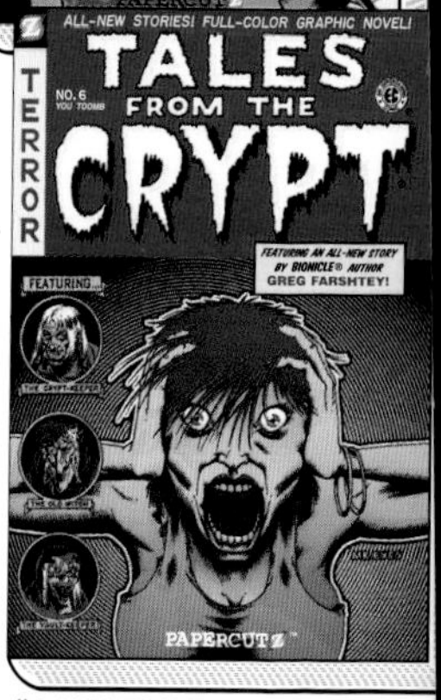
ALL-NEW STORIES! FULL-COLOR GRAPHIC NOVEL!
TERROR
NO. 6
TALES FROM THE CRYPT
FEATURING AN ALL-NEW STORY BY BIONICLE® AUTHOR GREG FARSHTEY!
FEATURING...
PAPERCUTZ

#6 YOU TOOMB

PAPERCUTZ™

www.papercutz.com

AN ENTERTAINING COMIC ®

ON SALE NOW AT BOOKSTORES EVERYWHERE!:

$7.95 each in paperback, $12.95 each in hardcover. Please add $4.00 for postage and handling for the first book, add $1.00 for each additional book. Send to: Papercutz, 40 Exchange Place, Suite 1308, New York, NY 10005
1-800-886-1223

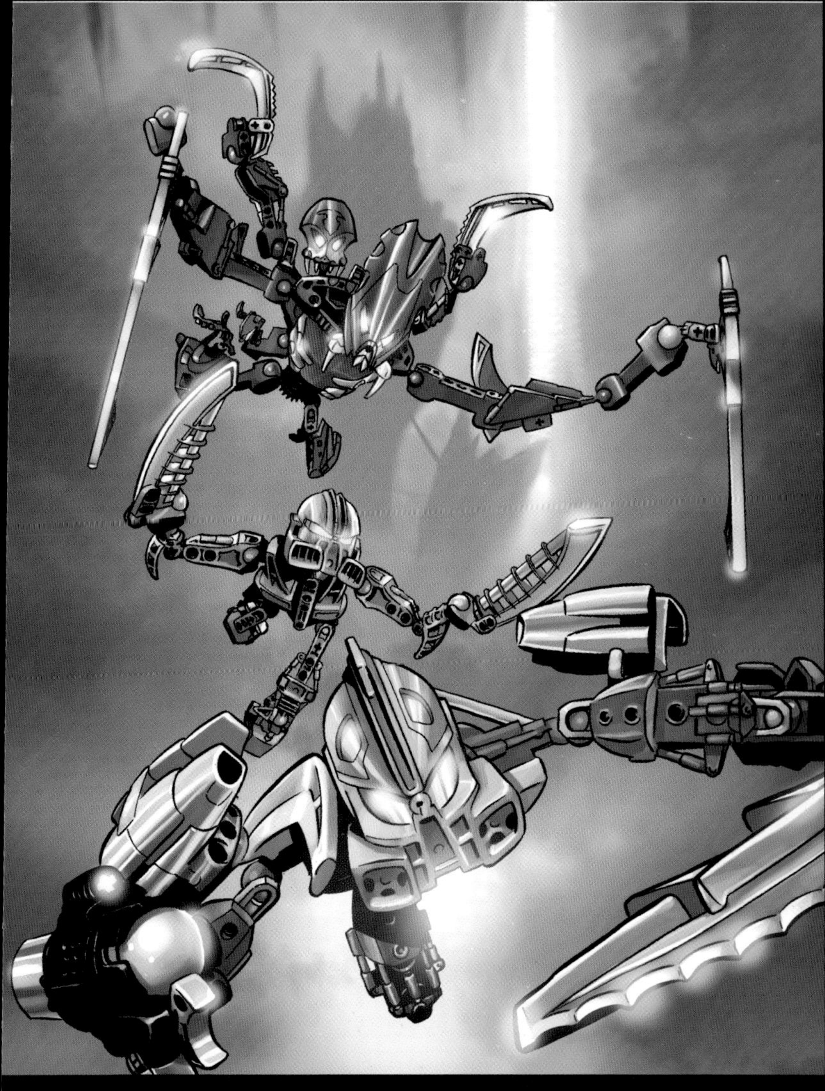

Special Preview:
BIONICLE Graphic Novel #7

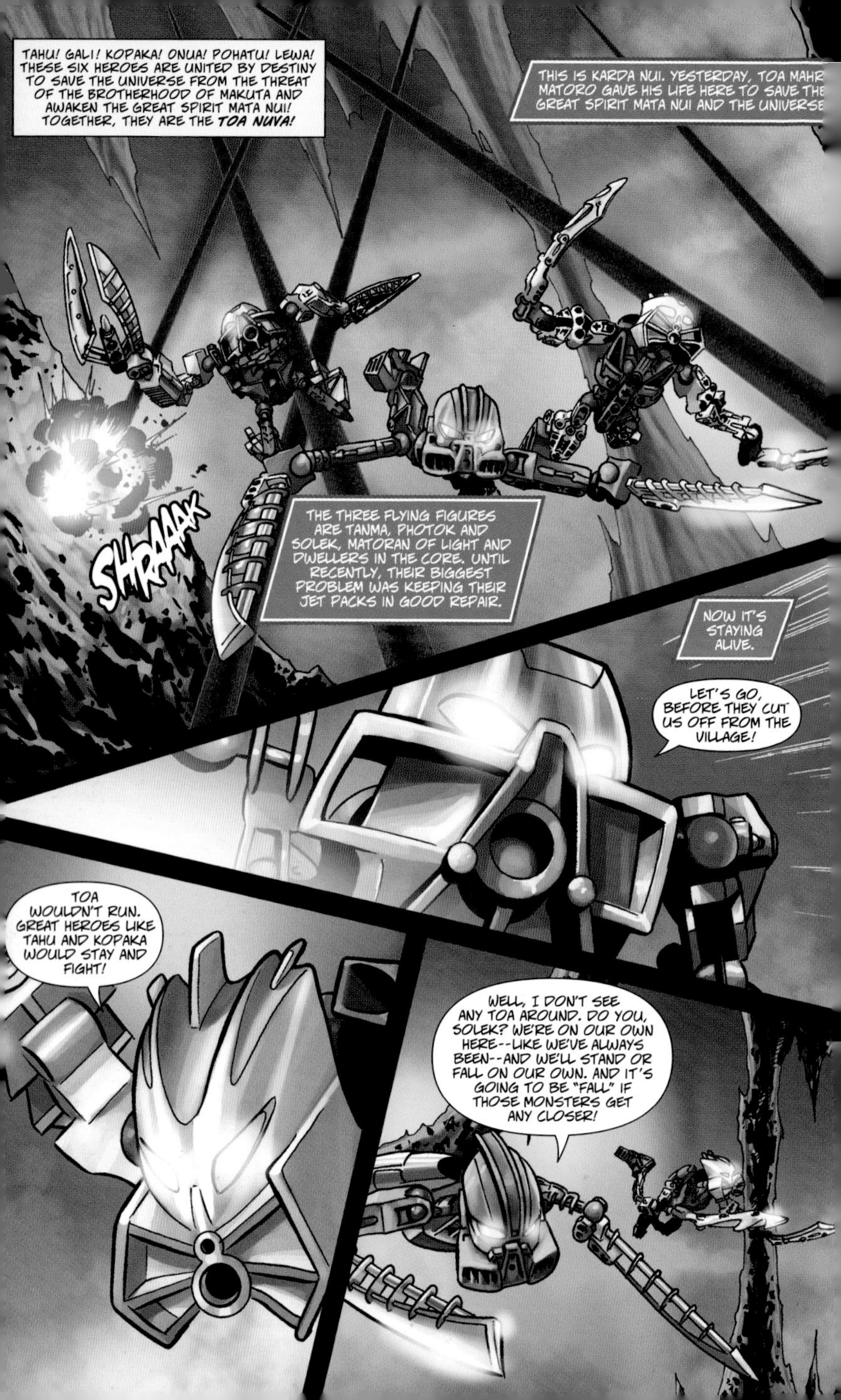
TAHU! GALI! KOPAKA! ONUA! POHATU! LEWA! THESE SIX HEROES ARE UNITED BY DESTINY TO SAVE THE UNIVERSE FROM THE THREAT OF THE BROTHERHOOD OF MAKUTA AND AWAKEN THE GREAT SPIRIT MATA NUI! TOGETHER, THEY ARE THE TOA NUVA!
THIS IS KARDA NUI. YESTERDAY, TOA MAHR MATORO GAVE HIS LIFE HERE TO SAVE THE GREAT SPIRIT MATA NUI AND THE UNIVERSE
SHRAAAK
THE THREE FLYING FIGURES ARE TANMA, PHOTOK AND SOLEK, MATORAN OF LIGHT AND DWELLERS IN THE CORE. UNTIL RECENTLY, THEIR BIGGEST PROBLEM WAS KEEPING THEIR JET PACKS IN GOOD REPAIR.
NOW IT'S STAYING ALIVE.
LET'S GO, BEFORE THEY CUT US OFF FROM THE VILLAGE!
TOA WOULDN'T RUN. GREAT HEROES LIKE TAHU AND KOPAKA WOULD STAY AND FIGHT!
WELL, I DON'T SEE ANY TOA AROUND. DO YOU, SOLEK? WE'RE ON OUR OWN HERE--LIKE WE'VE ALWAYS BEEN--AND WE'LL STAND OR FALL ON OUR OWN. AND IT'S GOING TO BE "FALL" IF THOSE MONSTERS GET ANY CLOSER!

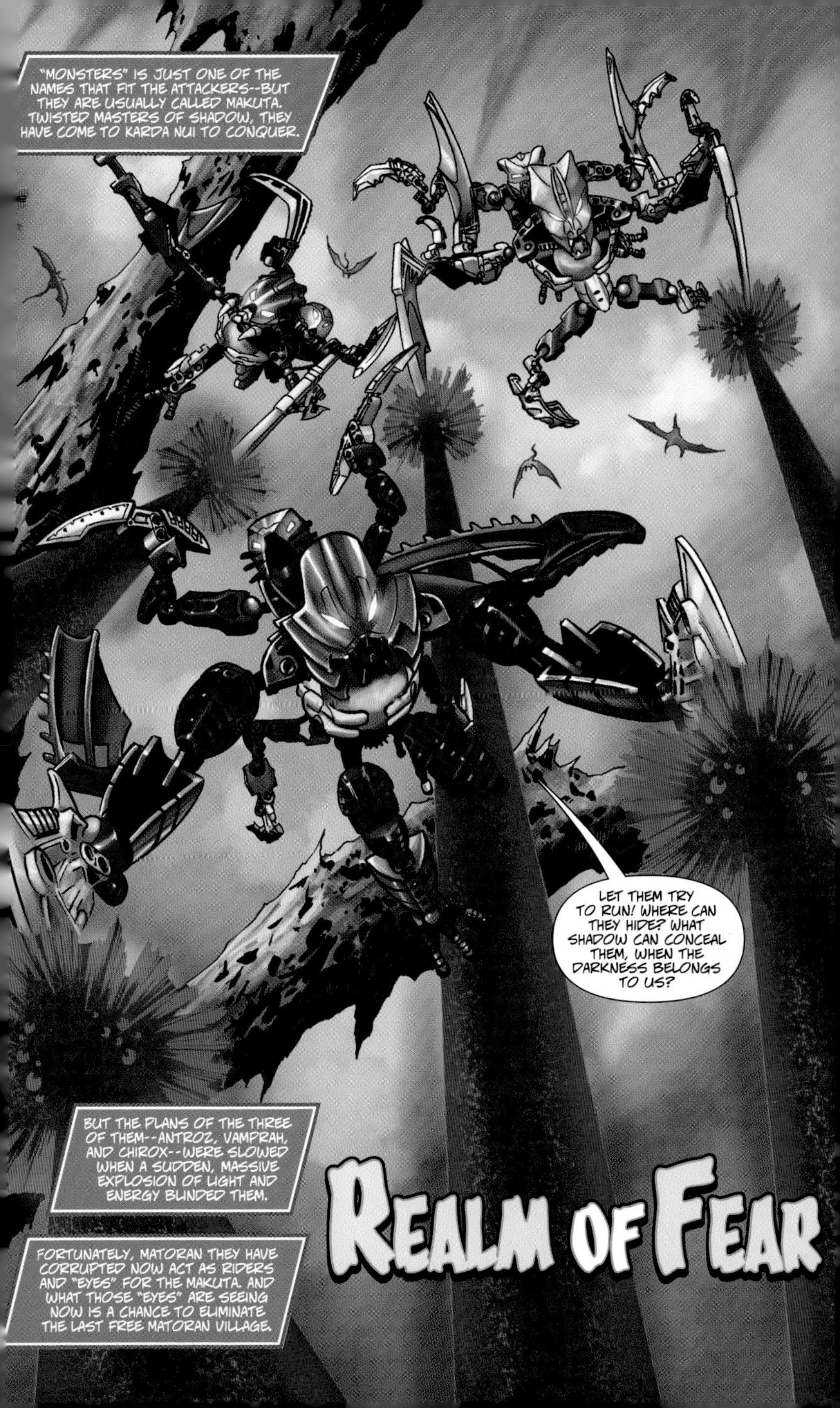
"MONSTERS" IS JUST ONE OF THE NAMES THAT FIT THE ATTACKERS--BUT THEY ARE USUALLY CALLED MAKUTA. TWISTED MASTERS OF SHADOW, THEY HAVE COME TO KARDA NUI TO CONQUER.
LET THEM TRY TO RUN! WHERE CAN THEY HIDE? WHAT SHADOW CAN CONCEAL THEM, WHEN THE DARKNESS BELONGS TO US?
BUT THE PLANS OF THE THREE OF THEM--ANTROZ, VAMPRAH, AND CHIROX--WERE SLOWED WHEN A SUDDEN, MASSIVE EXPLOSION OF LIGHT AND ENERGY BLINDED THEM.
REALM OF FEAR
FORTUNATELY, MATORAN THEY HAVE CORRUPTED NOW ACT AS RIDERS AND "EYES" FOR THE MAKUTA. AND WHAT THOSE "EYES" ARE SEEING NOW IS A CHANCE TO ELIMINATE THE LAST FREE MATORAN VILLAGE.

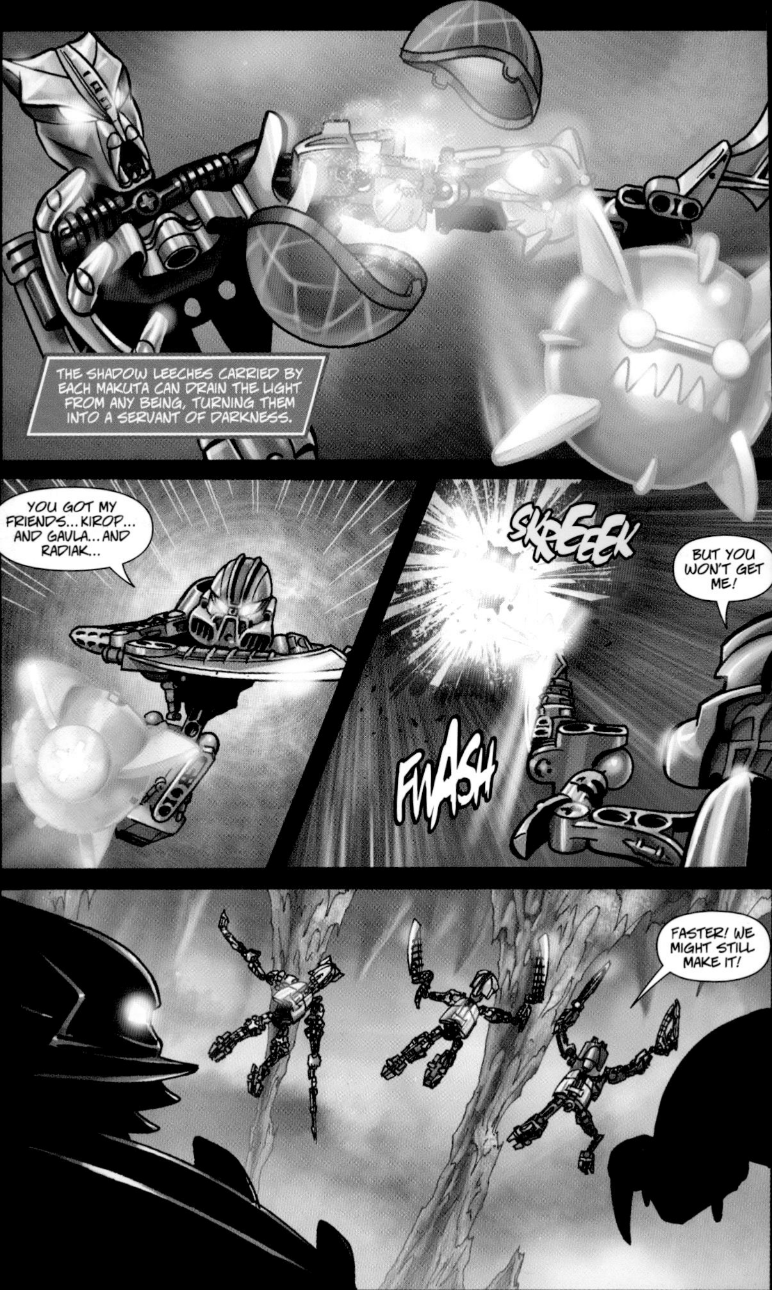

THE SHADOW LEECHES CARRIED BY EACH MAKUTA CAN DRAIN THE LIGHT FROM ANY BEING, TURNING THEM INTO A SERVANT OF DARKNESS.
YOU GOT MY FRIENDS... KIROP... AND GAVULA... AND RADIAK...
SKREEEK
BUT YOU WON'T GET ME!
FWASH
FASTER! WE MIGHT STILL MAKE IT!

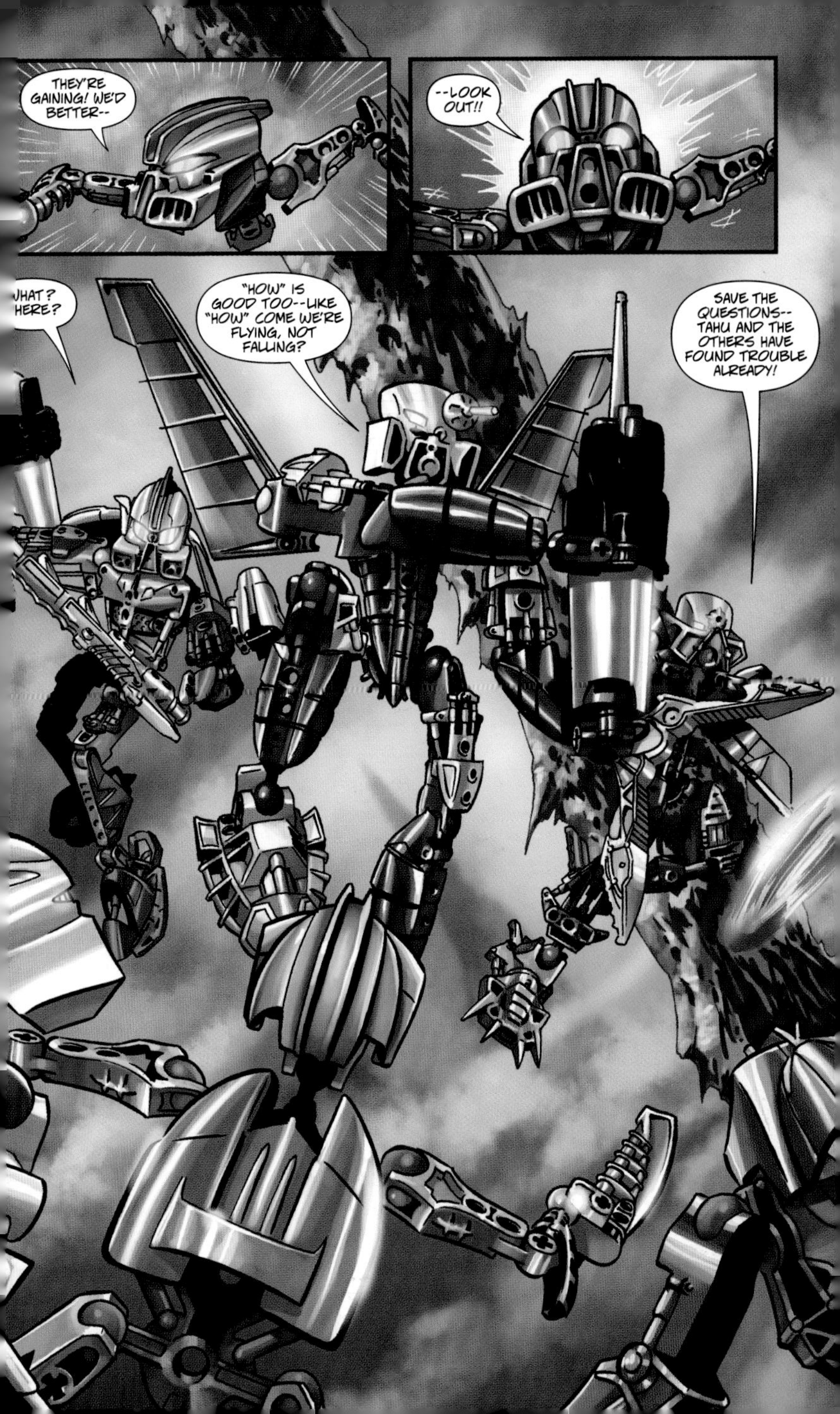

THEY'RE GAINING! WE'D BETTER--
--LOOK OUT!!
WHAT? HERE?
"HOW" IS GOOD TOO--LIKE "HOW" COME WE'RE FLYING, NOT FALLING?
SAVE THE QUESTIONS-- TAHU AND THE OTHERS HAVE FOUND TROUBLE ALREADY!

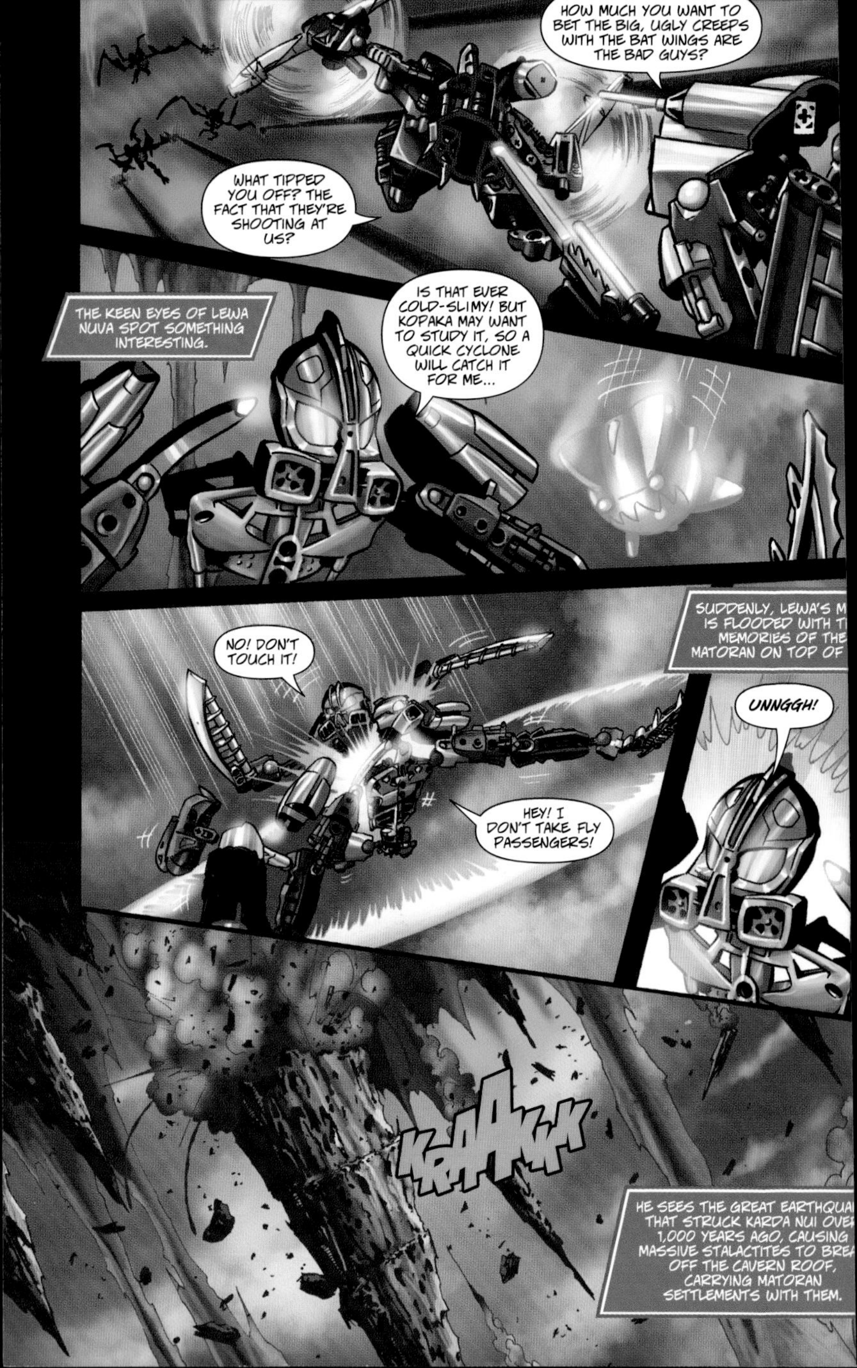
HOW MUCH YOU WANT TO BET THE BIG, UGLY CREEPS WITH THE BAT WINGS ARE THE BAD GUYS?
WHAT TIPPED YOU OFF? THE FACT THAT THEY'RE SHOOTING AT US?
THE KEEN EYES OF LEWA NUVA SPOT SOMETHING INTERESTING.
IS THAT EVER COLD-SLIMY! BUT KOPAKA MAY WANT TO STUDY IT, SO A QUICK CYCLONE WILL CATCH IT FOR ME...
NO! DON'T TOUCH IT!
HEY! I DON'T TAKE FLY PASSENGERS!
SUDDENLY, LEWA'S M
IS FLOODED WITH T
MEMORIES OF THE
MATORAN ON TOP OF
UNNGGH!
KRAAKK
HE SEES THE GREAT EARTHQUA
THAT STRUCK KARDA NUI OVER
1,000 YEARS AGO, CAUSING
MASSIVE STALACTITES TO BREA
OFF THE CAVERN ROOF,
CARRYING MATORAN
SETTLEMENTS WITH THEM.

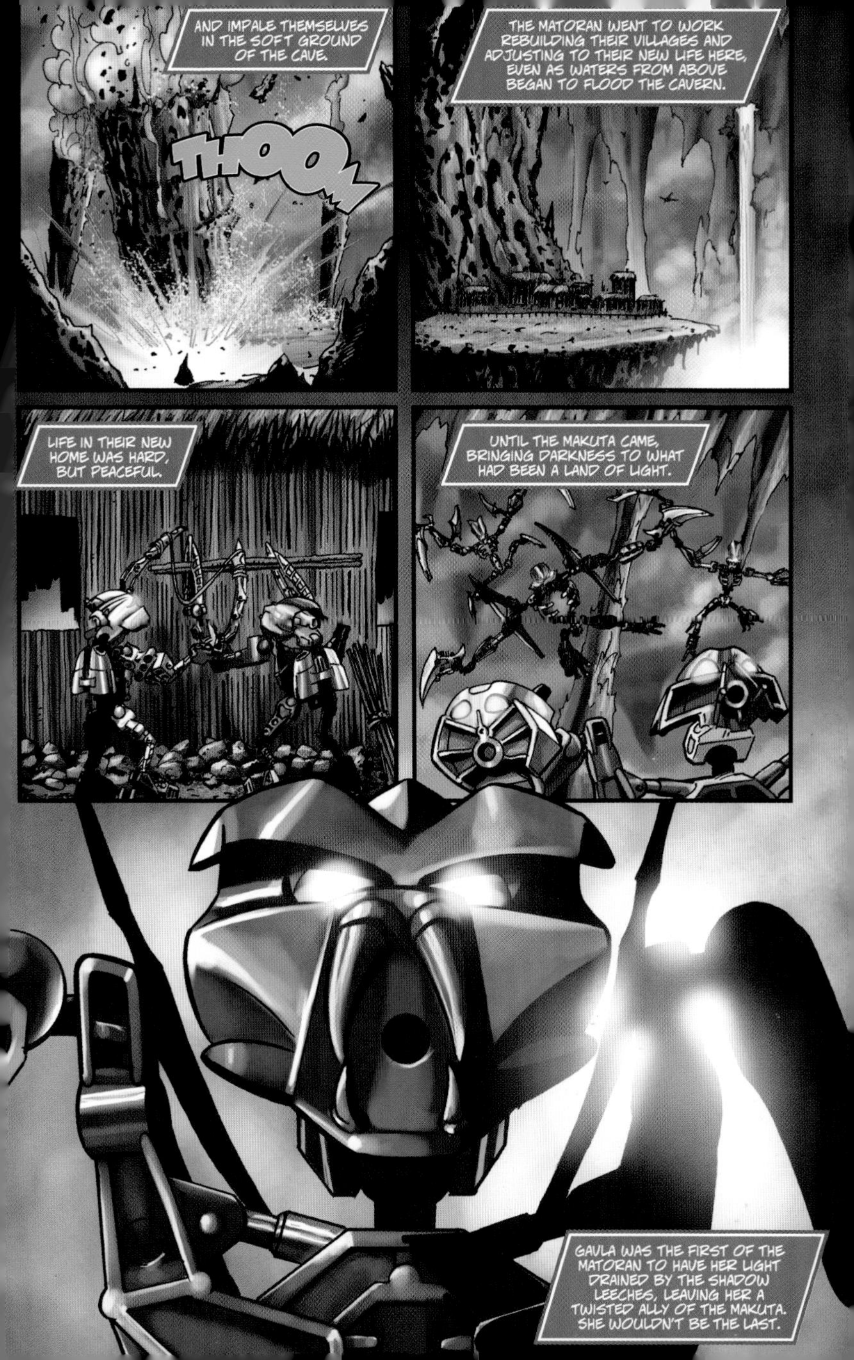
AND IMPALE THEMSELVES IN THE SOFT GROUND OF THE CAVE.
THOOOM
THE MATORAN WENT TO WORK REBUILDING THEIR VILLAGES AND ADJUSTING TO THEIR NEW LIFE HERE, EVEN AS WATERS FROM ABOVE BEGAN TO FLOOD THE CAVERN.
LIFE IN THEIR NEW HOME WAS HARD, BUT PEACEFUL.
UNTIL THE MAKUTA CAME, BRINGING DARKNESS TO WHAT HAD BEEN A LAND OF LIGHT.
GAVLA WAS THE FIRST OF THE MATORAN TO HAVE HER LIGHT DRAINED BY THE SHADOW LEECHES, LEAVING HER A TWISTED ALLY OF THE MAKUTA. SHE WOULDN'T BE THE LAST.

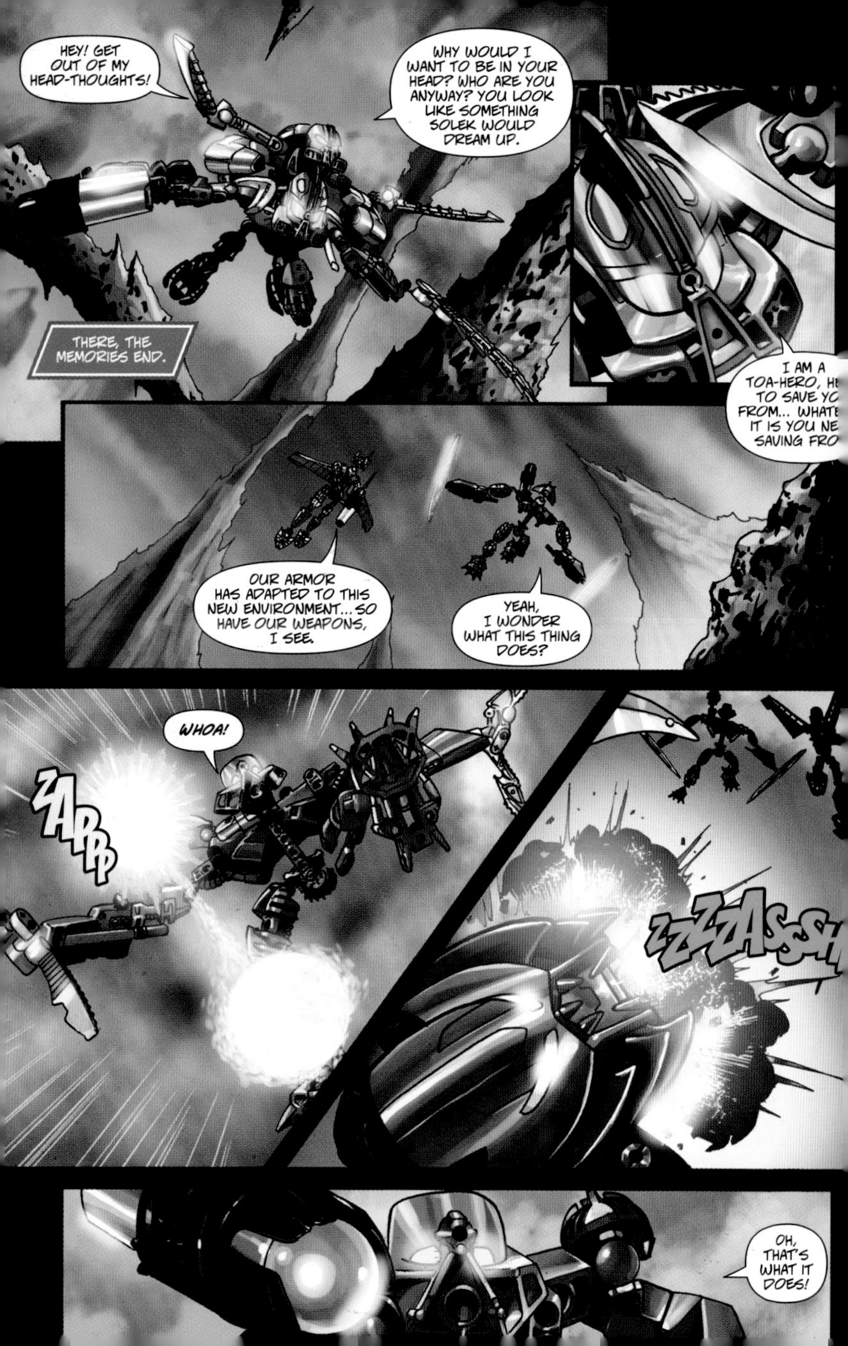
HEY! GET OUT OF MY HEAD-THOUGHTS!
WHY WOULD I WANT TO BE IN YOUR HEAD? WHO ARE YOU ANYWAY? YOU LOOK LIKE SOMETHING SOLEK WOULD DREAM UP.
THERE, THE MEMORIES END.
I AM A TOA-HERO, HE TO SAVE YO FROM... WHATE IT IS YOU NE SAVING FRO
OUR ARMOR HAS ADAPTED TO THIS NEW ENVIRONMENT... SO HAVE OUR WEAPONS, I SEE.
YEAH, I WONDER WHAT THIS THING DOES?
WHOA!
ZAPPP
ZZZZASSSH
OH, THAT'S WHAT IT DOES!

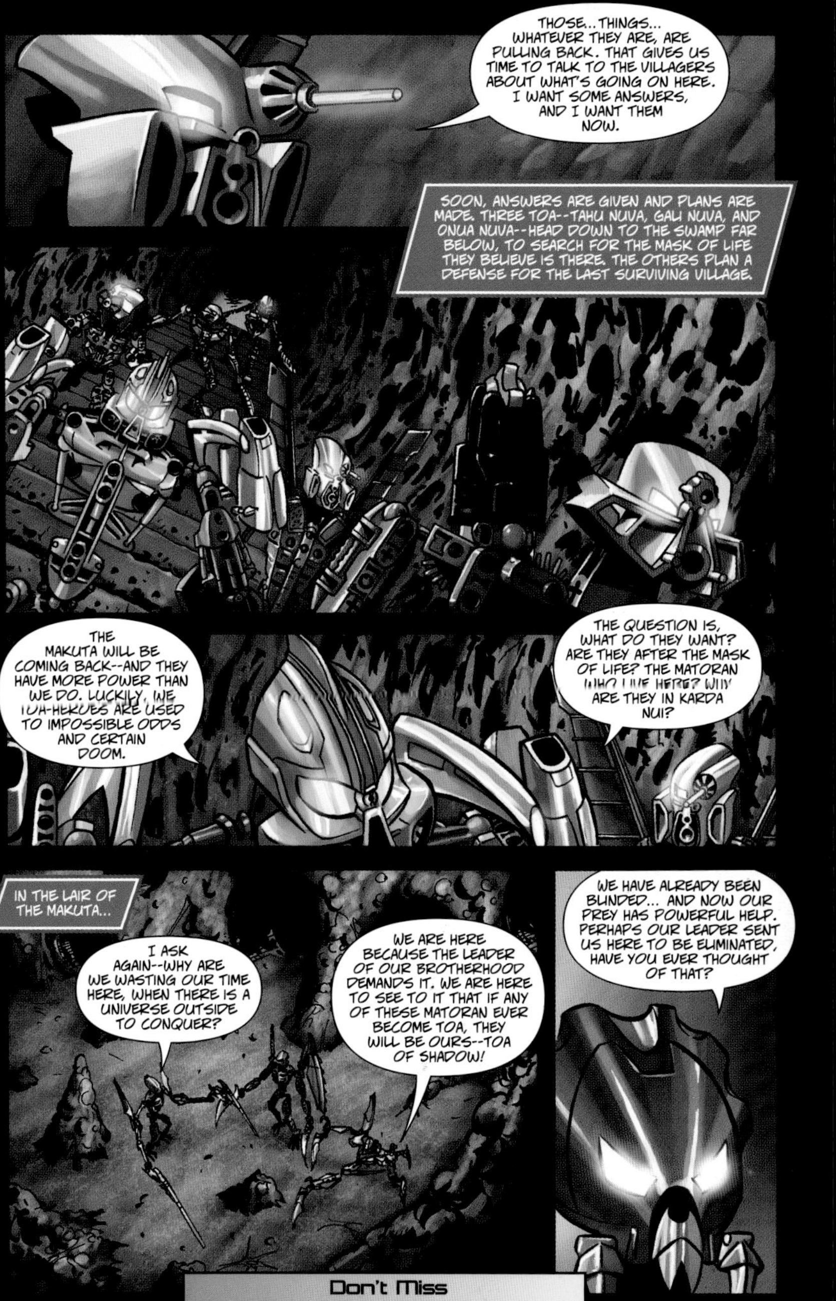
THOSE... THINGS... WHATEVER THEY ARE, ARE PULLING BACK. THAT GIVES US TIME TO TALK TO THE VILLAGERS ABOUT WHAT'S GOING ON HERE. I WANT SOME ANSWERS, AND I WANT THEM NOW.
SOON, ANSWERS ARE GIVEN AND PLANS ARE MADE. THREE TOA--TAHU NUVA, GALI NUVA, AND ONUA NUVA--HEAD DOWN TO THE SWAMP FAR BELOW, TO SEARCH FOR THE MASK OF LIFE THEY BELIEVE IS THERE. THE OTHERS PLAN A DEFENSE FOR THE LAST SURVIVING VILLAGE.
THE MAKUTA WILL BE COMING BACK--AND THEY HAVE MORE POWER THAN WE DO. LUCKILY, WE TOA-HEROES ARE USED TO IMPOSSIBLE ODDS AND CERTAIN DOOM.
THE QUESTION IS, WHAT DO THEY WANT? ARE THEY AFTER THE MASK OF LIFE? THE MATORAN WHO LIVE HERE? WHY ARE THEY IN KARDA NUI?
IN THE LAIR OF THE MAKUTA...
I ASK AGAIN--WHY ARE WE WASTING OUR TIME HERE, WHEN THERE IS A UNIVERSE OUTSIDE TO CONQUER?
WE ARE HERE BECAUSE THE LEADER OF OUR BROTHERHOOD DEMANDS IT. WE ARE HERE TO SEE TO IT THAT IF ANY OF THESE MATORAN EVER BECOME TOA, THEY WILL BE OURS--TOA OF SHADOW!
WE HAVE ALREADY BEEN BLINDED... AND NOW OUR PREY HAS POWERFUL HELP. PERHAPS OUR LEADER SENT US HERE TO BE ELIMINATED, HAVE YOU EVER THOUGHT OF THAT?

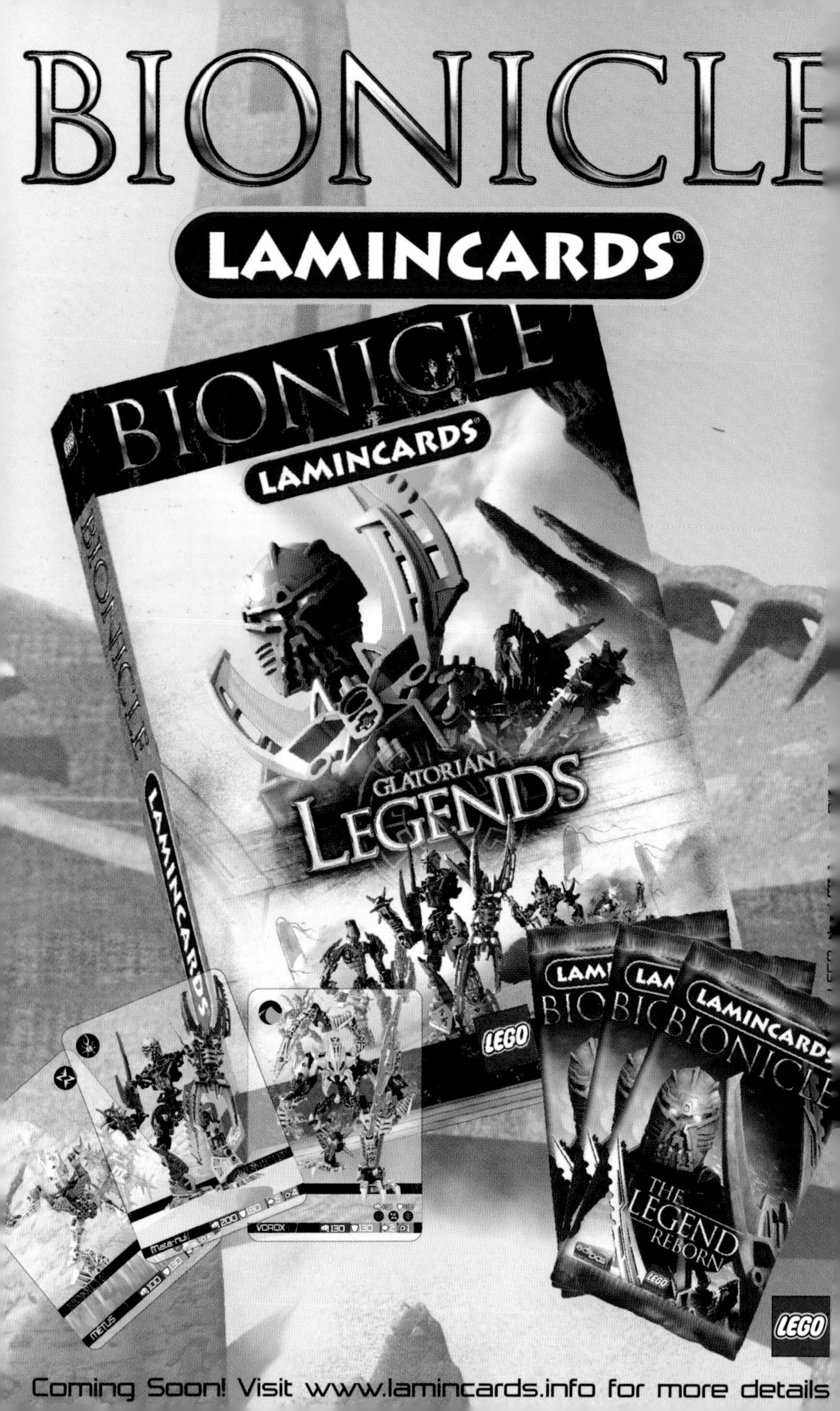
BIONICLE
LAMINCARDS®
BIONICLE
LAMINCARDS®
GLATORIAN
LEGENDS
LAMINCARDS
LEGO
LAMINCARDS
BIONICLE
THE LEGEND REBORN
Mata-nui
VOROX
METUS
LEGO
Coming Soon! Visit www.lamincards.info for more details

WATCH OUT FOR PAPERCUT𝗭

Welcome to the ever-popular Papercutz Backpages, where you can find all the latest news and previews of upcoming Papercutz graphic novels. I'm Jim Salicrup, your semi-humanoid guide and Papercutz Editor-in-Chief. This particular edition is so jam-packed with goodies, we better get right to it!

If you already picked up BIONICLE Graphic Novel #5 "The Battle of Voya Nui," then you have your exclusive B.I.O. code for a special free online sticker – if you didn't pick up BIONICLE #5, it's still available at booksellers everywhere. And now we have a special video game code available to you-- it's CUTZ96. Here's how it works:

🌀 Launch the Glatorian Arena game—either the web-based or downloadable version.

🌀 In the "ready room" (the default screen) there will be a character, and near the character is a post. Just click the post, and then enter the code. The code will provide you with a special enhanced ability in the game.

And what did you think of the all-new "Hydraxon's Tale" by Greg Farshtey and Christian Zanier? Both Greg and Christian are working on all-new stories for BIONICLE #8 "Legends of Bara Magna," which will be the first totally ALL-NEW Papercutz BIONICLE graphic novel. Tell us if you loved Greg and Christian's very first collaboration or hated it on our new blog at www.papercutz.com, Just post your comments, and you'll be able to interact with fellow BIONICLE fans and writer Greg Farshtey himself!

But right here we have a couple of special previews on the following pages. First up is TALES FROM THE CRYPT Graphic Novel #8 "Diary of a Stinky Dead Kid." We present here a few pages from one of the two non-wimpy tales created by writer Stefan Petrucha and artist Rick Parker. Also featured in CRYPT #8, is the sappy vampire romance to end all sappy vampire romances—"Dielite" by Stefan Petrucha and Miran Kim.

We've also got an excerpt from HARDY BOYS #17 "Word Up!" by Scott Lobdell and Paulo Henrique. Frank and Joe Hardy wind up risking their lives to save a controversial radio show host, because they believe that freedom of speech protects even people that voice unpopular views.

If all that wasn't exciting enough, just wait till BIONICLE #7 "Realm of Fear" is released. Don't let the title scare you — it's another bona fide BIONICLE classic by Greg Farshtey and artist Leigh Gallagher. But if it makes you feel better, it's okay to keep your Mask of Life close at hand!

Thanks,

October

Monday

My name's Glugg. It's always sad and scary whe a kid dies, especially if it's you. Funny, for the longest time I thought the scariest thing was m brother, Rock.

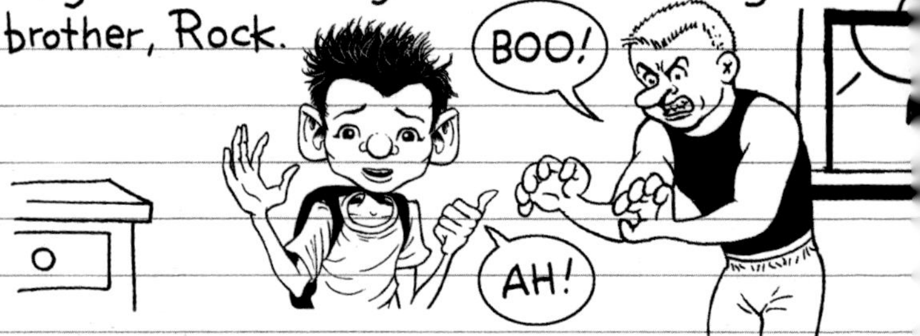
BOO!
AH!

He's twice my size and only has room in his brai for his band, bullying me and making fun of this journal. I think he's jealous I can write. Plus he wants a new drum set badly, and our parents made it clear we can't afford one.

Anyway, it turns out there ARE things scarier than Rock, just a couple, though, like death.

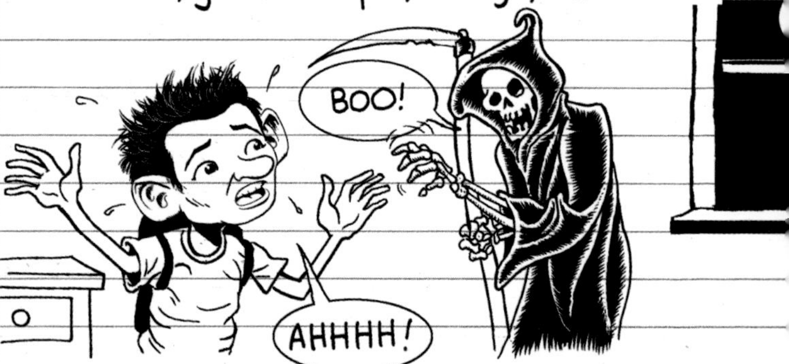
BOO!
AHHHH!

Have you ever just KNOWN the phone will ring and exactly who's calling and you feel really cool, like it's magic or something?

You'd think with something big as DEATH, you'd get the same kind of warning, but nope. Not me, anyway. No bells, no whistles, not even a vague sense of impending doom.

It sucks! I mean I was minding my own business, standing next to my pal Al Crowley at the train station with the rest of the kids, on our dumb school trip to the Museum, when...

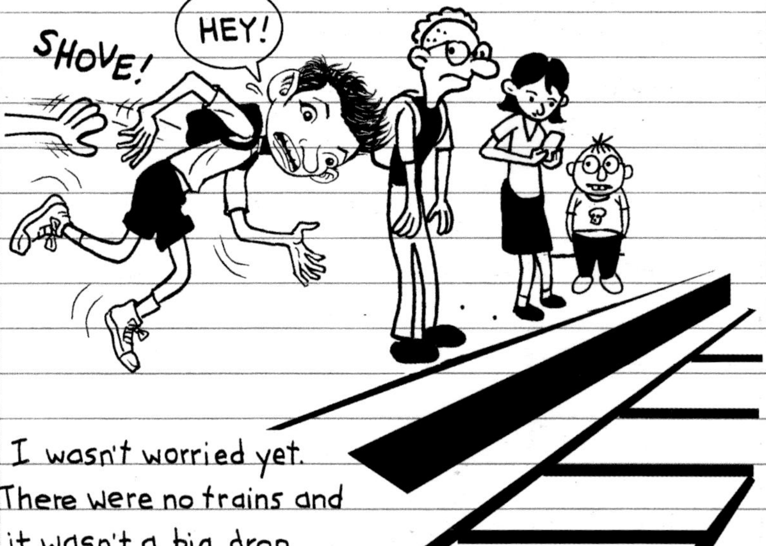
SHOVE!
HEY!

I wasn't worried yet. There were no trains and it wasn't a big drop.

After I hit bottom, I even managed to have a short chat with Crowley.

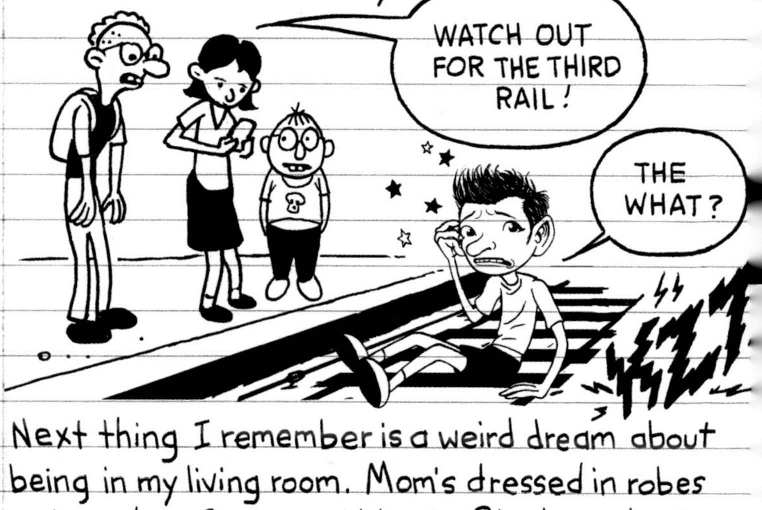
WATCH OUT FOR THE THIRD RAIL!
THE WHAT?
ZZZT!

Next thing I remember is a weird dream about being in my living room. Mom's dressed in robes and reading from an old book. She loves books.

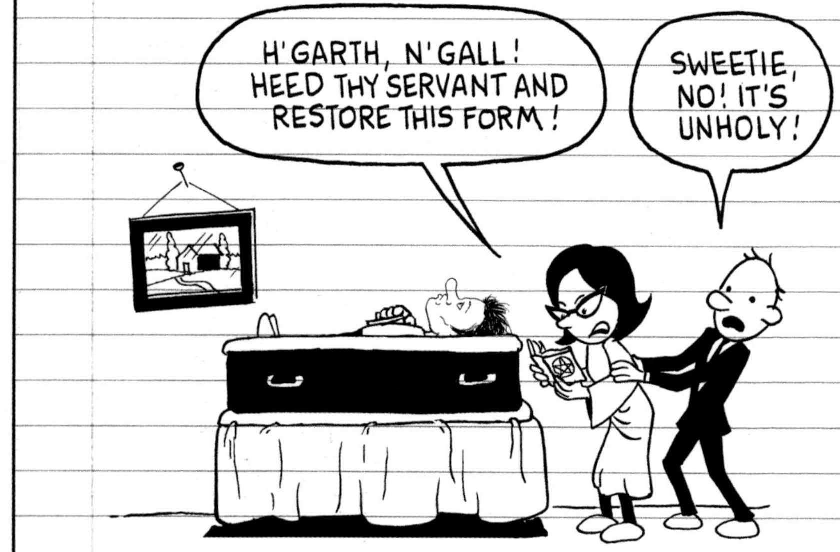
H'GARTH, N'GALL! HEED THY SERVANT AND RESTORE THIS FORM!
SWEETIE, NO! IT'S UNHOLY!

Me, I thought it was neat, but I guess Dad talked her out of it since it all went black again.

Tuesday

PART of the spell must've stuck, which made me REALLY wish Dad had let Mom finish.

I know people think it'd be cool to be at their own funeral, but I doubt they're imagining being totally paralyzed.

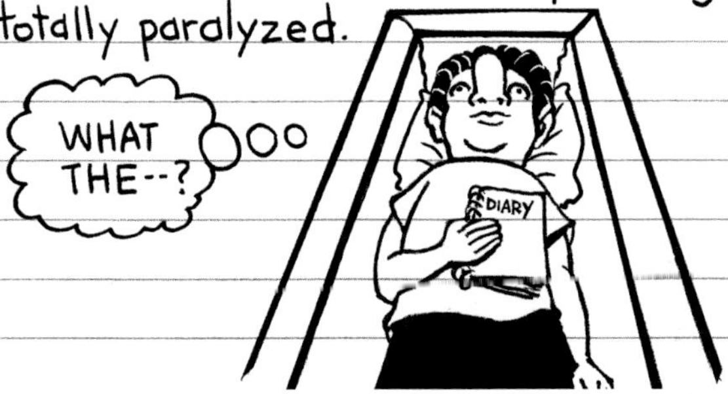
WHAT THE--?
DIARY

Worse? I could still SMELL! Uncle Garth, who always wears a gallon of awful cologne, leaned over my casket and said:

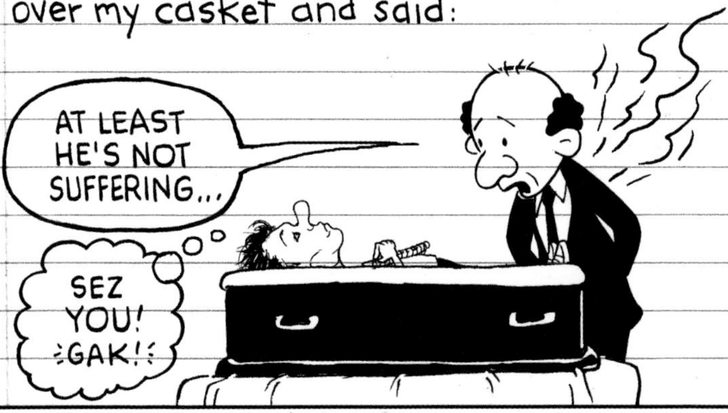
AT LEAST HE'S NOT SUFFERING...
SEZ YOU! GAK!

Don't Miss
TALES FROM THE CRYPT Graphic Novel #8
"Diary of a Stinky Dead Kid"

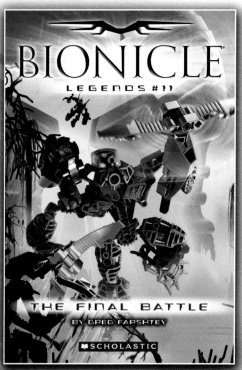

Special Preview of THE HARDY BOYS Graphic Novel #17 "Word Up!"

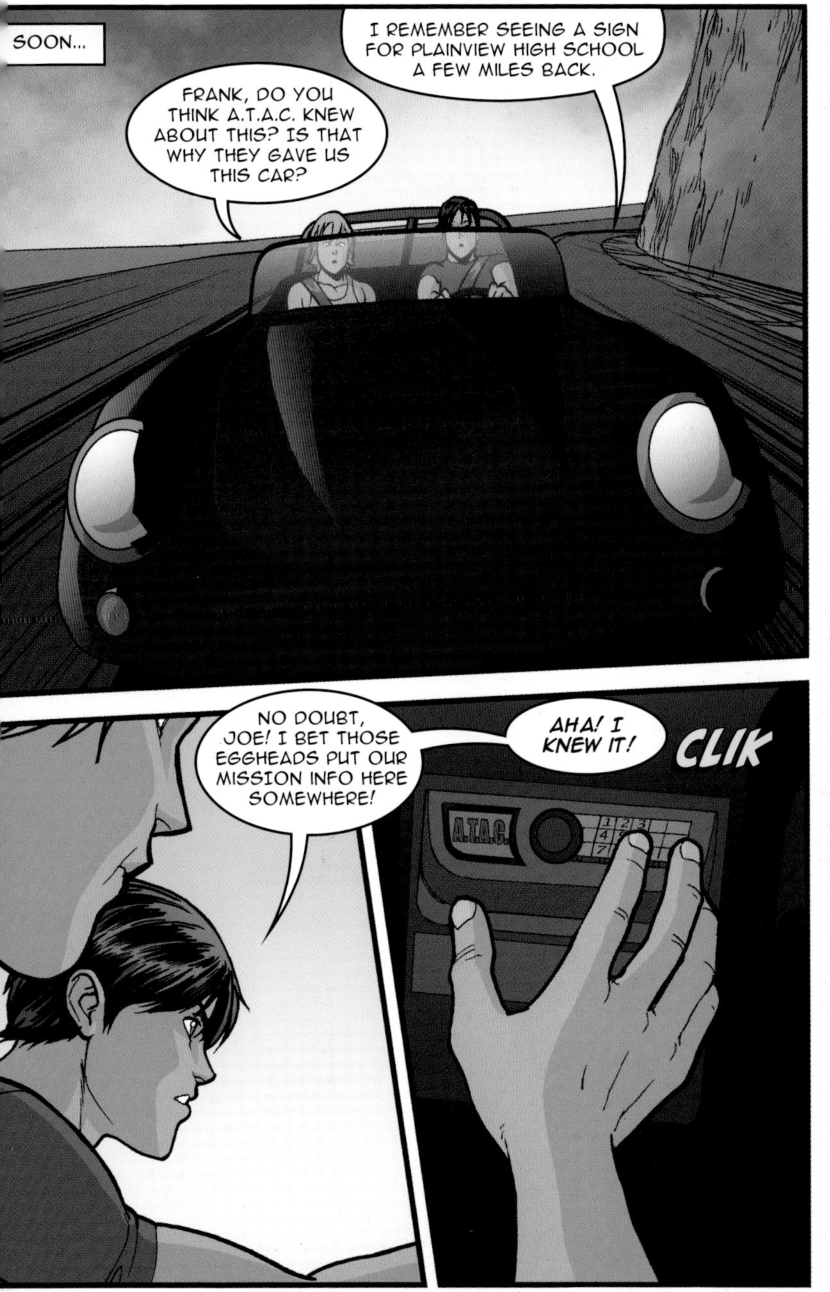
SOON...
FRANK, DO YOU THINK A.T.A.C. KNEW ABOUT THIS? IS THAT WHY THEY GAVE US THIS CAR?
I REMEMBER SEEING A SIGN FOR PLAINVIEW HIGH SCHOOL A FEW MILES BACK.
NO DOUBT, JOE! I BET THOSE EGGHEADS PUT OUR MISSION INFO HERE SOMEWHERE!
AHA! I KNEW IT!
CLIK
A.T.A.C.

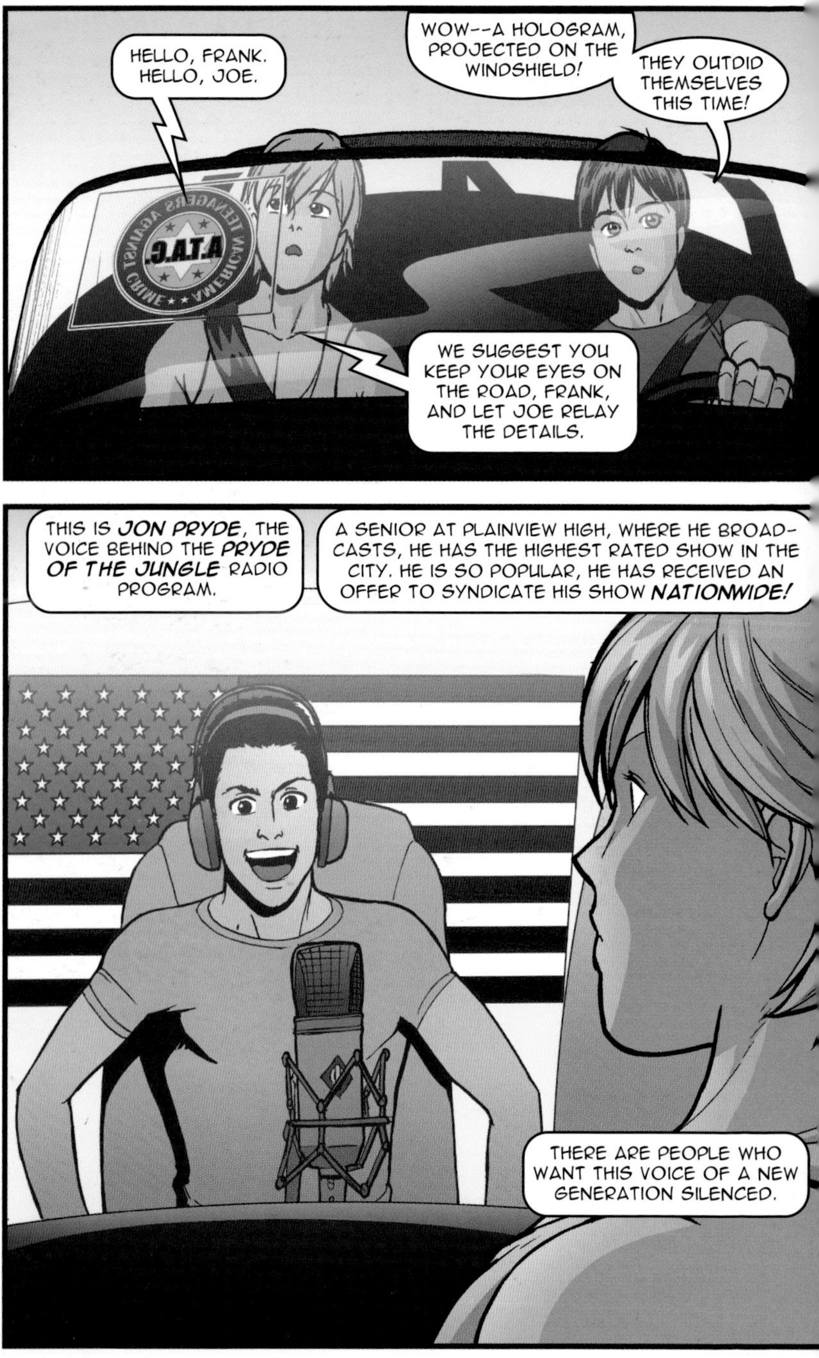
HELLO, FRANK. HELLO, JOE.
WOW--A HOLOGRAM, PROJECTED ON THE WINDSHIELD!
THEY OUTDID THEMSELVES THIS TIME!
WE SUGGEST YOU KEEP YOUR EYES ON THE ROAD, FRANK, AND LET JOE RELAY THE DETAILS.
THIS IS JON PRYDE, THE VOICE BEHIND THE PRYDE OF THE JUNGLE RADIO PROGRAM.
A SENIOR AT PLAINVIEW HIGH, WHERE HE BROAD-CASTS, HE HAS THE HIGHEST RATED SHOW IN THE CITY. HE IS SO POPULAR, HE HAS RECEIVED AN OFFER TO SYNDICATE HIS SHOW NATIONWIDE!
THERE ARE PEOPLE WHO WANT THIS VOICE OF A NEW GENERATION SILENCED.

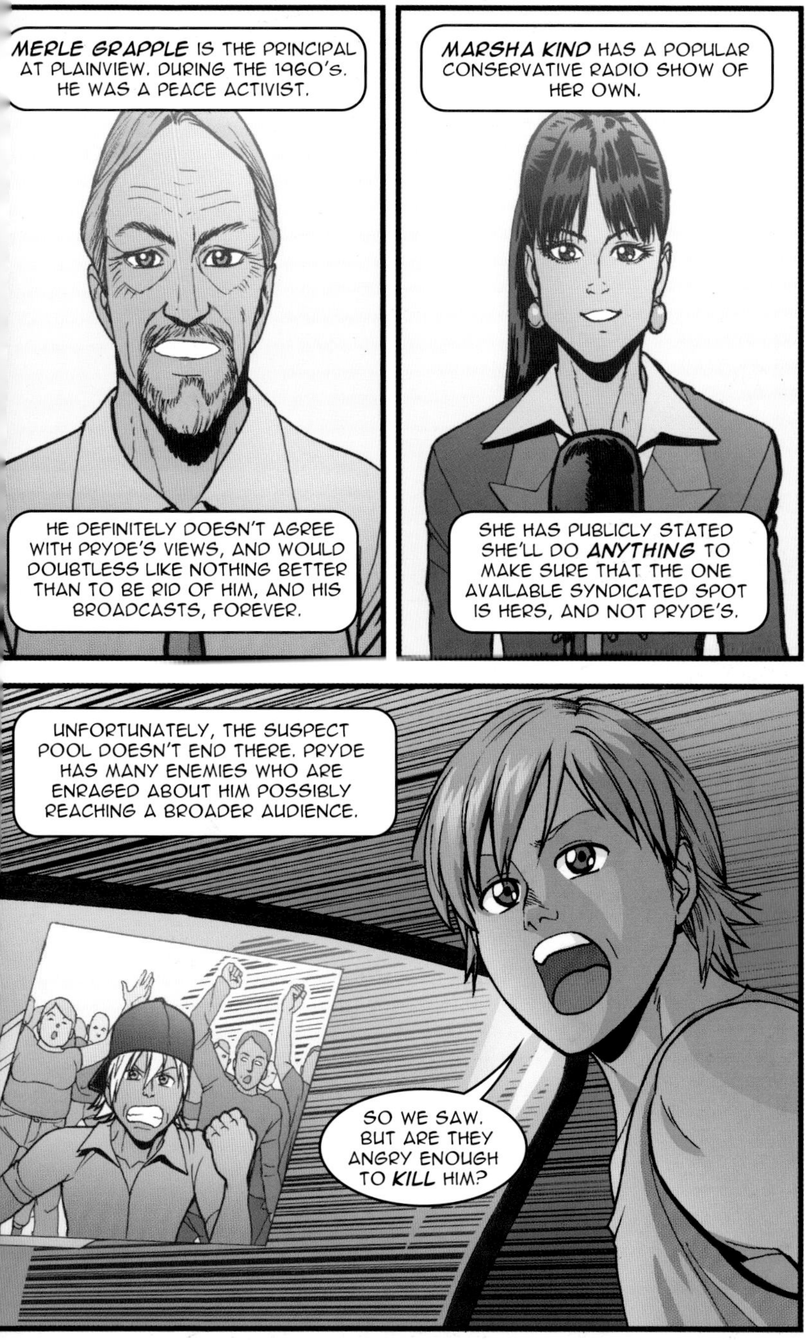
MERLE GRAPPLE IS THE PRINCIPAL AT PLAINVIEW. DURING THE 1960'S. HE WAS A PEACE ACTIVIST.
HE DEFINITELY DOESN'T AGREE WITH PRYDE'S VIEWS, AND WOULD DOUBTLESS LIKE NOTHING BETTER THAN TO BE RID OF HIM, AND HIS BROADCASTS, FOREVER.
MARSHA KIND HAS A POPULAR CONSERVATIVE RADIO SHOW OF HER OWN.
SHE HAS PUBLICLY STATED SHE'LL DO ANYTHING TO MAKE SURE THAT THE ONE AVAILABLE SYNDICATED SPOT IS HERS, AND NOT PRYDE'S.
UNFORTUNATELY, THE SUSPECT POOL DOESN'T END THERE. PRYDE HAS MANY ENEMIES WHO ARE ENRAGED ABOUT HIM POSSIBLY REACHING A BROADER AUDIENCE.
SO WE SAW. BUT ARE THEY ANGRY ENOUGH TO KILL HIM?

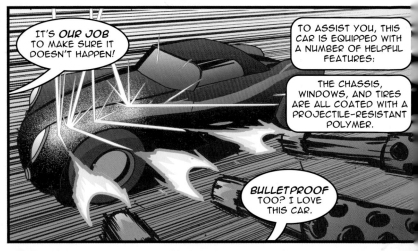

IT'S *OUR JOB* TO MAKE SURE IT DOESN'T HAPPEN!

TO ASSIST YOU, THIS CAR IS EQUIPPED WITH A NUMBER OF HELPFUL FEATURES:

THE CHASSIS, WINDOWS, AND TIRES ARE ALL COATED WITH A PROJECTILE-RESISTANT POLYMER.

BULLETPROOF TOO? I LOVE THIS CAR.

THE HIGH-BEAMS PROJECT AN ULTRA-LOW FREQUENCY INFRA RED EMISSION THAT TEMPORARILY INHIBITS ALPHA BRAINWAVES-- CALMING ANYONE IN ITS PATH.

TALK ABOUT "LIGHTS OUT!"

AS AN EXAMPLE OF WHAT A TEEN CAN DO WHEN HE SETS HIS MIND TO IT, PRYDE WILL BE APPEARING AT *AMERICA'S VOICE RALLY* IN APPROXIMATELY ONE HOUR.

THIS PARK IS CROWDED AND OPEN--THE PERFECT PLACE FOR A HIGH-PROFILE ATTACK.

WE'RE COUNTING ON YOU TO PREVENT IT.